SHATTER

LOLA TAYLOR

Copyright © 2015 by Lola Taylor
Cover designed by Kitten of Deranged Doctor Design.
Interior design and formatting by JT Formatting
Copy edited by Faith of The Atwater Group.
Proofread by Susie of Red Adept Editing

www.lolataylorbooks.com

First Edition: June 2016
Library of Congress Cataloging-in-Publication Data

Taylor, Lola
Shatter, a novel – 1st ed
ISBN-13: 978-0-9835131-4-8 | ISBN-10: 0-9835131-4-7

ONE

THE APARTMENT WAS a piece of shit. Anyone could see that.

But to Amy, it felt like seven hundred square feet of awesome.

It was *new*. Not "new, new." Nothing in this place screamed "updated!" It was "new" in the sense that she blissfully didn't recognize a damned thing in here: from the ramshackle, bright-green shag carpet, to the peeling, flowery wallpaper from the seventies. Every leaky faucet, every spiderweb-covered nook—hell, even the old, dusty sofa that the last occupant had neglected to move—was alien to her.

And that was what made it so wonderful. Here, she could truly forget about all the heartaches, lies, and bullshit that had come before now. She was officially rebooting her life, and she was going to enjoy every damned minute of it.

With a lightness in her step that had been absent for

years, she grabbed her first box of belongings and hauled it into her new digs.

Yeah, that whole thing about the apartment being cleaned before she moved in totally hadn't happened. Dust puffed up in the wake of her steps as she set her stuff down on the countertop, which also was covered in a light sheen of the gray fluff. Her sister would die in here. She was, literally, allergic to everything: cats, dogs, people. They'd both inherited some of their aloofness with the real world from their hopelessly starry-eyed, creativity-imbued mother.

Amy wished she could book a one-way ticket to La-La Land. She'd totally live there if she could.

Wishful thinking. She eyed the rectangular room. The kitchen, if you could even call it that, sat off in one corner; a bar overlooked the living room. A dining hovel—she called it a "hovel" because it wasn't nearly big enough to be considered a room—adjoined the kitchen. The only way it was marked off was by a block of mismatched tiles.

Classy.

At the opposite end of the living room was a small bathroom—with the emphasis on *small*—and a bedroom that reminded her of her college cell, er, "dorm." The weirdest thing about the apartment was that the bedroom had a concrete floor. That's right—*concrete*. Like a jail.

And yet, she stupidly grinned from ear to ear.

Who cared if it wasn't the most glamorous apartment in the city? It was hers, dammit, and she was going to own it. Starting with ripping down this dingy-ass wallpaper and slapping up some bright-yellow paint.

No more reminders of her past. No more wallowing in self-pity, and regret, and "God, why was I so stupid?"

If people could win an Academy Award for being a dumbass, she'd have stolen the vote. Her bestie, Becca, told her, "It's okay, doll, people make mistakes when they're in love."

But love didn't just make people blind—it made them dumb.

She gritted her teeth as determination lit a fire deep inside her.

She wouldn't fail at this. She could be on her own and enjoy it again.

Just as much as she had before all that crazy shit happened two years ago. The thought of it made her shiver, made her glance over her shoulder twice.

She was alone. There was something strangely comforting in that.

Her shoulders relaxed. *See? Things are already getting back to normal.*

She'd dreamed of a life where she wouldn't be afraid of her own shadow. She'd been there once, long before she'd met Michael, but she couldn't remember much of her pre-Michael life. Like her art, her life had gone through phases: pre-Michael, Michael, and post-Michael.

Post-Michael had been a bitch for about a year. Then she'd hit her stride and something miraculous had started to happen—she'd begun to grow, slowly stitching her life back together. One morning, she woke up earlier, and didn't wallow in bed all day. One trip to the grocery store, one smile at a stranger.

The first night she wasn't afraid to sleep in a dark room alone. Granted, she'd had a nightlight, but still. It was progress.

And the warm glow inside her told her things were

only going to get better.

The apartment was a turning point in her life. She could feel the pull of destiny, almost as if it were a tangible force.

Her life was about to change, and it was going to be epic.

It took all afternoon to haul her stuff in, mainly because she was doing it alone. Her sister and mom lived in another state, and Becca was still at the school, sorting out some drama involving her little brother, though Becca was supposed to meet her later to work out.

Ugh, couldn't she count the five flights of stairs she'd climbed over and over as a workout? The independence rah-rah train was grand until times like this, when you realized how fabulous movers would have been. If she could have afforded them, that is. Thanks to utilities deposits, plus the deposit and first month's rent she owed on this place, her bank account was pretty parched for cash.

Tired but not wanting to waste any time, she spritzed the wallpaper and peeled it off before she sanded the walls down and thoroughly cleaned them. She didn't even want to think about all the black crap that came off on the towels.

Yeah, this place definitely hadn't been cleaned. It broke her heart in a way, dumb as it sounded. Nobody had cared enough about this apartment to spruce it up. It was abandoned, just like she'd been after the incident that had nearly destroyed her. People tended to avoid negative things, and she'd been positively toxic. When she'd eventually tired of gargling her own negative thoughts and self-destructive behavior, she'd caved and seen a therapist on her mother's tab.

It had helped in more ways than one, mainly because she had someone to talk to. It was so much easier to spill your guts to a stranger than to your best friend, because you didn't give a damn what they thought. Besides, this stranger was paid to be nonjudgmental. Win-win.

Amy had already picked out the paint for the walls the afternoon she'd signed the lease, and got busy outlining the walls in green tape and throwing down massive drapes so the paint wouldn't get on the floor. She turned on the little stereo she'd brought to a local rock station. Rolling up her sleeves, she slapped on some fresh rubber gloves, grabbed the roller brush, and went to town.

For a few blissful minutes, she allowed herself to forget how she'd ended up here. It was just her, her paint high, and the sound of her voice belting out the lyrics to one 80s rock tune after another.

She'd almost forgotten where she was, when the radio abruptly snapped off. The silence slapped her back to her senses, seeming louder by its abrupt termination.

Yelping, Amy whirled; paint slung all over the floor. She swore and brandished the brush handle in front of her like some kind of cheap silver staff. Blowing her bangs out of her eyes, she lifted her head—and stared.

The man behind her kitchen counter was hot, at least from the torso up, because that's all she could see. The black T-shirt clung to his chest, revealing carefully refined muscles she'd love to run her hands over just to see if they were really as hard as they looked. Veins threaded along each arm, both of which were also impressively chiseled. The guy obviously took working out seriously, unlike she did.

She was a "work out only when I feel motivated"

kind of girl, despite her best attempts at staying fit. This or that got in the way, mostly herself, and she'd just never stuck with it.

If this gorgeous piece of man candy was at the gym, however, she might have to reconsider her routine. She could definitely find an excuse to get out of bed to look at *that*.

The power cord for her radio dangled from his hand.

Her eyes rose to his neck, and she slowly drank him in. If a man was delectable, she'd be eating him right up. Warmth rushed between her thighs, along with a dampness that soaked her panties. Sexual fantasies played out in her head, mainly where he said, "I've been waiting my entire life for a woman like you," swept her up in his arms, and made love to her on the countertop.

Holy shit, her hormones were out of control. It was a miracle she wasn't panting.

Then her eyes traveled up to his face.

He was gorgeous in every sense of the word. From the straight set of his nose to the slight dimple in his chin, he was H-O-T. Stubble shadowed his jawline, somehow making his full, sensual lips seem more pronounced.

Or maybe it was the flames that leapt in his eyes as he pinned her with an incinerating glare.

It would have been hot if she hadn't been so terrified. She gulped. *Uh-oh.*

He closed his eyes and took a deep breath, as if counting down. When he opened his eyes, a startling blue she could see from ten feet away, he looked no less pissed off.

"What the hell do you think you're doing?" he bellowed.

TWO

THE WOMAN STARED at him, her mouth snapping shut. She went from astonished to angry in a split second. With a flash of silver, she waved the roller brush at him. "Stay back. I'm warning you."

He raised a brow. *WTF?* Had he missed "mentally unstable" on her apartment application? "Or you'll what?" he said dryly.

"I'll..." The threat dried up on her tongue as that spark in her eyes flickered with doubt. With renewed determination, her gaze snapped up to his. She narrowed her eyes and gave him what he supposed was her "big girl" voice. "Who the hell are you, and what are you doing in my apartment?"

He glared at her and firmly shoved down the fact her assertiveness had sent a wave of heat through him. *She was probably a tiger in bed.*

He imagined her running her long, hot-pink nails down his back, whimpering with pleasure and crying his name as he thrust—

Whoa, boy.

God, if he didn't cool it soon, he was going to get hard. "I'm the building manager," he said flatly, trying to hide his arousal. "I was coming to welcome you to the neighborhood and give you more information on the area, since you're new."

She blinked. "Oh." She tucked the brush behind her back and composed herself, blushing. "I'm sorry, I didn't know what to think. I thought maybe you were—"

"A burglar?" he added with more than a dollop of sarcasm.

Her face went pale, and he mentally swore.

Wrong thing to say. She'd mentioned on her application about being an assault victim and having a restraining order out on someone. Apparently, the douche had taken out a restraining order on *her* after receiving his own. The one he'd taken out on her was eventually dropped once the court figured out he was just being a tool, but the one she'd placed on him had stuck. She'd written how the one he'd taken out on her had popped up on a background check before, so she liked to mention it up front.

He appreciated her honesty, which made him feel more like a dick for scaring her. He cleared his throat, stepped around the counter and extended his hand. "Scott Meyers."

"Amy Miles," she said meekly. Her firm grip surprised him; her delicate hands held an unexpected amount of crunch-power.

He handed her the packet he'd nearly squashed in a death grip when he walked in and saw the walls. "Here are some of the basics, as well as a copy of your lease and all the ground rules." He gave the drying paint a withering look. "I underlined number ten on page five about *not* painting the walls."

Her face turned a deeper shade of red. It was striking against her blond hair, which was obviously dyed. The hair color didn't look cheap or fake on her, though, unlike a lot of the women he saw around this area. Her hair looked... cute. Sexy, even. "Sorry," she said, "it's just the first time I've really been out anywhere on my own, and I thought since I signed the lease and paid the deposit and every-thing, we were allowed to paint."

"Did you buy the apartment?"

She stared at him. "No."

"Then you can't paint." He started to walk off. "It's sixty dollars an hour for my crew to come in and paint it back to neutral tones."

Her mouth flopped open in outrage as she gaped at him. "Neutral tones my ass! Did you even see that hideous wallpaper that was up here?"

"Oh, yeah, you're right." He gave her a thin smile. "Replacing wallpaper is a bit cheaper, about forty an hour. I'll add it on to your next month's bill." Almost as an af-terthought, he reached down and placed the lids on the open paint and primer cans.

Yellow. She had painted half the walls fucking canary, cheery yellow. If there was any color on God's green earth that deserved a slow, painful death, it was yellow.

But for some reason, he didn't seem to mind it so much on her pretty little head.

Even when she looked as if she was about to run him through with her roller brush handle. "What do you think you're doing?" she screeched as he hauled up the cans.

"Confiscating these before you do any more damage," he called over his shoulder.

Thundering footsteps vibrated the floor, and a moment later, he was jerked backward as she grabbed hold of a can and dug in her heels. "Like hell, you are," she said through clenched teeth. "Do you have any idea how much that paint cost? Sherwin-Williams is not cheap!"

"I don't care." He stared her down. Decorum be damned. He knew he was supposed to be professional and all, but honestly, sometimes the only way to deal with crazy was to dish up a little bit of crazy yourself. He yanked back, which only made her growl at him.

She *growled* at him, like a damned animal. Holy shit, she would definitely be a tiger in bed. Heat rushed through him, and blood pumped straight to his steadily growing erection.

"Give it back." She seethed.

His jaw ticked. If he wasn't holding back, he would probably hurt her. But he didn't want to. She seemed strong and fiery and yet perfectly breakable. Something in her eyes told him that, something that spoke volumes of the dark shit she'd been through.

He couldn't go there, wouldn't be the man who dredged that up for her. He could be an ass sometimes, but he wasn't a total asshole.

So, he held on without really trying, and said firmly, "No."

She stopped struggling and looked at him.

Scott stared down at the sassy blond. Her smartass attitude wasn't what surprised him. As building manager for the past year, he'd seen and heard a lot of crazy shit. "Interesting" didn't begin to cover some of the whack-jobs who had slipped under the radar and onto his turf. So, although dealing with crazies didn't catch him off guard, it was the rigidity in his sex that did.

It had been over an entire year since he'd felt an inkling of desire for the fairer sex. *Over a whole year.* That had to be some kind of record for any man who claimed to be heterosexual.

Now that she'd magically made his cock give a damn, he couldn't help but drink in her other features.

Wide hips with a little extra padding, which gave way to a pair of snug sweatpants. The material pulled along her thighs, which he imagined were just as plump and soft looking as the rest of her. He could hold on to her soft curves while he thrust into her, making her dizzy with ecstasy.

Her breath caught, and her eyes dipped to his lips. Thanks to their tug-o-paint-can, their faces weren't that far apart anymore.

A delicate pink tongue dipped out and *licked* her glossy bottom lip.

Oh fuccccccckkkk. His heart sped up as his desire for her doubled.

Just when he thought she might be thinking the same lustful thoughts, she shot him a sexy little smirk that made his heart skip a beat, and purred, "Have it your way."

Sporting uncanny swiftness, she swiped the lid off the can. In the tug-o-can, the can had shifted in his arms so the opening was tilted toward the ground. Yellow paint poured out the side and slopped onto the floor.

"Shit!" he spat as he scrambled to retrieve the lid, which she'd tossed onto the floor.

She smirked, with her hands on her hips, as even

more paint poured out. It covered his hands, making them slick, and the sides of the can even more slippery. It began to slide out of his hands. Like a man crazed, he grappled for it. The desperate movements caused it to shoot out of his hands. The now half-empty can banged against the floor and rolled toward the open door.

Scott ran after it, swearing the whole time as his shoes squished in a trail of fresh paint. In his haste to retrieve the can, the toe of his shoe kicked it and sent it flying out the door.

What happened next could only be described as something that would happen in a cartoon.

Yet, there he was, standing in the doorway with his jaw nearly on his chest, and watched as the can ricocheted off the wall and bounced down the stairs. It clanked loudly down them, one at a time, throwing up paint along its path.

Neighbors opened their doors and poked their heads out. A kid laughed and splashed in the paint as if it were a puddle.

The can landed at the bottom of the stairwell, at last drawing still.

The ringing still echoed in Scott's ears. Or maybe that was the steam that poured out of his head.

His temperature rose as his hands slowly curled into fists. He closed his eyes and took a deep breath against the rising surge of fury.

One, two, three, four...ah, screw it.

Whirling, he pinned Ms. Miles with a glare that would scare the shit out of the Grim Reaper. "You have two options: one, I charge you for the cleanup, or two, you clean it up. Either way, this gets fixed—now."

She stared at him wide-eyed. Both hands covered her

mouth, as if she couldn't believe what had just happened. "I'm—I'm so sorry!"

"Say you're sorry with a scrub brush and some cleaner!" he snapped and then stormed out of the room, leaving a trail of bright-yellow footprints.

THREE

O KAY, IN HINDSIGHT, pissing off her landlord—or hot-and-annoying-as-all-get-out building manager, or whatever the hell he was—
probably wasn't one of her brightest moments.

It had, on a lighter note, been hilarious—until she tiptoed to the hallway and saw the destruction the open paint
can had wreaked.

All she could see was dollar signs as her widening
eyes followed the path of canary-yellow paint. It was the
good stuff. As in, it wasn't going to come off anytime
soon. Plus, it was a special rapid-dry variety.

All that money—money she hadn't come across easily, considering her painting sales had slowed quite a bit
because she hadn't produced anything new in so long—
strewn across the stairwell...

Maybe if she'd flashed the expensive receipt in front
of her eyes, she would have thought twice about her little
lid-swiping maneuver. Still, seeing Mr. Hot Shit lose his

marbles over the out-of-control can had been good for a giggle.

People milled about, wondering what on earth had happened. It looked as if her neighbors were a collection of all sorts of people: the old, the young, the holy-shit-have-you-ever-brushed-your-hair-or-teeth?

After the sting of shock wore off, she'd erupted into hysterical laughter. Her neighbors stared at her as though she were insane. Which, apparently, she was. How else could she explain away what she'd done?

Brilliant, Amy. Really freaking brilliant.

Thirty seconds of uncontrollable giggling later, she abruptly slapped a hand over her mouth with a dramatic gasp.

Holy CRAP. What the hell had she been thinking? Mr. Sexy, er, Meyers had stormed out of her apartment like an angry bull. Granted, a very sexy bull. And she'd be lying if she said she hadn't taken the opportunity to scope out his ass. Damn, that man looked good in jeans.

He'd also probably look fantastic as he kicked her ass out on the streets.

Images of her living in a cardboard box, pushing around a shopping cart or a bicycle with a million bags on it, rushed through her head.

Oh God. She didn't have enough money in savings to afford another place. Her credit cards would get her by at a cheap hotel for a little while, but dayuuuuummmmm....

Like she said. Dumbass award.

She could imagine her sister yelling, "What the hell, Amy!" Inwardly cursing herself, she scrambled out the door and asked every person she could find where Mr. Hot Shit went. In her rush, she hadn't paid attention to where she was going. She slipped and slid on the barely dried paint and had to grip the railing when she nearly fell and tumbled down the rest of the stairs.

The cursing intensified when she saw the trail of yellow footprints she'd left on the stairwell. She looked around for something to wipe her feet off on. Exhaustion from moving all day had started to set in, so in her defense, she wasn't exactly thinking straight.

When people have something on the bottom of their shoes, they wipe their feet. As such, it should come as no surprise that she marched over to the first mat she saw, and wiped her shoes, leaving glaring yellow streaks.

Her mouth formed an *O* when she realized too late what she'd done. "Shit!" she screamed and stomped her foot.

The leasing office door behind the mat opened abruptly. Mr. Sexy stared at her with a perplexed frown. He was so big, he filled up the whole doorway.

Her sex throbbed as she wondered what other places he could fill up. He looked down and his expression hardened. "What the hell have you done to my mat?"

"What?" Blinking, she looked down. Her eyes widened as she sucked in a breath. *Shit.* She'd been too busy fantasizing about him to remember what she'd done. Her gaze jerked back up to a very angry Mr. Sexy. *More like Mr. Pissed.* "I-I was just, um, wiping my feet," she said stupidly.

"Clearly," he said, not bothering to hide his irritation. He squished his eyes closed and pinched the bridge of his nose. "I hope this isn't going to be a sign of things to come."

"No!" she blurted. Desperation crept into her voice.

"I'm just having an off day, I swear!"

He stared at her. His jaw—so perfectly sculpted and perfectly lick-able—was set in a hard line. "If this is an 'off' day, I can't wait to see a bad one."

She stopped breathing. Her heart hammered against her sternum. It felt as if her very life depended on his meaning, which it technically did. "You mean I can stay?" She made herself whisper, afraid to hear the answer.

He remained silent and studied her with his calculating stare. His eyes roved from head to toe slowly.

Oh shit. He was probably trying to decide whether her rent money was worth the trouble of putting up with her.

That's when she resorted to the only thing she had left.

Screw her pride.

With the weight of her prying neighbors' eyes on her back, she swallowed hard and knelt down on her knees.

Scott couldn't believe what he was seeing.

Was she...*groveling*?

The round globes of her ass, which looked damned good in the sweatpants she wore, made him yearn to stroke her. It didn't help that he could see a hint of a crimson thong peep above her waistline.

Damn. He hadn't been this hard in so long that it almost hurt. He cleared his throat, leaned against the door-frame, and crossed his legs in what he hoped was a casual pose. Anything to draw attention away from the noticeable bulge around his crotch.

"Please don't kick me out!" she begged, her face directed toward the carpet.

Oh, he could make her beg, all right. Beg for him to take her as he made her crazy with need while his tongue swirled—

Stop it. Right. Now.

These ridiculous fantasies had to stop. The girl didn't deserve a guy like him—she deserved better. Any woman did.

He was nothing but baggage wrapped up in a very male package. "Damaged goods," as it were.

He stood there, silent from concentrating so hard on suppressing his desire to do naughty things to her. His mind was so preoccupied that he almost missed what she said.

"Please," she went on, "I'll do anything."

"Anything?" He raised a brow. Damn, his voice sounded rough. He might as well say, "Want to sleep with me?"

She looked up at him. Those pouty lips opened slightly. He'd love to slip his tongue between them to see whether she tasted as sweet as she looked.

"Anything," she whispered.

That almost undid him. His mouth pressed into a firm line. "And what are you going to do to make it up to me?" His voice came out clipped. And low; rough, even.

She sucked in a tight breath. Briefly, her eyes drooped to his crotch and lingered there.

He caught his breath. Could she...? No. No way in hell would a woman that gorgeous want someone like him. He was "a plague upon women," or so one of his casual fucks had screamed at him on her way out the door.

If Amy knew what was good for her, she'd stay the hell away from him. And if he was any kind of a gentleman, he'd push her along.

"My face is up here," he said sternly.

She blinked as crimson flowed into her cheeks. "I—I wasn't—"

"It's fine." He tried to sound annoyed and sighed hard. "You can relax. I'm not going to kick you out."

Her shoulders fell as she released a huge sigh.

"That is," he added, "if you have the stairs cleaned by tomorrow morning."

She gulped and pressed her lips together.

Damn, she looked cute doing that, too. Wasn't there anything about her he didn't find attractive as hell?

Forbidden fruit always smells the sweetest...

He shrugged and started to go back into his office. "If you don't want to live here any longer, I certainly won't —"

"No, no, no!" She rushed to her feet. "I'll do it! I'll clean everything. I'll even get you a new welcome mat, something without yellow paint all over it."

Well, he did like the sound of that.

In her rush to her feet, her halter top had ridden down, revealing plump breasts just waiting to be squeezed. The lush, round mounds would fit nicely in his hands. And dear God, she hadn't worn a bra.

He had to get inside his office, *now*.

With a curt nod and a grunt, he turned and shut himself in the office.

His heart pounded as he leaned against the door. *What the hell?* You'd think he was going through puberty all over again.

Maybe he should kick her out. It would be better for everyone involved.

With his hands running through his hair, he almost jumped when a timid knock came from the door.

Immediately hoping it was her, and realizing too late what an idiot that made him, he rushed to open the door.

She stood there, clothes rumpled, hair a mess.

And far too tempting for his liking.

He needed to get rid of her before he dragged her into his office and did something they'd both regret.

She opened her mouth to speak, but he cut her off. "Do you have the stairs cleaned yet?"

She blinked, surprised. "No."

"Don't come back until you do."

Slam!

He felt like a douchebag for doing it, but so help him, he was desperate.

He froze and listened for her reaction. A few seconds later, he heard a growl, followed by a stream of curses as she stomped off.

He exhaled and slumped to the floor, harder than ever.

Hot damn. Her little temper tantrum had turned him on even more.

Houston, we have a problem.

FOUR

H ER LIFE SHOULD be a sitcom. Seriously, some producer somewhere should look into it. At least then she could get paid a shit-ton of money for having all this random shit happen to her.

She'd never had a door slammed in her face before, especially by a hot man, and it hadn't been a pleasant experience. Especially when she'd been about to thank him. In a huff, she'd turned and marched back up to her apartment for some supplies. It was going to be a long, miserable night.

A puzzling mixture of relief at him not kicking her out and anger at him dismissing her so rudely twisted her insides the whole time she'd cleaned. And when she got angry, she did one of two things—curse or cry. Sometimes both.

Feeling more on the cursing order, because she was too tired to cry, she cussed out the floor, the brush, and the rusty bucket Mr. Sexy had slammed down in front of her only to retreat to his office a few seconds later.

Seriously, what the hell was his problem? The guy was an asshole.

What was more irritating was that despite her knowledge of said assholery, she still found her panties to be stained with want once she'd finished cleaning, and it wasn't the cleaner that turned her on.

Her body seriously didn't know what was good for it sometimes. The generous love handles that clung to her sides were testament to that, at least when it came to food.

She sighed. She couldn't blame her body's lapse of judgment. She hadn't, after all, had sex with anyone in ages. Sure, she'd lusted after guys, but that's all it was— looking at pretty eye candy and never touching it.

But from the moment she'd laid eyes on Mr. Sexy, something carnal had awoken inside her.

And it was very, very hungry.

By the time she'd gotten the stupid stairwell all cleaned up, it was well into the night. Becca had texted her a gazillion times, wondering where the hell she was for their workout. Apologizing for being a terrible friend, Amy had changed and gone over to the gym. She hadn't even had time to shower and wash the paint off, not that she'd seen any point. She was about to get hot and sweaty all over again.

This was going to royally suck. Sweat + exhaustion + hunger = bitchy Amy.

Ugh.

The gym wasn't far, a short car ride a few blocks from where she lived. She got her membership at half off, thanks to Becca, who knew one of the trainers there. It was the only way Becca had needled her into joining.

Not that she was allergic to exercise equipment, but seeing all the skinny bitches running around, *flirting* with their overpriced personal trainers with their toned abs and tight asses, made her feel like shit. And, really, how the hell were they so skinny, doing *nothing*, when she worked her ass off and *gained* weight?

WTF?

Yeah, so, she'd let herself go. She blamed World War Michael. The devastation it had caused showed in the extra plushness around her thighs, arms, and ass. Changing her physique was all part of Becca's rehabilitation program for her.

"Burning up the calories (reminders) of her past." That was what Becca preached.

Easy enough for Becca to talk. She already looked like a supermodel. Amy felt like a hippopotamus next to her. Every time she saw Becca in a cute outfit, she couldn't help but think, "Wow, that's cute...but it wouldn't be on me for X,Y, Z reasons."

Low self-esteem about your body image majorly sucked.

So did being covered in super-expensive yellow paint that apparently had no plans to come off her body anytime soon.

She all but crawled into the gym, squinting at the bright lights. Even at eleven o'clock on a weeknight, there were a ton of people here. Were they battery powered? Or bionic? How did they still have so much energy?

Probably because they haven't been performing manual labor all day.

Casting them all begrudging looks for their effortless perkiness and toned bodies, she dragged her feet toward a petite brunette clad in hot-pink sweats. Her skin was lightly tanned—all natural, since she spent so much time outdoors—and her long, dark-brown hair was up in a ponytail. She was just tying her sneakers when she looked up at Amy—and frowned. "Why are you covered in yellow paint?" Becca asked. "Oh, wait a minute. Let me guess." She straightened and pretended to think. "You're doing a modern piece on canvas and decided to use your body as the paintbrush this time?"

"No, but I've thought about that." Amy stretched her sore legs with a groan before she hopped on the treadmill.

Becca didn't press her for details. It was something Amy loved about her. She didn't pry; rather, she let Amy tell her what was bugging her when she was ready.

The girls ran alongside each other. Well, Amy speed-walked. Sort of. "Speed-limped" was more like it. Becca did all the running. Amy didn't mind running—she actually kind of enjoyed it—but today was one of those days where she preferred to walk.

Or go to sleep on that comfy-looking bench over there.

"How'd the move go?" Becca asked after a moment.

"Eh," was all Amy said.

"That good, huh?"

Amy sighed. "It's a long story."

A few moments of silence passed between them. Becca cast her a guilty frown. "I'm sorry I couldn't help out with the move."

"It's okay," Amy said warmly, instantly giving her a smile. "I know you couldn't help it."

Becca scowled. "My brother can be a pain in the ass sometimes. I can't believe he got kicked out of school again. Do you have any idea how long I spent in the principal's office sorting his shit out?"

Becca, now twenty-five, had guardianship of her little brother, who was thirteen.

Amy gave her friend a sympathetic look. "Fighting again?"

"Nah. This time he's graduated to robbery. Took some kid's lunch money."

"Damn. That's low." Amy should know—she had some not so fond memories of being the kid who got picked on.

"Tell me about it." Becca's frown tightened as her eyes narrowed, and then she sighed. She punched the speed dial back on the treadmill until she walked at the same pace as Amy. Which, considering the shape of her aching legs, wasn't very fast. "I hate to see him acting out like this, but I don't know what else I can do. I've tried hobbies, sports, clubs...nothing sticks."

"What about his therapy sessions with his counselor?"

"You know, I'm not sure, considering he doesn't freaking go to any."

Amy's heart twisted for her friend. She was trying really hard. Despite her being only twelve years older than her brother, she did a damned better job at the "mom" thing than most older women could. The kid was damned lucky to have her. Now, if only he would realize that.

"It'll be all right," Amy said encouragingly. "Don't give up trying to get through to him. Some kids take awhile to see you're only trying to help."

Becca gave her a small smile. "Thanks, Ames." She stared at Amy's legs and then her arms and chest. "Jeez, that stuff isn't coming off, is it?"

True to the promise on the can's label, the paint really was water-resistant. And sweat- and soap-resistant, apparently.

Becca looked as though she could use a distraction to take her mind off her brother. She was constantly worrying about him, and Amy was used to being her sounding board.

With a deep breath, Amy explained everything about the encounter with Mr. Sexy, right up to her cleaning the entire flipping stairwell.

The story had the desired effect—Becca was nearly in tears by the end, she laughed so hard.

Hey, at least she was laughing. That made Amy smile and a warm glow fill her chest.

"Oh. My. God. I *have* to meet this guy." Becca dabbed at her eyes with the towel she'd brought.

Her own eyes stung from sweat, too, but Amy dotted her face with the sleeve of her shirt.

Classy.

Black splotches marred her shirt afterward. Oh, that's right. She'd actually worn mascara today.

Today, she had given a damn because she was rebooting her life.

So much for that.

On second thought, she smiled at her shirt. The fact she even wore mascara at all was a small victory. For the longest time, she'd forgone makeup, cute clothes, and doing her hair. Nothing mattered after what she'd gone through. It all seemed so...petty.

But now, it seemed normal. Though she had a long way to go, some small part of her had healed in those two years, and it craved normalcy.

Maybe I really am starting over. Maybe things are finally getting better.

She firmly squashed down her hope, afraid it was too good to be true.

Just as her therapist had encouraged, she had to resist the urge not to care because it was familiar and "taking the easy way out."

Happy people didn't understand it, and good for them. After going through hell, there was a certain numbness that could take over. A survival mode. Because it was easier to feel nothing than to feel all that damned pain. She'd hurt for too long, to the point it had almost destroyed her.

When you'd gone to the edge of the abyss and nearly fallen in, seeing the light, any light, was like an addiction.

"Amy? Did you hear me?"

"What?" Amy's head snapped around; a nerve in her neck caught. She winced and reached up to rub it out.

A mischievous sparkle shone in Becca's eyes as she slowly smiled. "Oh my God. I was right."

Amy blinked. "Right about what?"

"You're hot for him, aren't you?"

"I'm sorry, I'm hot for *who*?"

"Mr. Sexy, your building manager."

"I...I did not call him that."

"Oh, you most certainly did. Throughout your whole story."

Holy shit. Amy's face heated. She stopped her treadmill and stood there, panting. Even just thinking about him made her blood boil, and she'd be a fool if she thought the slickness in her freshly changed panties was due entirely to her very light workout.

Her gut wrenched. It was happening again. She was dangerously attracted to a male, and last time, that had *so* not ended well.

"I...I need to get home." Amy's voice shook as she got ready to leave.

Becca stopped her treadmill and caught hold of her arm. Her voice was gentle, understanding. "Don't be afraid to fall in love again."

Amy swallowed hard. It felt as though she'd swallowed a rock. "I...I can't go through that again," she whispered.

"You also can't be alone for the rest of your life."

Amy took a deep, resolved breath. "Sometimes alone is the safest place to be." She smiled at her friend, knowing the motion was halfhearted. She was exhausted. "Thanks for working out with me. Guess I needed to relieve some stress after all."

Becca beamed. "Anytime. I'll always be here if you need me."

Amy squeezed her hand. "Thanks, girl. You're the best."

After bidding her best friend good-bye in the parking lot, Amy got in her car and drove home.

The parking garage gave her the creeps, so she parked along the curb. It wasn't exactly safe either, but hey, her car could get jacked anywhere. And this block, though old, was reputed as being safe.

That fact comforted her as she walked inside—and nearly slammed into the chest of a very tall, and very drunk, man.

"Jesus!" he slurred. He staggered backward and

gripped the doorframe of his apartment. The door hung open behind him. Loud music and voices drifted out, along with a stout breeze of beer and marijuana.

Great. This guy was clearly going to be the "asshole neighbor," the one who partied at all hours and didn't give a damn about the people around him.

She gritted her teeth, ready to chew him out. In no mood for bullshit, she opened her mouth when he spoke first.

"Hey," he drawled. His eyes sort of zeroed in on her. "You're that sexy-ass fox I saw mopping up the stairwell. The new maid."

Maid? "I'm sorry, but one, this isn't the Hilton; two, I'm not a maid; and three, you need to shut your party down before I call the cops. Some people are trying to sleep."

He laughed. "Cops ain't gonna do shit, girl. You're tripping if you think they're going to come to this side of town."

She blinked. Leave it to her to believe everything she read on the Internet. The building's high ratings were probably skewed by fake ones.

Whatever it takes to make a buck, she thought, not without irritation. They should advertise: "Move-in special! Free mugging within a week upon arrival, or your deposit back!"

His oily gaze slid down her body from head to toe; her skin crawled. A sleazy grin spread across his face. *God, had he ever heard of a toothbrush?* "You got a nice ass." He grinned wider.

Amy snorted. "Wow, your girlfriend is a lucky woman."

"Don't have one of them bitches!" he said proudly.

Apparently, he didn't get any exposure to sunlight, because his skin tone could rival Dracula's. "Imagine that," Amy grumbled under her breath. Giving him as wide a berth as she could manage, considering the tight hallway quarters, she tried to slip past him. McSleazy had other plans, however, and made that clear by grabbing her arm.

"Ow!" She tried to jerk her arm free. She could practically feel her bones grinding together. "Let go of me!"

"No way, doll. You're too sweet to pass up. You'd be a big hit at my party. We like our women with a little extra meat on their bones." Sure enough, a whole group of gangsters eyed her from within his smoke-filled apartment.

Cold sweat broke out over her skin. She'd seen that look, right before everything went to shit two years ago.

It was the look of a sociopath eyeing his next victim.

Demons from her past rose up to taunt her, making her feel about as small and strong as a dormouse. "I-I said no," she said, her voice more feeble than it was before.

McSleazy yanked her toward the open door. "Come on, girl. Just come on in and have a beer to loosen up some."

"I'll loosen her up!" called one of his boys before he thrust his hips into the air several times. His friends busted out laughing, but Amy didn't find it funny one bit. In fact, she felt nauseated.

"Please, let me go." She fought to control her nerves. Her hand slipped into her purse and fished for her keys.

"Like to play hard to get, huh?" He reached around with his free hand and felt up her ass. "I like tough girls."

That was it. The feeling of him touching her, violating her, made something inside her snap. Anger took over, years' worth of being pissed off at living in the shadow of what happened to her.

Dammit, she was sick and tired of feeling threatened all the time.

She glared at McSleazy. "You like tough girls? Then you're going to love me."

She gripped her keys, yanked them out of her purse and squeezed the little metal bottle attached. Liquid shot out of the can and right into McSleazy's eyes.

He screamed and immediately let her go as he clawed at his face. "You—you BITCH! What the fuck is this?"

Amy grinned. "Pepper spray." She started up the stairs and then turned and smiled coldly at the creep. "Who's the bitch now?"

She ran up the stairs, not wasting a minute of her getaway opportunity. McSleazy's buddies raced out of the apartment as he howled.

"Get her!" he screeched. "I'm gonna beat her fucking ass!"

She raced up the stairs. Footsteps thundered after her, and her heart shot to her throat.

Just as she was about to clear the last step, someone grabbed her hand and yanked backward. She swore as her keys dropped from her hands. They slid through one of the openings between the stairs, falling to the next landing, right where about three of the guys in the apartment, including the one who made the crude gesture, were.

None of them looked as happy to see her as they had a moment ago.

Panic crept in as they closed in on her. The one guy still had hold of her wrist. He went to pull her to him, and she immediately went into self-defense mode.

Her brain shut off, and her fight-or-flight instinct flipped on. Without thinking, her self-defense training kicked in, and she threw her knee up into the guy's groin. He groaned, followed by a curse. The moment his grip loosened, she jerked free and stumbled up the stairs.

She couldn't get into her own apartment, so she did what any sane person would do—she banged on the next-door neighbor's door.

"Help!" she screamed. "Somebody open up! Please!"

Shouts rang from the stairwell, coming closer.

Oh God, they were pissed. If murder hadn't shone in their eyes before, it sure as hell did now.

Pounding harder, she screamed until her voice was hoarse.

Someone please help. Oh God, please don't let me—

The door swung open so abruptly she nearly fell forward.

"What the hell is going on out here?" a deep voice—one that made her blood boil with desire—thundered.

The smell of pine assaulted her nose, alluring and male, much like the half-naked man who stood in front of her. His dark hair dripped, and a towel hung around his shoulders.

Her voice dried up as she stared at his chest. He looked...unreal, as if all the muscles had been painted on. Tattoos of Celtic knots and other filigree twirled over his skin. A tiny lion head was inked just below his left ear, almost on the side of his neck.

Yum.

Holy shit. Mr. Sexy was her freaking next-door neighbor.

FIVE

FTER THE OFFICE incident, in which he'd nearly acted like a caveman by dragging Amy's sweet ass into the office and ripping her clothes off, Scott had done what any other overly horny man would have done.

He'd struggled through his mountain of work, waited until Amy was gone, and then hauled ass up to his apartment for a very icy shower.

His sex didn't seem to give a damn that the rest of him was freezing. It was still rock-hard.

Shit.

Fuck.

Damn.

Mother—

Loud banging on his door, along with frantic screams for help, jolted him out of his cussing spree. After he shut the water off, he nearly slipped and busted his ass trying to get out of the shower in such a rush. When said ass-busting was safely deterred, he pulled on some pants and went to the door.

"What the hell is going on out here?" he demanded.

His heart stopped. He'd like to think it was the sight of Amy, of her sexy, plump breasts nearly spilling out of her low-cut tank top. But it was probably more the fact she nearly broke his nose when he'd opened the door.

Yeah, that's it, bonehead.

Not so gracefully avoiding her fists, which were still trying to pound on the now open door, he cleared his throat as she stared at him wide-eyed. "What?" he said gruffly, all too aware he was painfully hard now.

Her mouth flopped open a few times. "I—that is, um—"

"Hey!"

They both looked back at the stairs as a group of men approached. They looked pissed. Scott recognized them. He gritted his teeth. If it were up to him, he wouldn't rent any rooms out to a single college kid. Too many parties, too much illegal shit going on. They were just too much of a liability. Then again, so were a lot of older people. It was amazing how innocent some of them seemed on their applications and background checks, and how they really were to live with.

Scott grabbed Amy's wrist and gently pulled her toward his door. "Stay behind me," he said quietly as he stepped forward and crossed his thick, muscular arms to shield her from view. "Can I help you gentlemen?"

"That bitch fucking assaulted us!" one screeched and pointed a finger straight at Amy, who cringed behind him.

Scott nearly hauled off and decked the guy right there. His knuckles cracked as he formed fists. The backs of his hands were callused enough from tons of fighting.

Old habits die hard.

"I seriously doubt she assaulted you," he said coolly. "I'd like to know what *you* did."

The guy blinked. "Me?"

Scott raised a brow. "I could always ask Amy." He looked at her. "Did these men bother you?"

Amy stared at them warily. "They tried to pull me into their apartment," she said after a moment.

"We were having a party, man!" the guy said. "Bitch said she wanted to come."

"No, I didn't!" Amy yelled. "I wanted you to leave me alone!"

"So, let me get this straight." Scott cut the dick off before he could argue. "Not only are you throwing another party, after I explicitly warned you not to last month, but you tried to take this young woman inside against her will? What did you plan on doing with her?"

Amy turned pale, like, white-as-a-sheet kind of pale. She hugged herself, but not before he detected a tremble in her arms.

Scott's brows furrowed.

"We weren't gonna do nothin'!" Homeboy said. "Just have some fun with her."

That did it. Scott growled, grabbed a fistful of Homeboy's shirt, and slammed him against the wall so hard a painting fell off. "Listen here, you piece of shit," he growled in the man's terrified face, "you're going to leave this girl alone, and you and your roommates are gonna pack up all your shit tomorrow. Consider yourself evicted."

"Evicted?! But-But—"

"Shut up!" he yelled, slamming his head against the wall again for good measure. "This is the third report I've had of you trying to victimize innocent women. And I won't even get into all the other shit you've pulled. You've fucked up." Disgusted, he shoved the man toward his buddies, who caught him before he could fall down the stairs backward. "Now get the hell out of my face before I decide to call the cops."

"Let's go, man." One of the guys pulled him down the stairs. Now out of Scott's clutches, the man turned and gave him a death glare all the way back down the stairs.

Scott's chest heaved as he watched them go. Anger pumped through his veins. The urge to punch something returned, but he firmly shoved it down. He hadn't paid for all those anger management classes for nothing.

"Thank you."

Her voice was so quiet, he nearly missed it.

Amy stood next to the wall, hugging herself and shivering.

No, trembling. She looked terrified. Her head was ducked; wisps of hair hid her gaze from him as she stared at the floor.

The rage in him instantly died, replaced by concern. "Are you okay?"

She nodded and looked up. *Were those tears in her eyes?* Still not looking at him, she said, "I'm fine. He didn't hurt me. He never got the chance, thanks to you."

"It's nothing." He ran a hand through his still-damp hair. "Look, if you ever need anything, don't hesitate to ask. Especially don't hesitate to report shit like that."

She nodded, not saying anything.

He looked her over again and glanced at her door.

"You get locked out?"

"When...when they were after me, I dropped my keys on the stairs."

Assholes.

He reached in his pants pocket, took out a ring of keys he always kept on him, and opened up the door. "Wait here and lock the door. I'll be right back."

He went downstairs by himself to retrieve her things, thinking she'd had enough. The poor woman looked ready to jump out of her skin. People didn't just get that way by accident. *Must have gotten that way from the assault, or whatever happened to her.*

Once back upstairs, he knocked, and she cracked open the door. He handed her the keys. "Do you have pepper spray? And a cell phone?"

"I have pepper spray," she said, a slight warble to her voice. "And I have a cell, but I left it at home. It ran out of juice, and I don't have a car charger."

"I see." He pressed his lips together. "You have an Android?"

"Yes?"

He went back into his apartment and returned with a cell phone car charger, which he handed to her. "Here. It should work on most Android phones."

"I can't take this."

"Sure you can." He smiled. "I have a spare. I'll get another one. They're pretty cheap."

He lingered in front of her door, not quite willing to walk away yet. The urge to remain, to protect her, wouldn't go away.

But she's not yours to protect.

His shoulders fell. And she never would be. He had

too much baggage, and she seemed like she had her own problems to deal with.

"Well, good night." He turned and forced himself to walk back to his door, every fiber of his body aware she watched him as he left.

"I can't believe you didn't screw him." Becca sipped her cup of coffee.

They were walking back to Amy's car a few blocks over from their favorite coffee shop. Amy had run out for some more art supplies the next morning and had met up with Becca afterward for their weekly breakfast ritual.

Amy nearly choked on the donut she'd been in the process of swallowing.

"Easy, there." Becca gave her a mischievous look and slapped her on the shoulder a few times. "It's not like it didn't cross your mind."

"Well, yeah," Amy admitted between coughs. "But I'm...I'm not..." She took a deep breath and pressed it out. "I'm not ready to go there yet."

And probably never will be.

She shivered at the thought of sharing her body like that with someone again. Would anyone ever be as gentle a lover as Michael? Sure, he'd screwed up in a lot of other ways, but sex with him had always been amazing. Tender. Loving. She hadn't been with anyone since the day she'd come home to find...

She shook her head. "How are your birthday party plans coming along? Any idea of a venue yet?"

"Yep." Becca grinned. "Chains and Daggers."

A nervous tremble raced its way up Amy's legs. *Of course she would pick a club.* "Seriously?" She tried to play it cool and not freak out. "It's full of nothing but a bunch of horny Gothic wannabes." Chains and Daggers was a big club chain across the country. They'd had one back in her college town, too. She'd never been in the place, but she'd heard it had a dress code requirement: you had to be dressed in leather, with some sort of chain jewelry. Amy had no idea where the "Dagger" part of the club's name had come from. Someone probably thought it had sounded cool and decided to tack it on.

"That's why it will be fun! Besides, I've been dying to wear this killer leather dress I bought on consignment."

Amy rolled her eyes.

"Please tell me you're coming," Becca begged, grabbing her arm and pulling.

Amy groaned. She couldn't say no. Becca didn't have a whole lot of family support: her brother was too young to come, her father was in prison, and her mother was dead. But the thought of being around all those groping men made her blood run cold.

And a club was where she'd first met *him*, aka "the greatest mistake of her life."

"You could find some hot man candy," Becca sang.

"As if I'm searching for any," Amy grumbled.

A construction crew was digging into the sidewalk across the street, right in front of where they were parked. They must have just started work. Amy had seen cones, tape, and equipment when they first got out of the car, but not any workers.

It was already turning out to be a hot, humid day.

Most of the guys had their shirts pulled up or wore sleeveless tank tops. With that much exposed muscle, Amy and Becca both gawked appreciatively.

Becca's eyes stopped on one man. She slowly smiled. "Speaking of hot man candy..."

Amy looked up—and stared.

One man was cussing and pulling off a shirt that looked as if it had been blasted by sludge. Three other equally handsome men stood around, laughing. One of them held a long, ribbed tube dripping sludge, the other end of which snaked down into a manhole.

As soon as the man took his shirt off, he looked up. His eyes widened, but they were hardly what Amy noticed.

She couldn't take her eyes off his naked chest, the same chest that she saw in her next-door neighbor's apartment yesterday.

Scott blinked and gave her a breathless smile. "Looks are free. I charge for you to lick it."

Oh...

Her tongue raked over her lips, a movement she realized she'd done subconsciously, to her utter mortification, a few seconds later.

Damn. Oh, hot damn. Shit!

Scott—who shall henceforth be known as "Evil Hotness"—grinned like a fiend now.

Becca leaned in. "Dayuuuuuuummm, he is all sorts of hitting on you right now."

Amy gulped. "That can't happen."

"Why not?"

"Because that's my building manager. The guy I've told you about."

Famous last words, Amy realized too late.

A calculating look came over Becca's face.

"Hi!" she said brightly, interrupting Amy's silent meltdown. She stepped forward and extended her hand. "I'm Becca. So you're the hot neighbor I've heard so much about."

"Becca!" Amy hissed.

Scott raised a brow, smiling tightly as he shook Becca's hand. "Nothing but compliments, I'm sure."

Amy crossed her arms and returned his tight smile. "I still have paint in places that shouldn't have paint, thanks to you."

He shrugged. "You're the one who took the paint bucket lid off, sweetheart."

"Look," Becca said, with her win-over-any-man smile, "I know this is kind of short notice, but I'm having a birthday party day after tomorrow, and my friend here needs a date."

Amy slowly pieced together where this was going. "No, Becca—"

"And she mentioned thinking about going with you, but she was too shy to ask." Becca smiled sweetly, as though she were doing the most darling thing by trying to help out her friend.

Amy's jaw dropped.

Scott slowly grinned and looked at her. "Yeah, sure, I'll be your date."

"It's not a date!" Amy stuttered, still trying to get over the shock of what Becca had just done.

"So, you'll be there?" Becca asked hopefully, holding her breath.

With his eyes still on Amy's, he grinned. It was a wicked, sexy thing that made her clench. Those eyes were full of challenge as he said, "I wouldn't miss it."

"Excellent!" Becca squealed.

Amy bit her lip to keep from cursing Becca out as she gave him the details of the party. "Just pick my girl up at seven-ish."

"Seven-ish it is." He saluted.

Becca said good-bye to him and hauled Amy off. "Well, that went well."

"I'm going to kill you."

"You'll thank me later—once he's pounding you into the wall of a bathroom stall."

"Ew, can you please get your mind off sex for one second?"

Becca cackled like an evil Cupid and chattered about her theories on how good he was in bed.

An itch started in the back of Amy's mind, urging her to look behind her.

He probably isn't even looking.

She slowly looked over her shoulder.

To her surprise, those blue eyes followed her, watching her with the hunger of a predator eyeing its prey.

And, even more to her surprise and dismay, it only made her sexual cravings more restless as she forced herself to keep walking.

SIX

EVERY NIGHT, AMY had a ritual before she went to bed—she checked all the locks at least twice and made sure nothing was out of place or missing.

And every time she did, her gut twisted a little bit more.

The apartment was supposed to symbolize a new start, her revival from the darkness that still haunted her dreams. Yet here she was, still stuck in the same routine, unable to break these habits and lay old ghosts to rest.

The itch to keep looking out the window wouldn't leave either.

She swore someone was watching her. Always.

Though it had been two full years, and she knew Nathan had been obeying his restraining order, she couldn't help but keep looking.

And looking and looking and...

When was it going to end? Would she ever not be afraid?

Exhausted from a day of painting, she crawled into bed...and then crawled out again thirty seconds later to peek between the blinds. No dark figures lurked on street corners or in open view below the streetlamp.

The blinds snapped shut, and she made herself crawl back into bed and stay there. This was getting old.

So was Becca trying to set her up with someone.

Since getting back home, she'd opened up her new art supplies and had immediately started painting. She had a gallery showing later on this month, and she still had a few extra pieces she wanted to exhibit. Plus, she could turn them into digital prints and sell them through on-demand printing services, adding to her rapidly growing digital portfolio. The hunger to create had returned with a passion a few months back, and she'd rarely stopped painting since. She supposed a year and a half of creative silence had been all her body could stand. After the incident, she had stopped painting altogether. She had been broken.

Something must have healed, her therapist had said, when Amy mentioned she had started to paint again.

She wasn't sure about that, because she still felt like a train wreck inside, but if the therapist said so...

Flipping on the TV, she turned to one of her favorite mystery channels. It was mostly true crime, which she found fascinating in a morbid sort of way. Once darkness like that touches you, it's hard to let go.

The host, a pretty blond woman, went on about the most infamous celebrity murders. Amy watched about half of the program, her thoughts drifting off and her eyelids getting heavier, until a familiar story aired.

"And who can forget the tragic murder of rising rock star Michael Stone in New York City just two years ago?"

Amy stopped breathing. She bolted upright, suddenly wide awake.

A picture of a handsome man in his early twenties—blue eyes, spiky black hair, and enough metal in his face and ears to trip a metal detector—flashed on the screen. He clasped the hand of a smiling brunette girl with a lot of dramatic makeup, her engagement ring catching the light of the camera.

Amy stared. She looked so different then, before she'd dyed her hair to help obscure her identity and gained about thirty pounds from comfort food binges.

She reached for the remote and fumbled with the power button as her hand shook.

"The couple, who were college sweethearts, were due to be wed the following morning, when tragedy struck."

She managed to hit power before the host could go on. Once the TV was off, Amy sat in the darkness, breathing heavily. Tears pricked her eyes.

Was there anywhere she could go where she wouldn't be haunted? If she hadn't been about to get married to a freaking rock star, the whole goddamned country would not have taken notice.

She'd wanted to stay out of the attention of the media, to forget and move on. But no, the media just loved a good story, not caring how it might be twisting a knife in the side of the victims.

Michael's gone. He's gone, and he's never coming back.

Rolling over and bunching her pillow, she cried until she passed out, the face of her dead fiancé burned in her mind.

45

Becca was officially on Amy's shit list.

It was the night of the party, and she had about a half hour left to get ready. The thought of setting foot in another nightclub made her nauseous, so she'd busied herself with picking out the perfect outfit. But because of the Epically Evil Invite, every piece of clothing in her wardrobe had suddenly become inadequate.

Nothing was nearly sexy enough to rival Evil Hotness's innate sexiness. Keeping up with the club's theme, she'd found a leather pencil skirt and a sparkly black-and-silver top at a discount clothing store. Thinking the two didn't go that well together after all, she'd tugged them off and tossed them onto the floor with the rest of her discarded pile.

Running out of options, she looked at her bed. A dress, if you could call it that, lay across her bedspread. It was made entirely of an inky vinyl so shiny she could see her reflection in it. Granted, it wasn't real vinyl; the material was way too supple, and actually quite thin, to be the real deal. She'd bought some black lipstick and had painted her toes and nails black to match.

But...it was so skimpy. She'd never worn anything that revealing before. It was a halter top, which she knew looked good on her body shape, but the neckline went down to the top of her stomach. It had a built-in bra—sort of, the padding was so thin—so she wouldn't need one of those. Which was probably a good thing, considering the back was completely open. The top of the zipper was at the small of her back. It showed off her curves and somehow made her waistline look smaller, both perks. But the skirt barely covered her ass, it was so short.

You only live once.

Sucking it up, she pulled the dress on. Her hair and makeup were already done, as was her jewelry. This was the final piece.

With a deep breath to yank her gut in, she zipped up the dress. It snagged within an inch on her black lace underwear. Becca had encouraged her to go panty-less, but Amy wasn't quite that brave yet.

Now, she wished she had been. She cursed as the zipper pulled at her panties and threatened to tear them. Swearing, she tried to angle herself so that she could see the snag in the bathroom mirror, when the doorbell buzzed.

She gasped. *What time was it? It couldn't be...* Never wanting to run late for anything, she had clocks everywhere. Glancing at the little one on her bathroom wall, she nearly swallowed her tongue. It was seven.

Scott. It had to be him.

And here she was, with her zipper caught on her underwear.

"Shit! Shit, shit, dammit..."

Swearing under her breath, she frantically tried to unlatch herself from the zipper but kept failing.

The doorbell buzzed again, and she jumped. She couldn't keep him waiting.

Not seeing any other way, she said, "Oh, to hell with it," and opened the door wide.

Hot. Damn.

Scott had worn black leather pants and a dark-blue satin button-up shirt. A silver chain drooped from his front pants pocket to his back. His hair had been spiked slightly on the ends, making him look younger—and hot as hell. A leather bracelet with silver studs was fastened onto his wrist.

The word "hi" dried up in her mouth as she stared.

It took her awhile to notice that it was silent.

That *he* stared *back*.

His eyes slowly raked over her, inch by inch. Her breath quickened, and heat pooled between her legs, making her clench deep within.

His gaze stopped at her arm, and he raised a brow. "Need a hand?"

"What? Oh, um—"

Before she could say anything, he'd stepped forward and turned her gently so her back faced him. He gripped the zipper, unsnagged her panties, and slowly slid it up. His fingers grazed her bare skin, and she sighed low as she leaned her hips into him.

It had gotten quiet. Really quiet.

The sound of his ragged breathing, coupled with the hot brush of his breath against the bare skin of her shoulders, made her hot with need.

Clearing his throat, he abruptly turned around. "Ready?" he said gruffly.

She wasn't expecting the wave of disappointment at his dismissal.

When she saw the slight bulge around his crotch, she understood why he'd turned around.

With a nervous, pleasant fluttering in her chest that hadn't been there before, she smiled. "Yeah. Bring it on."

SEVEN

H E'D GOTTEN HARD for her. Again.

Thank God he'd still had enough blood flowing to his brain to have the decency to turn around and hide his erection. If she'd noticed anything, she hadn't said a word on the drive over.

Or once they were in the club. Actually, she'd ditched him the moment they'd walked through the door, as if she couldn't get away fast enough.

Scott hung out by the bar, idly sipping his gin and tonic, and watched everyone grind on the dance floor. The party was huge. According to Becca, who was decked out in chains and purple leather, most of the people on the floor were there for her. Scott watched them laugh and act wild.

It must be nice to have that many friends. He wouldn't know. He hadn't exactly been the popular kid throughout his school years, not coming into his looks until he was well into his twenties. Suddenly, it wasn't hard to get a date. In fact, he had women begging *him* for dates. They had started to pay a ton of attention to him, but by then he'd been burned enough to learn to guard his heart.

Some techno tune with way too much ramped-up bass rattled the speakers and floor; his bones hummed. He couldn't even tell what the lyrics were. It was some weird mixture of rap and death metal; it was gonna take serious surgery for that singer—if you could call him that—not to completely eviscerate his vocal cords with that much screaming. Scott loved heavy metal—when done well. Hell, he had a whole collection of screamers at home, one CD of which he usually kept on repeat in his tricked-out stereo system he bought for fifty bucks off a buddy of his. But this shit...

He took a larger swig and flagged down the bartender. "Another, please, man."

"You got it." The buff blond guy went to work at mixing his poison. He cast Scott a wry look. "You here looking for some action? I'm still sending Molly that picture I took of you earlier, by the way. You look like you belong on a romance novel cover."

Scott snorted. The bartender, Jace, was one of his oldest friends. They'd gone to high school together, and Jace had even married his high school sweetheart, Molly. "Go ahead," Scott said. "But don't blame me—or my awesome leather pants—when she leaves your ass because I'm so good-looking. And no." He frowned as he searched the sea of people again. "I'm with someone."

Jace raised a brow. "Oh? You dating again, man?"

Scott's jaw ticked, and something inside him froze up at the word "dating." He shrugged.

Jace studied him, quiet for a second. "I'm glad you're

at least out and about. You need to be around people, and women, Scott. Not everyone is like Erika."

It was as if Scott had been shocked. Memories of a screaming match, followed by his knuckles beating the living hell out of every breakable thing in the room, started to resurface, but he firmly shoved them down. That mess was something he'd dealt with a long time ago.

He downed the rest of his drink. "I'm gonna go outside for a smoke."

Jace gave him a knowing look, which only made Scott want to run away even more. He couldn't stand people looking at him with sympathy. It was his own fault for what had happened. He should have seen Erika for the lying, thieving whore she was. He wasn't hurting from her betrayal, not anymore.

And so help him God, no one would ever hurt him that way again.

So what the hell was he doing here?

He turned to walk outside to the smoking area and had taken one full step before he nearly slammed into a petite blonde sporting too much spray-on tan. She had been standing right behind him. Her hand was still raised, her finger poised as if to tap him on the shoulder.

"Oh!" she yelped and blinked several times. "Hi, there!"

He winced. *Had she sucked helium?* Her voice sounded as if it belonged to a hamster.

"Hi..." Scott eyed her warily. *What the hell did she want?*

The girl was cute, in an over-the-top girly kind of way. She wore hot-pink leather with delicate diamond chains on her shoulders for straps and around her waist as a belt. A pink riding crop was secured on her belt, along with sparkly handcuffs lined in hot-pink fur.

If Barbie were into BDSM...

The girl waited a moment for him to speak. You'd think glitter was going out of style, she had so much of it on: in her eye shadow, in her powder, on her lips. Her face was so sparkly, it could rival a disco ball.

"Hi!" she repeated with a broad smile. Some of her glittery lipstick had rubbed off on her bleached-white teeth; glitter gathered in the cracks between her teeth.

All he could do was stare.

"Um, so, like, do you want to dance?" she said, that annoyingly perky smile still plastered on her glittered face.

He managed to smile back, though the motion felt too tight. "Sorry, but I'm here with someone."

"Oh?" She made a point of looking around. "But I haven't seen you with anyone all night."

His teeth gritted. If it was one thing he couldn't stand, it was pushy girls. "Sorry, but like I said, I have a date." He decided to let her off easy and not be such a dick. "I'm sure there are plenty of men here who'd love to dance with you," he added. Hell, he even put in more effort with the smile.

Wrong move. Barbie took that as flirting. "But I want to dance with you," she whined with a pout.

Oh hell no. She was probably some seventeen-year-old girl who'd snuck out of mommy and daddy's mansion, expecting to be obeyed and treated like a queen wherever she went. He leaned in and narrowed his eyes. "Well, we can't always get what we want, can we, cupcake?"

He started past her when she latched onto his arm. Her nails dug in. "Hey, you think you can just walk away?

No one turns me down!'"

"Sounds like he just did."

They both turned to find Amy a few feet away. Scott's heart fluttered. Dammit, he did not have time for this pittery-pattery shit. Warning bells went off in his brain, which his sex promptly ignored. He felt it lengthen and harden, squeezing against the tight leather of his pants. Good thing it was dark as night in here, save for Barbie's face.

His heart pounded harder as Amy sauntered near. He couldn't take his eyes off the sensual sway of her wide hips, nor deny how the way the leather pulled at her thighs was hot as hell. He wanted to ride her skirt up, see if her thighs were as smooth and creamy as he imagined they would be.

Barbie rounded on Amy. "Who the hell are you?"

Amy walked right up to him, stopped, looked at Barbie's nails digging into his arm, and pried her hand loose. She then nuzzled next to him and put a hand to his chest. "I'm his date, Tinker Bell."

Barbie stared, mouth wide open. Scott did, too, with much the same expression. Dear Lord, if he wasn't hard before, he positively throbbed with need now. The slight buzz he was riding didn't help his raging hormones any.

Amy grabbed his hand. "Come on. Let's dance."

She pulled him away as Barbie continued to stare. Scott was surprised he didn't see smoke come out of her ears; it looked as if her brain had fried.

Amy guided him through the throng of gyrating bodies, most of which were stuck together so tightly, you'd think they were trying to fuse into one person.

When they were well away from Barbie, Amy

dropped his hand. "You're welcome." She poked a finger into his chest. She turned and started toward one of the many bars in the joint.

"Whoa." Scott caught her wrist to stop her. "How many have you had tonight?" She'd started chugging wine, martinis, whatever she could get her hands on, the moment they entered the club.

"What does it matter?" she snapped, jerking her hand free. "You're not my boss."

"But I am your date." He stepped in front of her to block her path. "And I care what happens to you."

She blinked, looking surprised.

"That is," he added quickly as his face flushed, "what kind of a date would I be if I let you get roofied or something?"

She rolled her eyes. "Get over yourself, Prince Charming. You're not my date. You were just another victim of Becca's scheming." She started to go around him, but he blocked her path again. She glared. "Would you please move?"

"No." He grinned. "Not until you dance with me."

"Not happening."

"Come on. Just one?"

"No."

"But you just said you wanted to dance with me."

She sighed and rubbed her temples. "That was just an excuse to get you away from Barbie. I didn't actually want to dance." She glanced at the dancers. Longing briefly flashed in her eyes.

He studied her, a slight smirk on his face. "You sure about that?"

"Positive." She leaned forward. "I. Do. Not. Want.

54

To. Dance. How many times do I have to say it?"

"As many as it takes to wear you down." He pressed his lips together in thought and looked around. "I could always go fetch Barbie, or one of the other women." He caught a pair of brunettes eyeing him with wide, flirtatious smiles from the wall. They turned to each other when they caught him looking, and giggled. "Actually, I don't know how much longer this not dancing thing can last. The natives are getting pretty restless. I might not be able to fend them off much longer."

Her shoulders tensed, and she looked away. "Go ahead. I thought Malibu over there was getting on your nerves, and you looked like you could use rescuing. But hey, maybe I was wrong. Dance with whomever you like. I don't care."

She shoved him out of the way, or at least, she tried to. It did about as much good as trying to move a mountain.

Her palms were pressed flat against his chest. That must have been what flipped his "stupid switch." Or the alcohol. Either way, he sure as hell wasn't thinking straight.

He didn't waste a second. He seized her wrists and twirled her around. She yelped as her back smacked into his chest; he gripped her hips and rocked them to the rhythm of the tune.

"What are you doing?" She wriggled against him in a feeble attempt to break free.

The friction against his hardened sex only made him want to groan. "This is your payback," he breathed.

"For what?"

He lowered his head until his lips grazed her neck.

She gasped. He moved his lips along the curve between her neck and shoulder. Her skin was smooth, and slightly salty from the exertion of dancing. "For teasing me earlier with that stuck zipper. It was very clever."

"What the hell are you talking about? Are you drunk?"

"No. But from how you're starting to slur, it kind of sounds like you are."

"I am not!" It sounded more like, "Immanah!" He held on to her to keep her from falling over. Good Lord, heels that high should come with a health warning: *Likely to break an ankle or possibly fall on some pavement and crack skull open.*

"Easy," he murmured next to her ear. It didn't even bother him anymore that her hair was blond, he was so into her: her spunk, her soft, curvy body, and the way her breasts bunched in the tight, inky dress.

Beautiful.

All around them, couples let their hands rove over each other's bodies. Some hands found themselves in some very private places. He wished hers would.

She had relaxed in his arms some; her body molded against his and moved to the rhythm. Those beautiful, lush breasts rose and fell with her quickened breaths.

"Not finding me so vile anymore?" he asked.

She stiffened, and he mentally swore.

Spoke too soon.

"No," she said, "I still think you're an asshole. I'm going to have yellow paint caked under my nails for the rest of my life."

"And whose fault is that?"

She turned her head up to glare at him. It would be so

easy to tip his head, close his lips over hers...

Focus.

"Yours," she said, as if this should be obvious. "You pressed my buttons."

He grinned and pulled her closer. "And what kind of buttons am I pressing now?"

She blinked a few times, startled, and looked away. A haunted expression came over her face that bothered him deeply. "You can quit flirting with me now. It's not going to happen."

"What's not?"

"You. Me. Us. This. Whatever this is."

The brief sting of disappointment was quickly replaced by a spark of determination. "Come on. You can't tell me the leather pants don't turn you on at least a little bit."

"Nope. Not even a little."

Liar, liar. He leaned in, his voice a husky whisper. "That's not what your nipples are telling me." The fake vinyl material of the dress was actually pretty exposing, it was so tight. He brushed his palm over one tight knot at the crest of her breast. She sighed as she leaned into his touch, rubbing her breast against his hand.

He took it as an invitation. His breathing quickened as he continued to tease her nipples, one at a time. "Do you like this?" he whispered.

What. The. Hell. Was. Happening?

Her body was losing control. Well, scratch that. The

barrel of tequila she'd consumed in thirty minutes flat had wiped out whatever brain function she'd had, including her determination to stay away from Evil Hotness. She'd thought drinking alcohol like water would drown her worries about entering the club and being so close to Scott, but clearly, that little plan had backfired.

Way to go, genius. For the record, alcohol=horny.

The boldness of his caress had surprised her—and then set her blood on fire. God, she'd never wanted anything more in her life than to find a dark corner, rip his pants off, and plant her sex on the rock-hard erection that currently rubbed against her ass.

"Yes, I like it," she breathed, taking his hands to guide them to both her breasts. She cupped her hands around his, making him palm both breasts. "I also like this."

He groaned and squeezed, slowly kneading her lush, soft mounds. She sighed with pleasure and threw her head back as she began to rock against him. It felt so damned good to be touched. His touch made her feel alive. The thought that this was a bad idea nagged her at the back of her mind, but it was far away. She didn't want to let go of this sense of being wanted, of being desired. It was addicting.

How long had it been since she'd let herself go, to not worry, and just feel? After what happened, she thought she'd only be able to feel that way while painting. If she won the lottery next week, it couldn't be more unexpected than this.

She was so taken with him that she hadn't realized he'd slipped a hand under her neckline until she felt the hot, callused skin of his hand caress her breast. She mewled and writhed against him as he kissed her neck. His lips were hot against her sweat-dampened skin. Or maybe it was the rush of flames heating her blood that made her feverish. She felt herself grow wetter with need; her sex throbbed in rhythm to every hot pulse of her blood.

Speaking, let alone thinking, was incredibly hard while he worked his lip voodoo. "You must think me a wanton woman," she breathed.

"Not at all," he replied, his deep voice ragged. "And I'm in no position to judge if you were."

"I'm not." She wondered why she felt the need to justify her character. Good, sweet little Amy. Never strayed too far from the safety of the sidelines.

Never lived a little.

Her life was pretty gray. Dull. Boring.

Safe.

Her world had started to be painted in Technicolor when Michael literally crashed into it, and look how well that had turned out.

Now, it was happening again. Vibrant splashes of color started to appear in her gray world, in the form of the hot man whose touch scalded her.

The over-amped bass thrumming in her blood and the party cries of the crowd faded to a low hum, accented by the strong throb of her heart. She closed her eyes and savored the feeling of his hands touching her in places she never thought she'd let a man touch again.

She should have been scared to be that intimate. Or, at least, she thought she would have been.

But she wasn't. She'd like to think it was because he made her feel so relaxed, but it was probably just the alcohol.

"Come back to my place," he whispered.

She thought about it for two seconds. She wasn't that drunk yet, no matter how badly her body screamed, "Hell to the yes!" "Nah."

"Why not?" Another kiss.

She sighed. "Because I don't sleep with strangers. And I guess that's what you are, technically, since I don't know a thing about you."

He tensed. "You don't want to. I'm high-risk."

"Oh?" Sensing the mood was ruined, she stepped away from him and raised her brows. "Because you're so big and bad?"

"No." A cocky grin came over his face. "Because once you go Scott, you never go back."

"Dork. That doesn't even rhyme." She rolled her eyes and crossed her arms. "I bet you'd be a horrible date. You'd probably talk about yourself all night."

He raised a brow. "Have I been a horrible date to-night?"

"I don't count this as a date since I was forced into it."

"All right," he said after a pause, eyes glittering. "Want to find out?"

"Find out what?"

"How I am on a real date?"

She stopped and stared at him. "I thought you just said you didn't want me to get to know you. That it's too high-risk or something."

"Well, maybe I don't think straight around you."

She waited for another cocky grin, or some sign that he was messing with her. But the look in his eyes was dead serious.

60

Warnings went off in her head. Her self-preservation instinct kicked in. *Walk away!* it screamed.

She couldn't move. Unable to comprehend what he'd just said, she pressed her lips together and shifted her weight. "I thought you didn't like me."

"Correction: I didn't like you painting my walls without permission. And yellow, of all things." He shuddered.

"What's wrong with yellow?"

"It's hideous, for starters."

"And what would you prefer? Black?"

"Like my soul," he said in a deep, monotone voice.

She snorted and bit her lip. "I don't know..."

"Come on. One date. We don't even have to call it that."

"You're my building manager. Isn't that a conflict of interest or something?"

"I just think of it as convenient."

She rolled her eyes. Indecision weighed on her chest.

He held up a finger. "All I'm asking for. We can keep it casual. Lunch, maybe. Start slow, if you want?"

Slow.

Was she ready for slow? Was she ready for anything?

She shivered, both from excitement and fear. She hadn't had a date since Michael was taken from her. It had taken a long time for the gaping hole in her chest to feel like a heart again, for emotion to return, and for her actually to feel anything other than numbness and shock.

Remember, this is Amy 2.0. The old Amy would run. What would the new Amy do? What do you *want to do?*

Her therapist said, "Change doesn't happen by staying the same. Change happens when you take risks."

The answer became crystal-clear.

Praying this wasn't going to be a colossal disaster, she whispered, "Okay."

EIGHT

FOUR A.M. WAS an ungodly hour for most people, but not for the Watcher. His bedroom window was the only one lit up on the block. While his neighbors slept, he felt wide awake. More alive.

Except tonight. Tonight, he felt absolutely crushed.

The Watcher opened the worn leather journal and positioned the tip of his pen to the first blank line.

Entry 408

Amy didn't see me tonight.

She didn't even look my way once.

Goddamned bitch. How can she forget about me so easily? I might as well not even exist.

Tears stained the paper.

I am such an idiot. All this time, she hasn't seen anyone. I thought maybe...maybe she was waiting for me.

Does she know how much I love her? Does she know how badly I ache to be with her?

The pen in his hand shook with his rising anger. It

63

was always there, lurking below the surface, threatening to spill over into rage.

Bitch. After all I've done for her, how can she dismiss me so easily? She won't ever forget about me again. From now on, she'll look my way. I'll make her notice me.

I have to—because she's mine.

NINE

R ED OR BLACK?

It was a simple question, a choice really, and yet the hardest decision she'd had to make since leaving home.

Amy stared at the bra-and-panty sets laid out neatly on her bedspread.

Her date with Scott was tonight, in approximately two hours. She'd already showered and done her hair, nails, and makeup, just because she was anxious and couldn't help obsessing over every single microscopic detail. Because of this, the process of getting ready had taken twice as long.

Just thinking about tonight made the wine she'd drunk earlier threaten to come back up.

Nerves wracked her body. Why the hell did she agree to do this?

Take it easy, her subconscious said. *You're going on a date, not being shipped off to war.*

Amy groaned and fell backward onto the bed. She threw her arm over her eyes, shielding them from the overhead light.

She wasn't ready for this. Not now, not ever.

It didn't matter that two years had passed. When she closed her eyes, she could still feel Michael's arms wrapped around her, could still smell the cool, minty cologne he wore. In her dreams, she heard his voice.

The pain was still fresh, too. The night she'd found out his darkest secret, the one that sent her perfect world spiraling straight to hell.

January 14, 2013.

The day Michael Stone, formerly known as Michael Lewis, was murdered.

Her throat closed up as her heart pounded harder. Fear ran in icy currents down her veins.

She shouldn't have any reason to be afraid now. Nathan was across the country, under close watch of his parole officer. He couldn't hurt her anymore. He hadn't tried contacting her since he had gotten out of prison.

So why was she still so afraid?

Her therapist's words came back to her. *Work through the fear. Don't let it, or the past, control you.*

Recognizing that she was getting caught up in the past—and thus, that paralyzing fear that refused to release her—Amy forced herself to sit up and shake her head. Sweat had started to bead on her forehead and just underneath her eyes, making her face feel oily.

"Great," she muttered with a long sigh.

Hi, Scott. I decided to sport the crack whore look tonight. Sexy, huh?

Not wanting to let her makeup run, she hopped up

from bed and padded into the bathroom to spruce up her makeup. Coming back out to the bedroom, she'd done a quick round of "eeny, meeny, miny, moe" and tugged on the black underwear set, when there was a loud screeching noise from outside.

What on earth?

She went to one of the bedroom windows, the one with the lovely view of the garbage-riddled alley below, and looked down.

It was hard to tell, considering it was getting dark, but there appeared to be four teenage boys standing there. She recognized them. They lived in the next-door building, and they were all little shits. They'd woken her up one morning, putting graffiti on the side of her building with crude artwork. She also saw them picking on smaller kids and stealing their things.

Her blood boiled when she saw the source of the screeching.

It was a tiny kitten, solid black with white boots.

And the kids were apparently trying to light its fur on fire.

Shock made her immobile for a second. A flash of movement from the building across from her caught her eye; someone had looked out the window and had drawn their blinds.

Un-freaking-believable. They weren't even going to help a poor, defenseless kitten.

Her nails dug into the windowsill. Like hell she was going to just stand around and ignore it.

Knotting her robe, she slipped on some flip-flops, snatched her keys off the counter and an aluminum baseball bat from the living room corner, and hauled ass down to the alley.

The poor kitten's tortured wails seemed twice as loud out here.

An elderly couple walked by the alley, not even turning their heads to the noise.

Seriously, what the hell was wrong with people? Didn't anybody have the guts anymore at least to attempt to do the right thing?

She sprinted around the corner and lifted the bat. "Hey, assholes!"

They were all gathered around the kitten, snickering. One held it up by the tail, its little bloodied paws flailing about, while another held the lighter directly under its face.

Bile rose in her throat at the smell of singed fur, along with a heaping of rage.

Her fists shook around the bat, making her knuckles turn white. It took every ounce of control she had not to charge them and beat the living hell out of every single one of them.

They all looked up at her—and laughed.

"What are you doing, bitch?" The boy's voice was still high-pitched; he must not have undergone puberty yet.

Already off to a great start in life. Where the hell were these kids' parents?

She probably didn't want to know the answer to that question.

"Put him down," she barked. Her anger made her voice strong.

"Or you'll what? Club us?" one sneered.

"If that's what it takes," she hissed, never backing down.

The boys behind him whistled low and snickered.

"Kitten's got claws," the tallest boy said, the one who held the kitty by the tail.

"Last warning," she growled.

The boys shook their heads. One of them rolled his eyes and muttered, "Dumb bitch."

Her eyes narrowed. "Suit yourself."

She swung.

Whap!

"OW!" The tip of the bat nailed the tall kid on the wrist. His fingers flew open, and the kitten dropped to the ground. After it landed on all fours, it scampered to a nearby Dumpster.

The other three boys' jaws dropped as they stared at their howling comrade. He clutched at his hand, and tears formed in his eyes. "Bitch!" he screamed. "You frickin' broke my wrist!"

"Serves you right, for what you did to that poor kitten!" She hefted the bat. "Who's next?"

The others froze and gazed at her warily. The tall boy seethed, starting toward her, but one of the boys pulled at his arm. "Let's go, man. Bitch is fucking crazy."

"That's right!" she yelled as they ran away toward the opposite end of the alley. "Remember that the next time one of you little punks decides to mug somebody or abuse an animal! I'M WATCHING YOU!"

Her screams echoed down the alley, chasing the boys as they disappeared from view.

She waited a few seconds, breathing hard, before she lowered the bat.

The wind picked up at her back, and she heard the scrape of an aluminum can as it skittered across the sidewalk.

She instinctively looked over her shoulder in the direction of the sound.

Her heart stopped.

There, under the streetlamp, stood a tall, lean figure in a dark hoodie and jeans. Some kind of symbol was on the chest of the hoodie. It was hard to make out details from across the street in the low lighting, but his hair looked spiky. It would have been a little less creepy if his hair color had been anything other than red.

No, auburn. Just like Nathan's.

But that was impossible. Nathan was in New York, a whole country away. His parole officer said he'd been to therapy and hadn't violated the terms of his restraining order. That meant staying the hell away from her and her family.

See, Amy? It can't be Nathan.

A group of giggling teenage girls raced past him to a nearby bus stop. He didn't even move out of their way or flinch.

Instead, he continued to stare at Amy. His lips slowly spread into a wide smile.

Something glinted from his bottom lip...a lip ring?

The fear she'd felt earlier returned, making her blood run cold.

Nathan had had a lip ring, too, in that exact same spot. Or was it on his upper lip? She had to be drawing her own connections again. Her therapist had said when dealing with trauma, especially the fear of being stalked, that it was easy to see threats where there weren't any, leading to paranoia.

But this...this fear was palpable. Reasonable.

Deep down in her bones, she had the sense this man

wanted to *hurt* her.

Run.

She blinked as the bus rolled in front of her and blocked the man from view. The girls climbed on, and a moment later, the bus drove off.

With a heavy dose of apprehension, Amy's eyes lifted to the spot directly across from her, over on the other side of the street.

Her breath left her.

The man was gone.

A tiny, scratchy meow floated up from her feet.

Crap, that's right. She'd forgotten the reason she'd come out here in the first place.

As she cast one last look over her shoulder, she knelt to the kitten that rubbed up against her legs. "Hi, little fella," she cooed as she rubbed his back. She had a little flashlight on her keychain ring. Shining it on the kitten's head, her heart squeezed as she spied a patch of singed fur and blistered skin. It had to be in pain, but the little kitten's purr motor ran up a storm.

"Animal lover, I take it?"

She yelped and turned. Scott stood at the mouth of the alley, a brown paper bag full of groceries in one arm and a gallon of milk in the other.

As if it would calm her galloping heart, she placed a hand to her chest and heaved a heavy sigh. "You scared the shit out of me."

He raised a brow. "I can tell. Everything all right?" He approached her as he spoke.

The kitten trotted up to him and meowed.

He smiled. "Hey there, cutie. Sorry, I can't pet you. My hands are a bit full."

Amy went into the story of how she heard the kitten crying for help and had raced outside like a lunatic to save it.

Scott was laughing by the time she'd finished. "Good, I hope you did break that punk's hand. Teach him not to mess with defenseless creatures. I swear, those kids are gonna end up in juvie or worse."

The kitten wove in and out of Amy's legs, purring the whole time and arching its back.

She glanced at her watch. Her conscience tugged at her. Biting her lip, she said, "Do you mind if we postpone our date until a little later tonight? They burned this little guy, and I'd feel guilty just leaving him here to possibly get infected." She shuddered. "Or leaving him at their mercy, if they decide to come back and finish what they started."

Anger burned in Scott's eyes. "Like hell we're letting that happen, right?"

She smiled. "Really? You don't mind pushing the date back so I can take him to the vet?"

"Nah. I need to do more good deeds. Build up my good karma and all that." He winked. "Come on. I know of a place nearby we can take him. You have a cat carrier?"

She winced. "No."

"S'kay. I think I have one stashed away in the Lost and Found section in the office. A lot of people leave, trying to escape paying late rent, and they leave behind a lot of shit. You'd be surprised, sometimes, what they forget, or don't care, to take with them. I've gotten nice watches, sixty-inch televisions, CD collections..."

She scooped up the kitten and walked with him to the

front of the building. "Wow. Sounds like a waste."

"Yeah. I'm sure grateful for it, though." He grinned. "I've furnished half my apartment with all their unclaimed stuff."

She playfully shoved him. "I'm sure you are *very* grateful."

Once inside the building, they stopped by the office to get the cat carrier, and then he walked her to her apartment.

"I'm going to go put this up"—he hefted up the groceries—"then I'll drive us to the animal clinic."

"Sounds good." She shifted her weight. "You sure you don't mind going with me? You don't have to."

"I don't mind," he said instantly. "But I'd say later, you owe me a kiss."

He winked and left, leaving Amy standing there, her face hotter than the sun.

A kiss. Something so simple and sweet. A gesture most adults who'd regularly dated probably didn't place too much emphasis on.

Except, she wasn't like most adults. She had a dark past.

And she knew from experience a kiss could be the equivalent of aiming a gun at her heart and pulling the trigger.

TEN

THAT EVENING AND nearly two hundred dollars later, the kitten had received veterinary care, a microchip, and a whole heaping of love. All the staff at the animal hospital had fallen in love with the kitten, showering him with sympathies, kisses, and hugs.

The vet assured Amy and Scott the kitten—a little boy Amy had named "Braveheart"—had suffered no permanent damage, other than that to his coat. The fur on his head would probably never grow right, because the boys had singed the hair follicles. He may even have a bald spot the rest of his life.

Asshole kids.

True to his word, Scott drove her and the now-bandaged-up kitten to and from the vet. They stopped by a dollar store to buy a litter box, some litter, and other kitty essentials, before they headed back to the apartment. Once settled in Amy's apartment, the little guy made himself right at home. He purred and purred and followed Amy around, taking the opportunity to brush up on her legs when she was standing still. She already loved him to pieces.

So. Freaking. Cute.

Her sister would love him. She made a mental note to text her a picture later.

Wanting to be polite, she'd offered Scott a drink when they got back to her place. They both stood in the kitchen, sipping on ice water and soda. "So, you know," he said casually, "this building has a strict no-pets policy. Granted, people still try to sneak them in…"

Amy choked on her water. After a coughing fit that had her eyes burning, she wheezed, "Are you serious? There's a freaking no-pets policy?"

Panic set in. What would she do with the little guy? She couldn't send him to the pound, most likely to be euthanized. She didn't know anyone who could take him. Becca was allergic to cats. And sending him back onto the streets seemed cruel and would most likely end up in the kitten's execution, should those boys seek revenge.

Scott chuckled. Her eyes snapped to him, seeing that mischievous sparkle she saw earlier.

"What are you laughing at?" Amy said, distraught. "This is horrible!"

Scott calmly finished off his soda and deposited the can in the garbage bin. He backed toward the door. "I'm going to go finish getting ready, then I'll be over here to pick you up in fifteen minutes for our date." His eyes darted to the kitten and back to her. "It'll be the first time I've seen you all day."

Amy quickly caught on. Just to make sure she heard him straight, she said casually, "So you never saw me in the alley."

"No."

"And you never saw a kitten."

"What kitten?"

Her face broke out into a wide smile.

And just like that, she felt herself falling for him.

Scott tapped the side of Amy's half-empty mug. "I'm so ahead of you right now." He raised his frothy glass and downed the rest of his beer before he pitched a dart at the board in front of them. For at least the tenth time that night, the dart struck dead center. Amy had teased him that his darts were rigged. "I'm, like, two glasses ahead of you, and I'm just getting fuzzed."

Amy snorted as he went to pull his darts out of the board. "You mean 'buzzed'? And yeah, I'm not buying that for a second." She frowned. "It's not fair. Your aim seems to be improving the more intoxicated you get, while mine's going down."

He pretended to fling an air dart. "All in the wrist, baby."

She laughed. "You're a dork."

The bar they were in was a dive, no doubt: scratched-up, checkered flooring from the seventies, an old jukebox that barely lit up anymore, tables and chairs with broken legs, and about a gazillion motorcycle pictures plastered to the walls. Motorcycle parts hung from the ceiling, the chrome glittering in the dim lighting.

They were about half a block away from the apartment. Not wanting to leave the injured kitten alone for too long, they'd opted to stay fairly close. She'd almost told him that she didn't feel like going. Ultimately, she knew that would have been an excuse to chicken out. But once she was here and riding a little alcohol high...she was actually enjoying herself. Scott was surprisingly easy to talk to. Just like he'd promised, he'd kept the date casual. They'd played pool for about an hour and had been playing darts for the past forty-five minutes or so. It almost felt like hanging out with a friend.

A very sexy friend she'd like to ride.

Scott held up his glass. "Hey, Jimmy!" he called over his shoulder. "Get me another, would you?"

"Yes, sir," the young man behind the counter said with a grin and a shake of his head.

Amy smiled gently and sipped her beer. Her tolerance had gone way down since her drinking binge right after the incident. It had taken six whole months to finally give up drinking, after an intervention from Becca and her family. "So, how long have you worked here?" she asked politely. She tossed another dart at the dartboard. The tip hit the thing at an angle and bounced off into a nearby trash bin.

Scott went to retrieve her wayward darts. "Eh, on and off for about the past six months." He shrugged as he handed them to her. "Bartending isn't my dream job, but it's good supplementary income. It gets pretty crowded on the weekends, which is the only time I work, so tips are good."

Amy nodded. "Let me see if I got this right: you work business days at the apartment, work construction during the weekend days, and you bartend Friday, Saturday, and Sunday night?"

"Yup."

"That's...impressive. I wish I had that kind of work ethic."

His eyes narrowed slightly as he stared at the dartboard. "It's not easy."

"I'll bet." She wondered why he had to work so many jobs. Did he have bad debt? Oh God, what if he had a gambling habit, or a drug addiction, and needed the money to fund it?

"I have a lot of bills," he said with a sigh. "Leftover from an ex of mine."

That sucked, but at least it wasn't about gambling or drugs. "Oh?"

Jimmy brought over another glass and took away the old one. Scott's posture seemed noticeably tenser than before. "Yeah. I was her sponsor. Well, sort of. I tried to be, but neither of us belonged to any groups, so it was never official or anything. Not that I'm much better. She had a shitty childhood, and I took pity on her. She didn't have much, was living on the streets, actually. She'd gotten in deep with a few bad people. I felt sorry for her, so I loaned her some money to help get her on her feet. Turns out she was just blowing it on drugs."

"Damn, that's harsh. I'm sorry."

He shrugged but made no reply.

She pressed her lips together. The nosy part of her wanted to know more about this expensive ex. But, not wanting to come off as too inquisitive and force him back into his shell, she decided to keep her trap shut.

"So, you said you have an exhibit coming up at the end of the month?" Scott said, in a clear attempt to change the subject.

She nodded, eagerly launching into the type of art she was working on, what the exhibit's theme was, where it was. A full ten minutes had passed before she glanced at her watch and clamped her mouth shut with a gasp. "I'm sorry. Art is really the only thing I get chatty about. You're probably bored to tears."

"Not at all." He grinned, and his eyes twinkled with amusement. "I can tell you're really passionate about it. I like that in a woman."

"What other things do you like?" she said in a low voice, surprising herself.

"Well," he said huskily, coming up behind her and placing his hands on her hips. The heat of his body soaked into her back, making her thighs clench. She wondered how hot he'd feel inside her. He placed his mouth beside her ear. The feel of his lips brushing her earlobe, of his hot breath against her hair, made her sex tingle. "I like watching these. You do this cute, sexy little hip bop every time you toss a dart and don't make it. It's fun to watch. Makes me glad you're so bad at this game."

She laughed and elbowed him lightly. He reluctantly dropped his hands, though he was grinning. The sudden absence of his heat behind her made her wish he'd return, preferably without any clothes on.

"I blame the alcohol," she said, though she knew that wasn't the truth. She couldn't aim for shit. She glanced at her watch and frowned. "It's about ten. Little guy's been alone for about two hours now. I should probably go check on him."

"Yeah, I was just thinking the same." Scott cashed out their tab, paying for the drinks and the cheesy fries—or as Amy had dubbed them, "greasy fries"—they'd snacked on, before they headed out the door.

The bar was close enough that they'd just walked. Amy had enjoyed it, breathing in the fresh air and leisurely walking beside Scott. With him, she felt safe. It made her realize how stressed out and tense she was all the time by herself.

Maybe her therapist was right. She really had grown paranoid.

The hope that this was the beginning of something special, a new start, blossomed in her chest.

They knocked elbows on the way back, both lost in their own thoughts. Scott's hand lingered by the side closest to her, while the other was stuck casually in his pants pocket. For a moment, she thought he might try to hold her hand. His fingers started to reach for hers and then fell back at his side, as if he'd changed his mind.

It was a miracle she made it back to the apartment at all without face-planting on the sidewalk. The alcohol had hit her body hard; she'd stumbled and giggled the whole way back, Scott poking fun at her. After her foot caught in a deep crack in one of the stairs up to the front entrance and she nearly went down, Scott said, "All right, clumsy. No way am I making a visit tonight to the ER."

Before she could process what he was doing, he'd scooped her up into his arms and carried her up the stairs, like a knight out of a storybook. She clung to him as she eyed the stairs below them. "If you drop me, I'm taking you down with me."

He held her tighter. "Wouldn't dream of it, sweetheart."

Her heart fluttered, along with a rush of heat that made her thighs squeeze together.

Once in front of her door, he set her down but didn't let go. His hands lingered on her hips, with her back against the door. The hard muscles of his arms flexed under her fingertips. He stared at her mouth, his eyes dark with desire.

Inside her chest, her heart thumped against her sternum. She stared at his lips and instinctively opened her mouth when he leaned in and kissed her.

The kiss was sudden and hot. He crushed her to his chest, pressing her against the door as his tongue hungrily sought hers. With a moan, she wrapped her arms around his neck as he hoisted her legs up around his hips.

She couldn't think, couldn't breathe. Hell, she didn't want to, this felt too damned good. Ever since she'd met him, she'd wondered how he would kiss, and now she knew.

He was fucking phenomenal.

She could feel his erection rub against her sex, making her groan deep in her throat. He rocked gently and reached down between her legs, stroking her through her jeans. His thumb caressed the spot where her sex was, and she cried out. Wanting to reciprocate, she palmed him.

Holy shit. He easily filled her palm, his sex hard and strong against her hand. She suddenly had the urge to unzip him, to feel the hotness of his skin on hers. To pet him, to please him.

To make him, any part of him, hers.

Just as her fingers found his zipper and began to pull down, a door banged open across the hall. "Disgusting youth!" yelled an old woman, her cane raised in the air. "Fornicating wherever you please! I'm reporting this to the building manager!"

With a slam of her door, she disappeared. A moment later, the landline in Scott's apartment rang.

They both froze and then burst out laughing.

Holy shit, *she* was *laughing*.

Phone the president. Amy Miles was officially laughing.

"Oops." Amy bit back another laugh. Her face heated as she realized what she'd just done. Having sex, even if it was just hot grinding, in public wasn't something she normally did, but hell if it hadn't turned her on.

Scott grinned and took a deep breath, letting it out slowly. His hand rubbed over his face; he took a step back and pinched the bridge of his nose. "Jesus, sorry I assaulted you like that. That was dumb. And here I was trying to be a gentleman."

Amy bit her lip. "In case you hadn't noticed, I didn't exactly mind you being a scoundrel."

"Duly noted."

A beat of silence passed between them, and she glanced at her door.

If she invited him in now, it would go further. She knew it would.

What she didn't know was whether she was ready for it to. Now that her head was clearing from her lust-fest, she was grateful the old woman had interrupted them.

She gave him an apologetic smile. "I had a really good time."

"Me, too." He smiled at her gently and leaned in; his mouth hovered over hers. "Good night?"

She took a deep breath, let it out. "Good night."

He kissed her. It was nothing like the one before. This one was sweet and tender, making her heart squeeze.

Oh, heaven help her, she was falling hard for this guy.

Once they'd finally parted ways and shut their doors, a process that took a full minute because they kept glancing over at each other and giggling, Amy sighed with contentment and leaned against the door.

Unbelievable. It had to be fate that she'd been drawn to this building and had moved in here. It couldn't be a coincidence that she and Scott were neighbors. Finding love wasn't something she'd intended on in the least, but now that it was waved in front of her face, she found she couldn't resist.

She poured herself some water and took an aspirin and then padded to her bedroom to check on the kitty.

He sat on her bed, playing with her underwear.

It was cute for about five seconds until she realized she hadn't let him out. When she'd left, he'd been in his kitty carrier, and her underwear had all been tucked away in her dresser.

The sense of panic, of that ice-cold fear, slowly took over her body as she stared. Trembling, she took a hesitant step toward the bed, and then another. Soon, she stood directly over it, now able to read the message that had been spelled out on her comforter using her panties.

The glass of water slipped from her hand and shattered against the floor.

I'm watching.

ELEVEN

EVEN A FULL half hour after the police arrived, Amy hadn't stopped shaking.

I'm watching.

Upon reading those words, every hope she'd had at living a normal, peaceful life blew up in smoke.

He was keeping his promise. Nathan had been serious.

"I'll always be watching, Amy."

She could see him, in her mind, hauled off by the police. Her shoulders had started to sag with unbelievable relief until he'd looked over his shoulder, winked, and mouthed those words to her.

"Miss Miles?"

"Huh?" Her head snapped up, and she blinked, her eyes focusing on the cop in front of her. He looked young for a cop, fresh out of the academy maybe. He stood with his pen poised above his notepad. She shook her head and sighed as her hands ran through her hair. "I'm sorry. I didn't hear you."

"It's all right. I was just asking if the lotion was the only thing you've noticed missing?"

She blinked and nodded again. Her throat felt way too tight as she rasped out an answer. "Yes."

"And you didn't misplace it?"

"No." She knew she hadn't. Her vanilla-and-lavender lotion, which she slathered on after a hot shower, always sat on the rim of her bathtub. It had, everywhere she lived. That's how she'd noticed such a common item was missing.

Nathan's voice whispered through her head.

He leaned in to her neck. Amy trembled and whimpered beneath him as he inhaled deeply. "Vanilla and lavender...my two favorite smells."

"Miss Miles?"

Amy jumped. Squeezing her eyes together, she sighed and put her hand over her eyes. "I'm sorry."

He gave her an understanding smile and closed his notepad. "Understandable." Reaching into his pocket, he handed her a business card. "You've given us plenty to work from. If you can think of anything else, please give me a call."

She nodded and took the card.

He started to walk away and then paused. Glancing around at his partners, he said quietly, "For what it's worth, my son's still a huge fan of Leviathan 5. I'm sorry for your loss."

Amy stared at him, going completely still as tears pricked her eyes. "Thank you," she whispered, barely able to make her mouth move. It had been years since she'd thought about her dead fiancé's band's name. When he died, the band had, well, disbanded. The lead singer, Roxanne, had stopped singing altogether, but Amy knew Michael's death had hit her harder than the others for reasons she'd rather never think about again.

"Please don't say anything," she begged quietly. "About who I am."

He nodded. Those kind eyes gazed at her with understanding and sympathy. "Of course."

She closed her eyes and let out a sigh of resignation. This was exactly what she'd feared in calling the police— that someone would do enough digging into her background and would recognize her. It was inevitable, really. When they asked whether she knew of anyone who would want to hurt her, she had to say yes. That cop had thought to ask. The others hadn't. They'd thought it was a simple break-in, but he'd dug deeper.

So deep, he'd scraped the scars on her soul.

Her heart pounded at the thought of undergoing all that media attention again. That same fear had almost made her chicken out of calling the police in the first place, but she knew she'd sit there all night worrying if she didn't. It was a catch-22.

It also confirmed her worst fear: that no matter how far she ran or who she became, she'd always be known as the fiancée of a dead rock star.

She would never get to be her own person again, a truth that both saddened and angered her.

Twisting her shirt in her clammy hands, she worried she'd made a terrible mistake in calling the police, who seemed to linger now that she was freaking out inside. She imagined reporters, talk shows, and uncomfortable questions. Her face plastered all over some tabloid or on TV.

Angry fans who blamed her for the band's breakup, or for Michael's murder, which was insane. If anything, at least it could be said his fans were passionate.

Amy tapped her foot, wondering whether she could break her lease and move again.

The tiny voice of rationality talked her off the ledge, as it usually did. It also curiously wore the voice of her therapist. *Stay calm. Think it through. You* had *to call the police. Don't be foolish, and don't run from your fears.*

As they finished their inspection and finally left the apartment fifteen minutes later, Amy's phone chirped—Becca.

It was awfully late for her to be calling. Amy opened it, intending to say hello, but her voice wouldn't work.

"Ames? You there?"

"Yeah," she rasped. It was no more than air. She cleared her throat. "Yeah?"

There was a sharp intake of breath from the other end of the line. "Oh my God, Ames, what's the matter?"

Amy closed her eyes and forced herself to breathe.

In and out, in and out. See? Your lungs remember how to work. Now, let's see if we can get your brain on board.

With another deep breath to steady her nerves, she explained what had happened. The rehash was fresh on her mind, considering it was the exact same thing she'd just told the police.

"Holy shit," Becca breathed. "Do you think it's him?"

Amy went cold and gripped the phone tighter. It was a miracle her voice worked when she spoke. "No," she rasped, "I don't think Nathan would be that dumb. He doesn't want to go back to jail."

"Did you at least tell the police his name, you know, just in case?"

"Of course I did." Amy sighed wearily.

"Aw, I'm sorry, girl. I know how much you wanted to hide your identity."

"It's fine," Amy said automatically, though it was anything but. "I'll...be fine."

Amy could hear keys rattle and clothing whispering: the sounds of someone getting ready. "I'm coming over."

"No, don't bother. I mean, I kind of just want to be alone right now."

A long pause. "Are you sure?"

Hell no. "I'm sure. But thanks anyway. Oh! Did you call for something or just to say hi?"

"Well, some of my coworkers were going to hit up the late showing of that new slasher flick...but I'm guessing you don't want to see that, huh?"

It suddenly became hard to swallow again. "Nope," she whispered.

"Figured as much." Amy could hear Becca's nails drumming along the phone, something she did whenever she was thinking. "Promise me you'll text or call if you need me? It doesn't matter the time. I'll come over."

Amy smiled. "I will. I promise, I mean."

Becca was silent. "Scott is your neighbor, right?"

"Yeah?"

"Well, maybe you should go stay with him for the night."

"What? I can't do that! I barely know him."

"Weren't you just saying you had a date with him earlier?"

Amy pressed her lips together. "Well, yeah, but I

can't just barge in and ask to sleep over. He might take it the wrong way."

Someone banged on the door in the background, and Becca groaned. "Be there in a second! Look, Amy, I know you're afraid to move too fast, but seriously, what are you going to do if that creep comes back in the middle of the night?"

Amy nearly choked on her own breath. Oh God, what if he did? She knew self-defense, but what if he had a knife or a gun?

What would he do to her?

"Exactly," Becca said. "Trust me—you need to stay with Mr. Sexy."

"Stop calling him that," Amy said irritably.

"I will when you do." She made a kissing noise. "Love you. Stay safe."

After she hung up, Amy looked around her apartment. It was quiet. Too quiet. Putting in a movie—she didn't have cable—she started cleaning religiously, a task she did only when she didn't want to think about something. The smell of lemon disinfecting wipes and lavender-scented dish soap soon filled her nose. Every few seconds she'd pause, go to the door, and check to make sure the door-knob, dead bolt, and security chain were locked.

Once the kitchen, dining room, and living room were practically sparkling, she checked the door—and windows, this time—again before she hauled her things into her bed-room.

She froze at the threshold and stared at the bed. Her heart beat faster.

There it was, the message meant for her.

I'm watching.

The kitten pawed at its kennel and meowed at her. She'd put him away when the police came over.

The mop handle smacked against the floor, making her jump. She hadn't realized she'd lost her grip on it; her palms were sweaty, but it wasn't the hot she-just-worked-her-ass-off kind of sweat. This was the cold, clammy kind, caused by fear.

The oddest thing about the police's once-over of her apartment was that they couldn't find a point of entry. The door was still locked, as were all the windows. It was as if the intruder had literally walked through the wall.

Or right through the front door.

When was the last time the locks on this place had been changed? She and Becca always swapped keys to their places in case of an emergency, but Becca had been across town. No one else, aside from Scott, had a key to her place—that she knew of. But a number of tenants had to have lived here before her. Anyone could have made a copy.

She hugged herself as she shook. Looked over her shoulder. Looked under the bed, in the closet. Anywhere the boogeyman could be hiding.

Except, he wasn't there. He'd vanished, like smoke.

And yet, she still didn't feel as if she were alone.

Once again, she didn't feel safe in her own home.

A tear rolled down her cheek as she sank to the floor.

Exhaustion started to set in, but every time she closed her eyes, she saw Nathan.

Nathan, with that dark, wicked stare, mouthing, "I'm watching."

And that grin. He was always smiling in her memories, as if he found torturing her funny.

It took five more minutes for her to decide to go next door. Taking the kitty and his things with her, she grabbed her purse and padded over to Scott's place. After a quick buzz of the doorbell, she waited. No answer.

It was nearly one in the morning. Wincing, she buzzed again, feeling guilty.

There was no sound from the apartment.

She bit her lip and glanced at her door. Every muscle in her body tensed, and her stomach twisted into knots.

Maybe I'll knock. She hadn't heard a noise when she'd buzzed.

Lifting her fist, she knocked softly; after all, it was so quiet in the hallway and she was trying to be considerate.

A door opened downstairs.

Amy's breath caught. It sounded like the front door to the building. She could hear the lonely, eerie screech of the rusty hinges as the door closed and footsteps started up the stairs.

Screw this politeness bullshit. She hammered on the door.

Please be there, please be there, please, please, please...

Praying maybe it was a neighbor coming up the stairs and they would turn away onto another floor, she tried to calm herself down. She had to be freaking out over nothing.

Except, the person never turned off the stairwell.

They were still coming, climbing up the stairs, closer and closer.

Please, Scott, please...

He wasn't home, or he would have answered the door by now.

Trembling, she scurried back over to her apartment. The keys slipped out of her hands as soon as she grabbed them.

"Shit!" she hissed under her breath. The cat carrier banged against the door as she stooped to pick them up.

About that time, she heard the bolt next door click, and a few seconds later, Scott stood in the doorway.

His eyes were heavy lidded, and his hair was all over the place. He was also shirtless. The zipper to his blue jeans was only pulled halfway up, exposing indigo boxers. Two lines near his groin curved down past the loose waistline of his pants and disappeared into a shadowed area she'd very much like to explore.

He slowly grinned, his voice groggy from sleep. "Let me guess, you were dreaming about me, but dream me couldn't compare to real me, right?"

The words tumbled out; the last word stuck in her throat, making her voice squeak. "I don't have anywhere else to go, and I don't know anyone else here."

"Of course." His brows furrowed in concern as he opened the door at once. "What happened?"

She stepped inside, kitten in tow, and he shut the door.

His place was...nice. A mess, but nice. It had a lived-in feeling Michael's place often lacked.

The layout was the same as hers. Sure enough, his walls were a drab beige. Posters of rock bands hung all over the place. The biggest stereo she'd ever seen sat against one wall and dominated most of the entertainment center. The stereo was by far the nicest item in the room. All the furniture was hand-me-down; that much was clear from the ramshackle fifties upholstery and chipped wooden frames. Windows took up most of the living-room wall. The drapes were pulled open, showing the dilapidated, abandoned building next door. At least one of her bedroom windows faced the street. Being on the corner of the building had some perks.

Stars twinkled in the night sky above, and moonlight shone onto the large fur rug that covered most of the floor space in the living room.

A kingdom of beer bottles and cans lay scattered across his coffee table. Bottle caps littered his carpet. She hoped he wore socks or slippers inside his apartment; that stuff couldn't be comfortable to walk on.

He noticed her staring. "I haven't touched another beer since we got back from the bar." He gestured. "And I didn't drink all of those at once. They just kind of accumulate because I'm rarely home, and as you've noticed, I'm kind of sloppy."

She attempted a smile. "I think your place is nice."

His shoulders relaxed. "You, however, look like you could use a beer."

Could she ever. "Yes, please."

He went to the kitchen and grabbed two cold Bud Lights before they sat together on the couch. The cushions smelled faintly of dust, probably because they were so old, and cigarette smoke, probably from the impressive triple stack of cigarette butts in his glass ashtray.

"Do you mind if I let Braveheart out?" she asked.

He shook his head. "Not at all."

The latch clicked open as she pressed the levers and opened the metal door to the carrier. Tentatively, the little guy emerged to explore his new surroundings.

They sipped on their beers for a while as the cat ran

around and played.

"Does your doorbell work?" she finally asked. It was a lame question, but she needed an icebreaker. Despite the fact they'd practically had sex through their clothing earlier, she suddenly felt shy around him. Sitting alone together in his apartment felt way more intimate.

"Nah," he said. "I keep forgetting to call the electrician, since it's more than our resident handyman—aka me—can fix. Besides, it's not that big a deal to me." He cast her a sheepish look. "Sorry it took me so long to come to the door. I was in a coma. I pulled a double last night, so I didn't get much sleep."

She stared. "And you still wanted to go out with me?"

"That I wouldn't miss for the world."

It was the beer warming her belly. Nothing. Else. "The police came by earlier, but I think you might have been sleeping," she finally said.

He sat up. "The police?" His eyes narrowed as he studied her. "Are you okay? Did something happen?"

The tremble started back in her hands almost immediately. "No," she whispered. "No, I'm not okay, and I haven't been for a very long time. Sometimes, I don't think I ever will be."

His expression softened. "What happened?"

She pressed her lips together.

Could she tell him about that night, about what happened to Michael and who she really was?

No. Not yet. Some monsters could never be tamed; they could only be caged.

Slowly, she opened up about the message on her bed and what the police said about not finding a point of entry. She left out the part about the stalker and her real identity.

Well, more like the lump that formed in her throat prevented her from talking about it.

The kitten was at their feet, batting the bottle caps around with his little bandaged paws.

"Jesus." Scott ran his hands over his face. "I'm so sorry I didn't come to the door." He slammed his fist against the table. "Goddammit, if I could just stop drinking!"

She tensed. "It's okay, Scott. Nothing happened."

"Doesn't change the fact it could have. And I would have been too passed out to do anything about it."

Amy rested a hand on his forearm. His skin was hot, the hairs along the back of his arm coarse. A shiver of desire to keep trailing her hand along his arm, toward that deliciously lick-able chest, rolled through her. "It's fine. I'm fine. Don't be so hard on yourself," she said quietly, before she tried to pull her hand back.

He caught her hand and clasped it as he twined his fingers with hers. Her heart stuttered, and her breath caught.

"I promise I'll get the locks changed tomorrow. And I'll reinforce the windows however I can."

"Thank you." She smiled. Her heart beat faster when he didn't let go.

"You can stay here tonight, if you like." His deep voice had gotten quieter, huskier.

She found herself leaning in without really meaning to. "Thanks," she whispered.

Though she felt anxious, it wasn't from fear, not when she was with Scott. That comforting feeling of safeness settled over her like a blanket. Before she knew what she was doing, she leaned in and planted her mouth on his, reacting more to her body's instincts than what her brain was screaming at her.

He blinked, caught by surprise, and then wrapped his arms around her with a groan. He fell backward and she on top of him; her breasts rubbed against his bare chest. She pressed her tongue against his, moaning when he answered with a lick of his own. His hands squeezed her ass, and she mewled, arching her back.

His touch was like a drug.

The hard grind of his cock, sheltered from her sex by a thin layer of cotton boxers, had her fumbling to undo the rest of the zipper.

She couldn't stop herself, though distantly in her mind a little voice kept saying, "No, no, no."

There wasn't time for regret. She needed to finish what they'd started in the hallway. As she ran her hands over the hard muscle of his bare chest, all she could think about was how much she wanted him.

"Amy," he murmured, kissing her neck and cupping her cheek.

She stared up into his eyes. They were dark with lust, but there was a sparkle of something else there.

Need.

In that moment, she forgot how to breathe. It had been ages since she had needed someone and they had needed her, too.

And that alone scared the hell out of her.

TWELVE

S HE SHOOK HER head, placed a finger to his lips.

He hesitated, a question in his eyes.

Adrenaline hummed in her veins as she rasped, "I don't want to think right now. I just want to forget." *Forget about Michael, forget about the fact I'll probably never be truly safe, forget about the past. Just help me forget.*

It was about more than that, though. She needed to feel human again, to feel normal. For the past few years, her life had been a circus. The rumors, the gossip, the looks of surprise on people's faces when they recognized her on the streets, despite her best attempt at hiding her identity. Even worse were the too personal, invasive questions that spewed out of their mouths once they recovered from their shock.

Oh my God, did you really walk in on them having sex?

Why the hell did you call off the wedding? He was a

*fricking rock star! You could have been famous and rich!
Who cares whom he screws on the side, so long as you get
your diamond and your mansion, girl!*

Was his throat really slashed wide open?

*Did you actually slip and fall in the blood before you
saw it, or was that something the media cooked up?*

Yes. She needed this, needed Scott. She wasn't living
in the past anymore, and she desperately didn't want to be
haunted by it.

And yes, she may or may not still have been a little
intoxicated. She'd had to have been to be so bold, a dangerous combination of beer buzz and desperation.

Scott held her so gently; she wondered how he'd be
inside her. Would he be a gentle lover? Or the kind who
liked to let his passion blaze?

Pulling back, he looked her in the eyes as he studied
her. "Are you sure?"

She barely hesitated. "Yes."

That was all the answer he seemed to need. With a
quick tug, he had her breasts pressed against him once
more, his hands already reaching for the hem of her shirt.

She stopped thinking and just went with what her
body told her to do. Lifting her hands above her head, she
let him tug the shirt free and toss it on the floor. Her
breasts felt too full, as though they were about to explode
out of the lacy number she had on for a bra. Scott's eyes
immediately dropped to her breasts and widened slightly.
Leaning forward, he teased a nipple through the lace. She
moaned and threw her head back, pressing her breast
against his mouth as he worked her nipple to a hardened
point. When he was satisfied with his work, he started on
the other, sucking and licking and teasing. His mouth was

so hot. She wondered what it would feel like on her sex.

Breathing hard, he reached back and unhooked her bra with practiced ease. That probably should have been a warning sign, but hell if she cared.

Impatient, they tugged the bra off together, and he immediately seized her breasts. He scooped them together, pressing and kneading the soft mounds as he kissed her nipples with as much passion as he had kissed her mouth. The whole time, she kept her eyes closed, wanting to feel everything without the help of her eyes to ruin it. Tension drained out of her body, making her languid in his arms. Scooping her up, he got her pants loose, and before long, those were on the floor with her bra—as was she.

He delicately laid her against the rug. It had some kind of gold-and-black striped pattern, like a tiger.

She reached for his zipper, but he caught her hand. "Soon." He smiled. Snagging her underwear with his teeth, he pulled them past her hips and down her legs but kept his eyes locked on hers the whole time.

This was definitely a man's apartment; she could tell from the temperature drop the moment she walked inside. The cold was even more pronounced without any clothes on. Goose bumps broke out along her skin, and her wetness tingled from the chill in the air. She was thankful for that chill a few seconds later when his hot breath blowing across her sex made her sigh. The contrast was nice, sexy even.

He lowered his chin so it brushed the girlish, dark curls above her sex. She knew what was coming next, and she arched her hips in anticipation.

In a ghost of a kiss, his lips whispered against her most sensitive spot. She moaned out loud and writhed against his mouth. A growl of satisfaction came up from his throat.

He ducked his head and kissed her, lavished her with his tongue. "God, you taste so good."

She could tell he was holding back. Whimpering with need, she rasped, "Take me."

He paused for only a second. Clamping hold of both her legs, he opened her wide and claimed her with his mouth.

She practically screamed; she would have if she hadn't had enough brain function left to clamp down on her bottom lip.

His hot tongue raked her, lapping at her in quick, searching strokes. They quickly built up a rhythm, rocking her hips against his mouth. His fingertips dug into her thighs, turning her on even more, but she didn't think it possible to be any wetter than she already was.

Then he sat up, jerked his zipper down so harshly she heard denim rip, and stepped out of both boxers and jeans.

Holy. Shit. Her imagination had been right on the money. He was big; the moonlight shone against his proud sex, highlighting a vein that ran along its side. She licked her lips as he slowly put on a condom and lowered himself over her. She tensed and bit her lip in deliberation.

When he had one knee on the floor, she sprang up, wrapped her arms around him, and rolled him so his back was on the floor. His eyes were wide with surprise. "Amy, what are you..."

She poised herself above him, smiling like a queen. "Returning the favor."

She sat straight down, her legs open wide to receive him. She took it slowly, as her walls stretched, adapting to the extra girth. Bit by bit, she took him in, releasing her held breath as she did.

A cry of pleasure rang free from Scott's mouth, driving her wild. She rocked; the rest of him slid inside her as she relaxed. God, it felt good to have sex again.

He was hard and hot. She bucked, squeezing her aching breasts to keep them from bouncing against her chest, reveling in the power of her sexuality. She'd never felt bolder, never this much in control.

And deep down, she knew that's what this was about—being in control.

She saw something she wanted—aka *him*—and she took it without doubting herself.

That's when it hit her. From the beginning, being with Scott had never been about a choice.

She'd already made the decision to sleep with him the moment she'd laid eyes on him. Her body had wanted him.

So did the woman, whose heart was perhaps more mended than she'd dreamed.

He slid inside her easily now, gliding in and out from tip to base. He brought his hips up to meet hers, grunting every now and then.

She could feel the explosion coming, that sweet release of ecstasy. She touched herself, frantically rubbed her thumb along her now-throbbing sex. She moaned.

"Come for me. Come for me, Amy."

A scream exploded from her mouth, and she desperately rocked herself along his shaft as she orgasmed.

She'd come since the incident, but not like this. Not with a man inside her. It was as if the past two years' worth of tension and anxiety washed away from her in a deluge of release. Her insides turned to goo, and she would have collapsed on top of him had he not caught her and rolled her onto her back.

"What are you doing?" she breathed, delirious with the liquid pleasure that coursed through her veins.

He smiled before he placed a gentle kiss on her lips. "Showing you how I feel."

He slowly lowered himself onto her again, still rock hard. With care, he pushed himself inside of her, inch by inch, until he was fully sheathed. She sighed in contentment as he began rocking gently. Where her lovemaking had been wild and passionate, his was tender and sweet.

It didn't drive her any less wild; the heat slowly built deep in her belly. She whimpered as his thrusts became harder, more urgent. Tendrils of fire curled out from between her legs, making her toes curl. "Yes, Scott...just like that," she breathed against his ear.

"Come for me, baby," he said. "I want to hear you moan again, feel you writhe around me."

That did it. The second orgasm slammed into her with twice the power of the first. Her back arched, her breath left as she screamed, and a moment later, Scott grunted deep in his throat, thrusting a few more times before at last he went still.

He propped himself up on his elbows, which straddled her neck. Their breaths mingled, and sweat shone across their bodies, shining gold with the streetlamp light that had kicked on sometime while they were preoccupied.

At last, Scott reached up and pulled at some of the wisps of golden hair plastered to her face. He kissed her forehead. "How do you feel? Are you all right?"

She thought about it. After two years, she'd finally had sex with a man.

She never thought this day would come, where she'd open up to someone again.

Yet, here she was, tangled up in the arms of a warm, loving man, who was everything she'd ever dreamed of.

Please, don't let it be too good to be true.

She smiled, so wide her face hurt. "Amazing."

And she meant it. She was happy, really damned happy, right now.

Which was why she should have known it wouldn't last for long.

THIRTEEN

THE WATCHER LICKED his lips as he watched the blonde throw her head back in ecstasy. A streetlamp kicked on just outside the apartment window, highlighting the contours of her body in dusty orange light. Reckless fools, leaving the blinds open like that. They screwed like two animals in heat, so they probably hadn't been thinking about having an audience.

All the better for him.

The apartment building across the street was supposedly boarded up and closed off.

To all but those who knew how to get in, those lonely creatures who went bump in the night.

No one would see him watching from the dark window, with its yellowed blinds innocently opened as if the last occupant had forgotten to close them. The shadows hid him well as he zoomed in with the binoculars, trying to memorize the lines of Amy's beautiful body. He could tell from the fit of her clothes that she'd put on some more pounds.

Good. She'd been too damned skinny to start with. He liked a little extra meat, and the softness it provided for fucking.

Just like a velvet cushion.

He licked his lips. A flutter of excitement went through him.

He took his time memorizing the details of her body. The mole on her back that she'd always been self-conscious of; how her hair faded to brunette closer to the roots. Her skin was smooth and flawless. He knew it was soft from the bottle of lavender and vanilla lotion he'd swiped at her apartment earlier. He'd rubbed some on his hands every time after washing them, so Amy could always be with him. The scent was clingy. Even through the gloves, its sweet scent tickled his nostrils, and he inhaled deeply.

She'd kept the bottle by the shower, meaning she probably rubbed it on those long, creamy legs after bathing.

What he wouldn't give to massage the buttery liquid onto her skin...

Amy's mouth flew open as her body bobbed up and down. He imagined the blissful sigh releasing from those lips, the ones he'd lined the walls of the apartment with pictures of. How many times had he stood in front of those drawings and photographs, tracing the contours of her mouth with his thumb, leaning in to kiss them while wondering whether they were more like satin or velvet.

Then that begged the question—what did Amy Miles taste like? The thought sent a sharp pang of heat straight to his loins.

Oh, the things I could do to you, Amy.

He always thought seeing her with another man would drive him mad with jealousy. Oh yes, the jealousy was there, coiling deep within his gut like a viper waiting to strike. But with those dark feelings of possessiveness and desire lurked an unexpected surprise—pleasure.

God, it made him hard to watch her in the throes of ecstasy. She hardly ever let loose like that. Since the tragedy that had shattered her world, he'd longed to show her how to feel alive again. That love wouldn't hurt, that it could make you feel so damned good. He'd dreamed of her mounting him like that, with her full breasts bouncing, nipples erect, inviting him to suck them. He'd tease them until she'd beg him to take her, and then he'd take her into his mouth and show her pleasure like she'd never experienced before.

He knew what was best for her, the things to do to her that would really please her. He'd done his homework, paid attention to what turned her on.

Amy's hands raked up her chest, cupping her own breasts, and he went utterly still with wonder. It was like watching a preview of things to come. He imagined himself being the one on the bottom, watching his Amy as she rode him.

Shit, this was making him restless. If he didn't have her soon, he was going to come undone.

He'd tried being patient all these years, had looked the other way when she'd dated other men. He'd punched a wall the night she'd gotten engaged to Michael.

He grinned. *Hope hell is as hot as they say it is, asshole.*

Michael had been a fool. Had he not been generous

when he warned Michael to stay away from Amy? That no one ever had a right to claim her but himself?

Amy disappeared from the window, and he shifted his weight to get a better view. She was sprawled on her back now, the naked ass of a finely sculpted man rocking back and forth over her as he drove himself into her. And she looked as if she was *enjoying it*.

A growl ripped from his throat. Another fool in the making. But no matter. He, too, would learn it never boded well to touch his things.

Amy belonged to *him*. They were soul mates, destined for each other since the moment they'd met all those years ago. No one else had ever seen him for who he really was, had ever looked upon him without judgment.

Amy was perfect. She was an angel, a queen, and she deserved nothing but the best.

Even if he had to raise hell itself, she was going to belong to him.

FOURTEEN

S HE WAS RESTLESS.

Amy twisted in the sheets, which were partly tangled around her naked body and partly dripping onto the floor of Scott's bedroom.

Her body was sinewy, her muscles completely free of tension for the first time in years. It had been a long time since she'd slept this deeply, the kind of deep, dark sleep where even her nightmares couldn't touch her.

That's probably why it took her a whole minute to realize there was a tongue probing at her sex.

Still half asleep, she writhed as it slowly licked her, making her whimper. "What are you doing?" Her voice was scratchy, partly from just waking up and partly from screaming her head off last night as they made love well into the morning.

The living-room rug, the couch, the kitchen counter, the kitchen table, and finally the bed: was there any surface in here they hadn't had sex on?

Scott's head looked up at her, a cheeky grin on his face. "Waking you up so we can play some more."

She sighed as he stroked her sex with his thumb in long circles. Her hips rocked against his hand, and he cupped her; his fingers slid in and out of her as his thumb continued to work.

"Mmmm...play sounds good," she purred. His fingers glided in and out more easily now; she got wetter by the second.

His rigid sex soon replaced his hand, and thirty seconds later, he had her back up against the wall, her legs wrapped around his torso as he thrust into her. Thank God there weren't any neighbors on the opposite side. It was a miracle no one had called the cops again because of all her screaming.

The head of his arousal stroked her sweet spot, stoking the fire building deep within her. "Harder, Scott," she breathed, nipping at his earlobe.

He obliged, lifting her up slightly so he could go deeper. She was coming undone, becoming nothing but a network of skin and nerves floating along a current of bliss. The orgasm rocked her, making every bone tingle and every muscle feel soupy with relief. Sighing, she sagged against him as he finished, coming hard. They both fell against the bed and cuddled, panting.

A few minutes passed while they lay there in each other's arms. He doodled a design against her cheek with the tip of his finger. "What are you thinking about?"

She smiled and stretched, snuggling closer. "I was wishing that I could wake up like that every morning."

He chuckled and kissed her forehead. "Amen to that. You hungry?"

As if on cue, her stomach gave a loud growl. She flushed. "Guess all that sex worked up an appetite."

"Yeah. I was getting kind of scared. Your stomach's been going off for the past half hour. It was what initially woke me up, all that growling. I thought maybe Braveheart had turned into a tiger and was going to eat me."

She punched him in the arm. "You are so silly."

"You like it."

She grinned. "I do." She pressed a finger to his nose as he leaned in to kiss her, stopping him. "But don't let that go to your head."

"Me? Never." He pressed his lips to hers in a long, lingering kiss.

She groaned as they forced themselves apart and winced as her stomach gave another audible growl. "Guess I should feed the monster before it decides to eat me instead."

He grinned, sat up, and stretched his arms above his head.

She openly gawked at him. He couldn't have more beautifully sculpted muscles if they'd been painted on. With all the jobs he carried, when did he have time to work out? She felt incredibly lame. Here he was, busy as hell, and she couldn't even find time to exercise with one job—plus, she worked from home.

"Want to go out?" He got up and retrieved his pants from the floor. "I know the people who own this little diner around the corner."

"Let's stay in." She pulled the sheets up to cover her chest in a useless attempt at modesty. Her nipples, puckered from the chill and her afterglow, poked at the material. "I can cook."

"Ugh, that sounds great." He gave her a sheepish look and ran his hands through his bedhead. "Except, I don't have any food here, really, to cook with. Unless you count boxed dinners and soup as cooking."

"That's okay." She got up and started to dress. "I have stuff at my place. You want to freshen up and come over?"

He raised his brows. "All right, cool. Sounds good."

She gave him a quick peck on the cheek, resisting the urge to wrap her arms and legs around him and pull him back to bed. Being wrapped up in sheets that smelled like their lovemaking was tantalizing.

While he brushed his teeth and combed his hair, she rounded up the cat. About five minutes later, he was ready. On the way out his door, he spanked her ass, and she yelped.

"Careful." She winked at him. "You're going to make me horny again."

"Already there, sweetheart," he said. Sure enough, there was another bulge around his crotch.

Shaking her head and smiling like a fiend, she opened the door and stepped into the hallway.

Someone rushed past her, nearly knocking her into Scott, who was trying to lock the door. Braveheart gave a screech as she nearly dropped the kennel. "Hey!" she snapped, catching the kennel before it could fall to the floor. "Be careful..."

Her voice died as she took in the back of the tall man. He had on jeans, expensive sneakers, and a black hoodie with a Gothic cross emblem emblazoned in the middle across the back. He raced down the stairs, keeping his head down. The hood was drawn up, concealing his face.

She froze; the hand that gripped the carrier handle had turned white at the knuckles.

"Jerk," Scott grumbled, watching the guy with a frown. He looked at Amy, and his brows stooped in concern. "Hey, Amy, you okay? Did he scare you?"

She barely heard him. Yesterday, a man had watched her from across the street. Or she thought there had been. It had only been for a few seconds, and it had been getting dark. Maybe she didn't know what she was seeing. He'd literally vanished when the bus pulled away, meaning he very well might not have even been there at all.

Her mother had always said she had an active imagination. Sometimes, she was so wrapped up in her own little world that she had a hard time distinguishing between reality and dreaming.

Besides, it would be stupid for Nathan to be here. It had taken nothing short of a miracle to get him out of prison—or a quietly bribed judge. *Coming from wealth has its perks,* she thought bitterly.

A door slammed across the hall, and she jumped.

It was the cantankerous granny who'd yelled at them after they'd stumbled in from their date.

The old woman's beady eyes looked between them before she sneered at Amy. "Have a fun time last night, little whore?"

Feeling cheeky, Amy grinned. "Yes, ma'am. I sure did! There's nothing like hot sex to take your mind off your problems."

The woman's jaw practically fell off. Amy bit back a giggle as she turned around, grabbed Scott's hand, and let them into her apartment.

It didn't feel nearly so scary coming back inside as it

had when she'd left last night, but she'd be in denial if she didn't know it was because of Scott.

He gave the place a quick sweep, as if expecting someone to jump out from a corner at any second.

She let the cat out and wrung her hands, suddenly nervous. "Um, make yourself at home. I'll, er, get you something to drink."

She scampered off to the kitchen while Scott sat down on her sofa. Braveheart had scurried off to the pantry, most likely eating right now. The little fella sure loved food.

About halfway to the kitchen, Amy paused, smacking her forehead with her palm while making a face. She turned around. "I'm sorry, I didn't ask what you wanted to drink."

"Whatever you're having is fine." He gave a casual wave of his hand and a smile that had her feeling slick again. She had a feeling if he was within five feet, she'd be doing a whole lot of underwear changing. Fine by her; any excuse to shop for more cute undies was a good one.

Fixing them two iced waters, she handed Scott his, nearly dropping it in the process. She'd been a little clumsy while trying to pour it, getting water on the sides of the glass.

"Whoa." Scott caught his glass just in time. "You feeling all right? You're not feeling shaky, are you? I have an aunt who's hypoglycemic."

"No, no," she said quickly, blushing. "It's just, this is the first time I've had a boy over."

A boy. Oh Jesus. What are you, twelve?

"I mean," she blubbered, "it's the first time since Michael that I've had a man over. Here, that is. In my home.

Where I live. Well, not here, obviously, since I just moved here." *Shut your mouth. Now.*

Her lips pressed together, she looked away. Thick silence followed her word vomit. Scott stared at her, glass poised mid-sip and one eyebrow raised.

She let out a huge breath and smiled too wide, giggling. "I'm, uh, going to go do that cooking now."

Before I make any more of a fool of myself.

The oven had never become so interesting. With her back turned to Scott so he couldn't see how red she was, she furiously beat the eggs and scrambled them, pressed fresh juice from oranges, and miraculously managed not to burn the toast.

Scott entertained himself by walking around the living room/art studio and checking out her paintings. "You're really good," he said as she set out their plates.

"Thanks," she said, glad for the icebreaker. "Like I said—it's my passion. And my living."

"You just paint?"

She nodded, and they sat down beside each other at the bar to eat. "I do galleries and live classes from time to time, but most of my income is from the Web, selling prints, mugs, anything I can think of, really."

"Wow. That's awesome. I'd kill to have that kind of life."

She smiled softly. "I hear that a lot."

They ate in silence for a beat. "So who's Michael?"

Amy nearly choked on her egg. Coughing roughly, she forced down a big gulp of juice. "Wow, blindsided."

"Sorry." Scott blushed. "I couldn't help it. I figured it was someone you used to date, and that made me curious. Sometimes I talk before I think, as you've noticed."

"Join the club," she muttered, dabbing her mouth to get rid of the juice that had dribbled down her chin. She tucked her hands on her lap and stared quietly at her plate. "Michael was my fiancé."

Scott froze. "Oh Jesus. I'm sorry I brought it up."

"It's fine," she said automatically. She was so used to saying it by now that she almost believed it.

Scott studied her. She could see the curiosity in his eyes, which was why she wasn't surprised by his next question. "What happened?"

She pressed her lips together. "He died."

Scott's face fell. "Oh my God, Amy. I'm so sorry." He took her hand and squeezed.

She shrugged and tried to smile. Her mouth more or less twitched. "It was a long time ago."

"What happened, if I may ask?"

Her throat locked up, and her heart began to beat faster as she was pulled into a memory.

She stood at the bathroom doorway, staring. The entire bathroom was white, which made the red pool of blood Michael lay in all the brighter.

She jumped, abruptly pulled back to the present as he squeezed her hand again. "It's all right. You don't have to tell me."

Amy smiled sadly at him, grateful for the understanding. "Maybe someday."

Scott changed the topic to other things, mostly getting her to talk about her art. It put the shine right back in her and made her heart ache. Michael had been the only other man to understand her passion. Probably because he had been so passionate about music.

Had been.

It had taken awhile to get used to referring to him in past tense. Because that's where he would always remain—in the past. A memory, one she was scared she was going to forget altogether someday.

They cleaned up, her washing dishes while he dried and put things up. He said he'd get her dishwashing machine fixed right away. In an attempt at playing the part of the polite hostess, she asked whether he wanted to see the rest of the place. It didn't dawn on her that the message was still on her bed until they walked in her bedroom.

Scott froze in the doorway, staring. Amy sucked in a quick breath and immediately picked up underwear as quickly as she could.

Silently, Scott helped her, not saying a word the entire time. A muscle twitched in his jaw, and his shoulders looked stiff. "I'll be right back," he said, an edge to his voice.

After he'd stepped out of the room, she straightened up a bit and joined him in the living room a minute later.

"No, two thirty is fine. There was a recent break-in, and I need to get the locks changed as soon as possible for my tenant's peace of mind." After saying "thank you," he snapped the phone shut.

Amy leaned against the doorframe and crossed her arms, smiling slightly. "You mean, for your peace of mind?" Though it was true, changing the locks would make her feel a heck of a lot better.

He took a deep breath and let it out through his nose, but he still didn't look very calm. "I just can't stand the thought of something happening to you."

Amy's heart squeezed. "Thank you."

He nodded gruffly. "Do you mind if I use your restroom?"

She smiled. "Considering my apartment is the same layout as yours, you know where to find it."

He glanced down the hall and then back at her. A slow grin spread across his lips. "You know, we haven't had sex in a shower yet. And since neither of us has showered..."

Her sex tingled in anticipation. "No, we haven't. We should change that."

He kissed her forehead and grinned. "I'm gonna grab a fresh change of clothes from my place. Be right back."

He left, and she hummed in excitement as she locked the door behind him. Sweet, thoughtful, sexy Scott. Always changing the subject to make her feel better, usually on one of her two favorite topics—art or sex.

A knock at the door interrupted her thoughts. "That was quick!" she yelled, practically bouncing to the door. It felt silly locking it, but she had to play it safe. Dark thoughts were far away, though, with the promise of Scott returning and doing sexy things to her. She felt so light, she could float away. She flipped the lock and opened the door. "You just couldn't wait, could—"

Her heart dropped into her stomach, and all the oxygen in the room evaporated.

Her brain froze, as did her lungs.

All she could do was stare at a face that haunted her nightmares, a face she thought she'd never see again.

"Na-Nathan," she whispered.

FIFTEEN

NATHAN STARED BACK at her, his gray eyes just as cruel as she remembered. "Hey, doll. I was in the neighborhood and thought I'd drop by. Miss me?"

Her brain was still frozen. No words would come out of her mouth.

As she stared at those hardened eyes, the same eyes that stared back at her in her nightmares, she could feel the calluses along his palms, grating against her wrists as he pinned her to the bed...

Ice-cold fear washed over her, and spots fired around the corner of her vision. *Oh God, please don't let me pass out, not here.*

Gripping the doorframe, she sucked in a deep breath. "Nathan, you should go."

He smiled. A few years ago, she would have thought it sexy. She *had* thought it sexy, back in college. Nathan was attractive, so she'd chosen to ignore the gleam to his smile that set her on edge. His smile, just like his eyes, was too hard, too plastic.

Too fake. He was a predator, a wolf who'd learned to blend in among sheep so as to be able to pick them off easier.

Nathan pouted. "Aw, don't be that way, sweets. I just got here. Don't you miss me?"

"You asked me that," she rasped. "And hell no, I don't fucking miss you. Leave."

The smile dropped off as if a switch had been flipped, replaced with anger. He stepped forward. "I came all this way to see you, and you don't even invite me in? What a bitch."

She backed up and grabbed the doorknob. Was she fast enough to shut the door and lock him out?

"I want to hear you say you missed me." Nathan's voice went frigid.

Amy bit down on her lip to keep from whimpering as he leaned in, towering over her as he placed his palms on either side of the doorframe.

His face came closer. Those frosty eyes chilled her to the bone as they looked at her dead-on, without blinking. "Don't make me ask again."

Her voice wouldn't come. Neither would her breath. She struggled to form a sentence, to form a thought, anything, but she was paralyzed.

"Hey!"

Nathan's jaw ticked. "Go away. This is none of your business," he said without looking at the source of the voice.

To Amy, it was the best sound in the world, practically sent from heaven.

Apparently, Scott didn't like Nathan's answer, because he grabbed Nathan by the shoulders and yanked him backward so hard he stumbled and nearly fell into the opposite wall.

Scott promptly put himself between a pissed-off Nathan and Amy.

"Look," Scott said, "I don't know who the hell you are, but you stay away from her."

Nathan straightened and adjusted his hoodie with the casual grace of a cat. He raised a brow. "You got a badge?"

Scott's jaw ticked. "No."

"Then I don't guess you can do anything to stop me, can you?"

Looking at Amy, he winked and made a kissing motion before he strutted past them and knocked into Scott purposely before he went down the stairs, whistling the same tune he had when the cops had hauled him away two years ago.

"Here's your tea, miss." The waitress set a darling, steaming teacup in front of Amy.

She and Scott sat in a corner booth at the little diner he'd spoken of earlier. After half an hour of pleading with Nathan's parole officer, who insisted he was there in New York, Amy was exhausted and hysterical. Which, in turn, had made Scott grab the phone and cuss the officer out for daring to hint Amy was crazy and "off her meds."

Both of them had needed to get away from the building for a while.

Scott didn't say anything, patiently sipping his coffee while Amy calmed down. He leaned forward on the table and restlessly toyed with a napkin. A pile of little paper pieces he'd torn off sat beside the silverware he wouldn't be using.

The tea helped her nerves; it was her go-to relaxation method. Nothing beat hot herbal tea with an extra shot of fresh lemon and honey.

When she finally felt as though her heart wasn't going to burst out of her chest, she said quietly, "His name is Nathan Hawke. I"—*deep breaths*—"went to college with him." She swallowed and took a sip of tea to help ease the growing lump in her throat. "He was in the same band as Michael, so we hung out a lot."

"But he wanted it to be more?"

Amy nodded and pressed her lips together, cradling the half-empty teacup so it would warm her clammy hands. "I'd always suspected Nathan liked me, but I was so over the moon for Michael I never gave it much thought. One night, we were at a party. I'd gone to the bathroom, and when I came out, Nathan was there. We were just talking, and then he started coming on to me. I was drunk, so I couldn't do much to fend him off. Before I knew what had happened, he'd shoved me in a bedroom, pinned me to the bed, and started taking my clothes off."

Scott had gone still; his breaths were rushed. His fist was wrapped around the butter knife so hard that his skin stretched stark-white against his knuckles.

"Michael was looking for me. I started screaming when I heard his voice outside the door. Michael about broke it down trying to get in. When he did..." She shook her head and squeezed her eyes closed. "I'd never seen him so angry. He and Nathan got in a fight, a bad one. I thought he was going to kill him."

"Too bad he didn't," Scott muttered darkly.

Amy took a sip of her tea. "The police arrived. Michael urged me to confess, to press charges against him. The other band members didn't want me to, because they knew they'd never find another killer drummer like him. Nathan is a lot of things, but the one thing he's superior at is playing the drums."

"Did you press charges?"

Amy nodded. "Yeah." She sighed and stared glumly at the bottom of the teacup. "Nathan was carted off by the police, and there was a big...fuss over it. Michael couldn't stand to look at him, so he kicked him out on the spot. Everyone blamed me for breaking up the band."

"What did Michael think?"

Amy smiled sadly. "He supported me all the way."

Scott nodded and leaned back against the booth. He sighed hard and ran his hands down his face. "I can guess what happened next. The fucker went to jail and somehow got out on parole. Next came all the restraining order bullshit you told me about on your apartment application."

"More or less, yeah." Amy took a deep breath and let it out slowly. "Wow. I haven't told anyone about that but Becca and my therapist. Everyone else thought it was some love triangle gone wrong." She'd tried to bring it up to her mother, but with her mom's anxiety attacks, it was hard to talk to her about difficult situations like this. So, she'd stopped bringing it up. As far as her mother knew, she'd been assaulted and it had traumatized her. That's all there was to it.

But there had been so much more. And the scars ran deeper than she'd ever let her mother know.

Scott studied her.

Amy smiled, though it was worn. "Go ahead, ask. You're too quiet."

Scott chuckled and leaned forward again, crossing his arms over the table. His voice was gentle. "You mentioned being on meds back at the apartment..."

Amy nodded. This, she was used to talking about by now. "Yes. Antidepressants. Well, I used to be. I've been off them for a few months now. My therapist felt I was ready to, you know, cut the cord."

Scott's eyes softened. Standing up, he came over and sat beside Amy, wrapping her up in a fierce hug.

It felt so good to be held by someone, to know that someone cared and didn't blame her for what had happened.

For once, *she* was what mattered. Not the band's fame. Not Michael's death. Just her.

She hugged him back. They were quiet for a while, holding on to each other.

"I swear it, Amy," he breathed into her hair, "I'm never going to let that son of a bitch hurt you again."

She wanted to believe him. Really, she did. For so long, she'd yearned for a world where she'd finally be safe, a world where she could forget the past and move forward. But if she'd learned anything two years ago, it was that if Nathan wanted her, there was truly nothing capable of standing in his way.

SIXTEEN

NOT EVEN A whiff of Nathan was seen or heard in the next week. Amy started to let her guard down around day four. Since Nathan had shown up on her doorstep, she'd been sleeping over at Scott's. And by sleeping, she meant she'd practically moved in.

Most of her pajamas, her toiletries, and other essential items were at Scott's now. Her apartment was basically a studio. Not wanting to completely invade Scott's space, Amy had left her painting items over at her own place. So far, there was no evidence of anyone having entered her apartment. The building owner had immediately shot down Scott's suggestions for video surveillance of the building, so Scott had installed security cameras himself in her apartment. No one had been by, which set her nerves at ease, some.

She'd tried calling Nathan's parole officer one more time, but the woman wasn't picking up. And she never returned the voice mail Amy had left her.

Amy snapped her phone shut in agitation as they pulled up to the club. Scott had taken the night off to spend it with her. He'd been doing that a lot lately. Amy was worried it would set him back financially, but he insisted he had a lot of savings and that he'd be fine. The fact he cared so much to want to watch over her was touching.

"No answer again?" Scott put his car into park.

"No." Amy growled a sigh as they got out of the car and walked up to the door. "It's so weird. She used to be really good at keeping me posted and watching my back. Now, it's like she's turned against me or plain stopped caring. It's frustrating."

Scott looped an arm around her shoulders and pulled her to him. "It'll be okay." He kissed her temple. "If need be, I can call the chief again tomorrow."

Amy snorted. "As entertaining as it was listening to you berate him for half an hour straight, I don't think that's going to solve the problem. She'll still be a bitch."

Scott's eyes narrowed in thought. "You still sure you don't want to get the local police involved? Or we can go back to the apartment and forget about this whole thing…"

Anger, mixed with fear, surged up in her. "No," Amy said firmly. "I won't hide. I can't. He can get me in the apartment just as easily as out in public if he really wants to. I think we're safer here, anyway. The crowd should keep him from trying anything too stupid." She pressed her lips together. "And no, thank you, I'm sure about the local authorities."

No press, no cops, no drama. She wasn't getting them involved unless she absolutely had to. Maybe Nathan would get bored and leave on his own.

If only she believed he would.

Scott remained silent; his jaw tensed. He took her hand and squeezed, letting her know that though he doubted her decision, he would support it all the same.

Being one of the hot social spots in town for people their age, the club—dubbed Midnight—was booming. Literally.

The music was so loud that the floor shook as they walked in. Unlike the last social establishment they'd visited, Midnight didn't have a dress code. Amy wore a simple red-and-white paisley-patterned dress, and Scott had on a striped button-down and nice jeans.

Though she was apprehensive about the club, her nerves weren't nearly as bad as last time, not with Scott there. His presence brought peace to her soul, wrapped her up in a sense of safety she'd missed all these years.

Becca and her latest boy toy, Brad, were dressed about the same as Amy and Scott, only more chic. Becca somehow always managed to make casual look sophisticated.

"Nice to see you again, Scott!" Becca said brightly, jumping up to give him an unexpected hug. Startled, he awkwardly hugged her back as Amy and Brad shook hands. "I'm so glad you guys decided to come. I thought, with all the drama, you two could use a night out on the town."

Amy did her best to smile. She'd wanted to go play putt-putt, but the club scene was more Becca's style. Hell, anything that involved drinks, dirty dancing, and loud music was Becca's style. And if Amy had learned anything, it was that Becca always got her way. Amy thought she could be a bit spoiled at times, but she didn't judge her for it, not after everything Becca had done for her. If it weren't for her unwavering, patient friendship, she wasn't sure she'd have lived through the mess that became of her life after Michael died.

"Thanks for inviting us," Amy said politely as she and Scott crammed into the booth.

A waitress came by and got their drinks, depositing a basket of tortilla chips and a cup of homemade artichoke dip on the glossy black table.

They all promptly dug in.

"So, you two have known each other since college?" Scott asked between mouthfuls of salty chips and gooey cheese.

Becca nodded. "We ended up as roommates, via that whole dorm application thing. God bless Amy for putting up with my shit."

"Let's just say our room was the party room." Amy winked. "I'm glad I got paired with Becca, though. She brought me out of my shell."

Becca beamed. She reached across the table and squeezed Amy's hand. "You were good for me, too. You made me want to try harder at school."

"Bookworm?" Brad seemed nice enough, with a soft-spoken voice, skin the color of chocolate, and a Ralph Lauren polo. He looked hot, and though he was polite, he actually seemed a little too nice, at least, for Becca's tastes. She usually went for the party boys.

"Yeah, a little," Amy admitted. "I was in the studio a lot, painting."

"She was determined to take over the world with her art," Becca said conspiratorially. "Said she had a message. It was all I could do to drag her out of the studio to go socialize."

Amy stuck her tongue out at her, flushing a little.

Judging from the empty daiquiri glass beside Becca, they'd gotten here early. She pointed a finger at Amy. "Admit it. You owe me big. Without me, you never would have met Michael."

It was as if the air had been sucked out of the room. Dead silence followed as Scott swore and Amy grew quiet.

Becca gasped and covered her mouth. Brad looked between them. "What?"

"OhmyGod," Becca breathed. Her shoulders deflated. "Amy, I'm so sorry. I never should have said—"

"It's okay." Amy quickly flashed her a smile. "I'm fine. You're right. I never would have met him if it hadn't been for you, and I don't regret that one bit." She squeezed Becca's hand. "So, don't worry about it, okay?"

Becca continued to spew apologies for the next three minutes straight. Amy drummed her nails along the table. Sensing the conversation was killed at least for now, Amy stood and turned to Scott. "Mind if I get by? I have to go to the ladies' room."

"Oh, um, yeah. Sure." He stood up to let her out, and she rushed past him.

People bumped into her, but she didn't care. Her heart strummed at a rate of a million beats a minute.

She never should have come. Why the hell did she always let Becca push her into situations she didn't want to be in?

Because she's the only friend you have left who knows what really happened, and you don't want to lose her.

It was pathetic but true. She'd become very closed off from the world after dealing with a shit-storm of publicity.

Even she wanted to forget who she was after most of her "friends" turned on her, telling her she was overreacting to Michael's infidelity and blaming her for the band's breakup. It became apparent the only way to forget about them was by burning bridges. And her life, though lonely at times, had been better without them to criticize and judge her.

Amy thrust past the drunk girl who stumbled out of the bathroom. "Watch it, bitch!" the girl yelled, but Amy didn't care.

She shut the door and leaned over the sink, closing her eyes.

Just breathe. It'll be okay. Just breathe...

The door started to open. She swore, realizing she'd forgotten to lock the door, when Scott stepped inside and locked it.

Amy blinked. "What are you doing in here? This is the girl's restroom."

"Actually, it looks like an anybody restroom, considering there isn't a gender label by the door." He crossed his arms and leaned against the wall. "You okay?"

"Yeah, I'm fine."

"You don't look fine."

She shrugged and shook her head, about to lie, but something stopped her. Finally, she turned around to face Scott, but she didn't readily look at him. "When I told you earlier I didn't want to go clubbing, it's not that I don't like it. I do—I think it's fun, I mean. It's just that I met Michael for the first time at a club. Becca was dating a guitar player in a band that was becoming pretty popular around campus, and she'd set me up on a blind double date with Michael."

"Shit. Well, that explains why you were drinking like a fish the last time we were at a club. I thought maybe you just couldn't stand me. You should have said something, babe," he said gently. Scott ran his hands over his face. "We never should have come here. I'm gonna tell her we have to leave."

"It's okay." Amy rushed forward and placed her hands on his chest to stop him. "Please, we can stay."

"Why? Obviously you're not okay with it." His eyes narrowed. "Is it because of Becca pressuring you?"

Amy bit her lip. "No."

Scott shook his head. "Don't let someone make you do something you don't want. She'll get over it, or she won't. If she doesn't, she wasn't that good a friend to start with."

Amy's heart sank.

"Hey," Scott said gently; he rubbed her arms and ducked his head to try to see her face. "I don't mean to be a dick, but I'm just trying to protect you. I care about you so much, I just don't want to see you hurting."

A warm glow filled Amy's chest, and she smiled.

She'd been wrong—Becca wasn't her only friend, not anymore. Now, she had Scott.

"Thanks, Scott," she said softly.

A smile touched his lips. "Anytime," he said, a bit distractedly.

His eyes dipped to her lips. She was already on her tiptoes, leaning in to meet his lips.

His kisses were hot—they always were—and she found her thoughts drifting away. Scott gently walked them back to the wall and pressed her against it. He rubbed his crotch, which was quickly hardening, against her sex, and she groaned. Reaching down, she palmed him, squeezing his hard length as he grunted in approval and ground harder against her.

Someone banged on the door, followed by, "Hurry the fuck up!"

Amy groaned. "Do we have to stop?"

"Nah. Fuck 'em." Scott leaned in again, but the pounding continued. The doorknob rattled so roughly, Amy thought it would snap off.

Amy raised a brow and looked at Scott's crotch. "On second thought..." She gave him one last squeeze. He groaned deep. "Maybe we shouldn't stay. Maybe we have someplace else to be right now."

"Sounds good," he breathed, his voice dark and husky.

Briefly tugging their clothes into place, Scott took Amy's hand and opened the door. A guy who looked to be in his early twenties stood there, a leer on his face. "'Bout fucking time!" he snapped and then disappeared into the bathroom with a slam of the door.

Amy bit back a laugh. "Someone's having a bad night."

"Ah, he's probably just not finding an easy lay." Scott winked.

Amy shook her head. "I never understood why men wanted to pick women up in a club or a bar. Talk about jailbait." Some of these girls didn't look old enough to be eighteen, let alone twenty-one. Either the bouncer must look the other way when cleavage was involved, or someone was making a killing off some extraordinarily realistic fake IDs.

Amy squeezed Scott's hand. "I'm going to go grab

my purse. Meet you at the car?"

Scott paused.

"It's okay." Amy gave him a shove toward the door. "I'll be two seconds."

Scott reluctantly started toward the door, and Amy rushed back across the room to their booth.

Only it was empty. *Becca and Brad must be out on the dance floor.*

Her purse wasn't under the table or sitting out in plain sight, so Amy set out to find Becca, assuming her purse was with her.

She meandered through the dense dance crowd, eyes scanning for Becca's sparkly hoop earrings. The music was so loud it rattled her brain.

People were getting very friendly, rubbing up in places only Scott was allowed to touch. Gritting her teeth, she kept searching.

Aha!

Brad and Becca were off on the other side, dancing slow and steamy in a shadowy corner. Brad's back was to Amy, kissing Becca's neck as his hands roved her body.

Blushing, Amy stopped behind him and tapped him on the shoulder. He spun around, startled, and Becca looked up with a gasp.

Only it wasn't Becca. It was some random girl Amy had never seen before.

Amy stared between them. "Where's Becca?"

Brad had the decency to blush. He ran a hand through his hair, not quite looking at her. "She said something came up with her little brother and she had to bail."

"Oh." Amy frowned for a second and then felt stupid and guilty. After all, she, herself, was about to leave, thus the whole point of scouring the dance floor for an apparently absent Becca. "Do you know if she took my purse?"

"No clue." He eyed the girl pawing at him with a flirtatious smile.

Amy pursed her lips. "Okay. I'll just, um, leave."

Brad didn't say good-bye as he immediately turned his attention back to the girl.

Ass. She made a mental note to tell Becca next time she saw her what a jerk Brad was.

Amy's stomach twisted with nerves as she fought her way through the crowd and toward the door. *Please, please, please let Becca have taken my purse.* That's just what she didn't need right now...to have her driver's license, birth certificate, and credit cards stolen.

"Looking for this?"

Amy's foot had been mid-step down the stairs to the exit. Gasping, she clutched the railing to keep from falling as she righted herself and turned.

Nathan stood at the top of the stairs, smirking at her with his head cocked to the side. From one raised hand dangled her purse.

Shit.

"What are you doing here?"

Nathan's brows furrowed as he slowly approached her. "You seem incapable of asking me anything else. How about, 'How are you doing?' 'What have you been doing?' 'Are you as mind-blowing a fuck as I remember?'"

"I don't remember anything about that, because Michael beat your ass before things got that far."

"Yes, he did," Nathan hissed. He stopped in front of her, and his eyes turned to stone as he glared down at her.

"You're pretty happy about that, aren't you, you little bitch? That band was going places. Now, Michael's in the ground and Leviathan 5 is dead because of you. My *career* is dead because of you."

Amy's hands fisted at her sides as angry tears stung her eyes. "Your career is dead because you have a record now, and a reputation for being an asshole and hard to get along with."

Nathan laughed. "Those are my better traits." He shook the purse. "I've also become adept at bargaining. Like, how you're going to blow me for this."

"I'm not doing shit for you."

He raised a brow, a wicked gleam in his eyes. "You will if you don't want me to go to the press and reveal your true identity."

Her heart literally stopped beating.

He watched her for a moment. That malicious grin spread wider. "What do you say, Amy?"

"You...you wouldn't do that." Her voice was barely audible. It was all she could do to speak, her throat had become so tight.

"Oh, dear, sweet, *innocent* Amy." Nathan trailed a finger along her jawline, making her shudder. "There isn't anything I wouldn't do to make you pay for what you did to me."

"Son of a bitch!"

Nathan looked past her. His eyes widened.

Amy started to look when Scott swept past her and dove for Nathan. The two went to the ground; Nathan tried to knock Scott off while Scott beat the ever-living hell out of him.

Shock made her immobile. Numb, she stared as people gathered, cheering and placing bets. It wasn't until someone knocked into her in an effort to see the fight better that she came to her senses.

"Scott, stop!" she screamed, running to him. She grabbed his arm and pulled, but it was useless. His arms were as hard as rocks.

Pure rage burned on his face, twisting his features into something feral she had never seen before. It shook her to her core.

For the first time, she was actually afraid of Scott.

"Sc-Scott?"

His fist froze an inch away from breaking Nathan's nose, and he looked at her. His eyes widened as he took in her trembling form.

Blinking slowly, as if snapping out of a trance, he turned to look at Nathan. His face turned red in places where he hadn't managed to block Scott's blows. A nice-sized knot was forming on his forehead.

Scott, breathing heavily, looked at his hands. Smears of blood stained his knuckles. He went stark-white. "No," he mouthed. "Not again."

Leaping off Nathan as if he had burned him, Scott frantically wiped his hands on his pants.

Amy watched, mesmerized and horrified. Questions burned her tongue, questions she couldn't ask—wouldn't ask—until they were alone.

Starting with who the hell Scott Meyers really was.

SEVENTEEN

H IS FACE HURT like a mother, but hell if he was about to let Amy know. Nathan didn't throw a bad right hook. The guy might be smaller than Scott, but damn, was he fast. The son of a bitch had gotten a few hits on him. Blind rage had made him sloppy, as it had in the arena all those years ago.

He could still hear the crowds cheering, feel the coins and money being thrown at his feet as he strutted through the arena while people called, "All Hail the Lion! All Hail the Lion!"

Something ice-cold pressed to his face, and he jumped.

"Sorry," Amy said sheepishly, wincing. "I said your name, but you looked like you were somewhere else."

Scott looked around. Nope, still looked like his shithole apartment. After getting her purse back, they'd bailed, at Amy's insistence. She'd seemed desperate to get out of there before the police could show up. "Yeah, I kind of was," he admitted.

"You want some ibuprofen?" She headed for his medicine cabinet.

He grinned, liking the fact she knew where it was. "Wouldn't hurt." Ibuprofen had been his best friend a few years back, along with a mixture of other drugs. He'd really had his head up his ass back then. It was amazing how much clearer he thought now, how sharp his mind was. Or what was left of it.

Amy returned with the pills, which he gratefully swallowed. "Thanks."

"Yeah."

The clock on his wall clicked away at the time, accenting the silence in the room.

Amy stood a foot away, her arms crossed over her chest.

His chest tightened. "You okay?"

"Yeah, yeah," she said quickly, shifting her weight. "Just rattled." She pressed her lips together and looked down the hall. "I'm, uh, just going to take a long, hot shower to try to relax."

Scott smiled sadly. "Go ahead. Take as much time as you need."

"Thanks." She gave him an anxious smile back.

He watched her quickly pad away to the bathroom. After the door shut, he heard the door lock and the fan click on.

His shoulders sank. She never locked the door, ever.

Dammit.

His suspicions were confirmed. She was afraid of him, had to be. She hadn't been right since they'd left the club. The way she'd stared at him, so frightened and pale...

It had been like dumping a bucket of ice water over him.

He never, ever, wanted to see her that scared again.

Which meant he needed to do something about Nathan, and fast. The prick's parole officer sure as hell didn't seem too concerned by him, when he was clearly a threat.

Asshole.

He wished she would go to the local cops. It still puzzled him why she refused. He wasn't blind; he knew she was scared to. He'd seen the fear and panic in her eyes every time he mentioned it.

What happened to make her this way? He could relate to mistrust. He could count the people he fully trusted on one hand. But this…this was more than simple mistrust. This kind of fear had been branded on her, possibly scarred her for life. It broke his heart. He couldn't— wouldn't—let her live the rest of her life in fear.

Restless and agitated, he started to get up, when his eyes landed on Amy's purse.

He paused. Normally, snooping through his girlfriend's stuff wasn't something he liked to make a habit of.

The shower kicked on.

He had to act now, before the window of opportunity slipped away.

After he grabbed her purse, he dug through it until he found her phone and perused her contact list.

Programming the number into his own phone, he texted Becca.

Hey, Becca, it's Scott. This might seem kind of out of the blue, but I'm worried about Amy. Do you mind if I meet you for lunch tomorrow to talk?

He started to set his phone down, figuring he'd get a response later, when his phone chirped before it had even left his hand.

Sure thing. Sorry I had to bail. Little brother stuff. Let's meet at my place for lunch, around noon.

An address followed.

Relief filled him. *Okay, thanks,* he texted back.

Before he forgot, he arranged Amy's things back the way they were and returned her purse to where she'd left it. Only a minor twinge of guilt remained.

See? No harm done. Quit being such a baby about it. It wasn't like you were going through her diary.

He was trying to help, really he was.

Now, let's just hope I can.

Amy was gone by the time he woke up the next day. Not wanting to freak her out more, he'd slept on the couch, waking to find a note from Amy waiting for him on his coffee table.

Gone back home to paint. Gala in a week. See you to-night—Amy.

His spirits picked up at reading that last part. If she was coming back over tonight, then she couldn't be too weirded out by him.

As he got dressed, he stewed the whole time over what to do about Nathan. Leaving was a bad idea. What if that asshole came back and he wasn't there to protect Amy? The thought distracted him so much that he put his shirt on inside out at first, not seeing his mistake until he glanced over his appearance in the tall body mirror that leaned against his bedroom wall.

After tying his shoes, he locked up and went over to Amy's, pressing his ear against the door. Muted music, orchestral this time instead of rock, filtered over to his ear through the door.

She must be working. Last night, she'd said she had a lot to do today to finish getting ready, something about all her paintings being due at the museum two days early so they could prepare the room.

Not wanting to disturb her, he sighed and dropped the fist he was about to use to knock and got out his phone instead.

Hey, gotta run some errands. Don't answer the door for anyone, and call me immediately if anyone comes by, he texted.

Already locked up the extra deadbolt you had in-stalled =), she messaged back a few seconds later.

He smiled.

Gazing at her door with trepidation one more time, he forced himself to go down the stairs; otherwise, he'd be late meeting Becca.

She lived in a nicer part of town. The apartments were all new, as was the two-thousand-square-foot town-home she lived in. From what Amy had said, Becca came from money and was a super-smart IT grad.

She didn't strike him as the studious type, but he knew, all too well, people often weren't what they seemed.

The townhome was stucco tan on the outside, with indigo shutters and black iron filigree baskets containing stems of lavender.

Can we say ritzy?

A tall stone wall surrounded the property, and a matching iron gate faced the sidewalk. He rang the buzzer, and a moment later, Becca's voice came over the intercom. "Who is it?"

"Scott."

The bolt clicked open a second later. He let himself in and walked up the sidewalk to her front door. She opened it before he got there. She looked slick, with a white button-up blouse, an indigo pencil skirt, and heels. Her straight, glossy hair had been swept up into a sophisticated, clean ponytail. She smiled. "Hi, Scott. Come in. I'm afraid I don't have much time. I ended up getting another assignment dumped on me at the last minute, and I'm going to need to head back to the office sooner than expected to get a head start on it."

Scott started to purse his lips and then stopped himself. Couldn't she have texted or called him before he drove over here to say she didn't have much time for him? *Don't be a dick. At least she agreed to help you.* "That sucks. Thanks for still meeting with me."

"You bet. Have a seat. You want anything to eat?"

"Just water is fine."

The interior was just as fancy as the exterior, with warm brown-colored walls covered in rows of delicate pearly fleur-de-lis, potted orchids in expensive vases, state-of-the-art electronics, new furniture...

Must be nice.

An oversized black hoodie lay on the floor near the sofa he sat on. Some sort of pattern was printed across the front, but it was hard to tell with the way it was wrinkled. Something tickled the back of his mind—that the pattern was familiar somehow—but the sunlight spilled through the blinds and cast hundreds of rainbows all around him. Startled, he lifted his gaze to the opposite wall. She had these cool solid-crystal bookshelves mounted all along one wall, right above her electric fireplace. Tons of pictures in different types of frames sat in neat rows along the shelves. Most, he noticed, were of Amy and Becca. A scattering of photos featured a teenage boy, which must be the little brother he'd heard about. Off to the corner was a picture of a man, woman, a little girl, and a newborn baby. Judging from the similar coloring, Scott guessed it was a picture of Becca's family.

He stared at the woman. "This your family?" He pointed as Becca returned.

Becca nodded as she handed him a chilled bottle of water. "That one's my favorite. My brother had just been born."

Scott pressed his lips together as he studied the woman. "Sorry to say, but your mother looks really familiar. Amy said she was sort of famous?"

Becca tensed as she sat down in her oversized chair to eat her salad. "She was. So what kind of questions do you have?"

He blinked from the topic whiplash. He guessed talking about her mom was off-limits. Hell, he'd also half expected her to ask how Amy was.

If he didn't know any better, he was starting to get the impression she didn't like him, didn't want him here, or maybe both. She was a hard girl to read. "Well, I was wondering if you could tell me what happened to Amy's fiancé."

"Nice try." Becca smiled tightly. "But I've sworn to carry that secret to my grave. Next question?"

Damn. "Okay, well then, can you tell me about Nathan?"

"That I can." She took a sip of her water. "He was the drummer for her fiancé's band before they split. He comes from old money. His family is pretty deeply rooted in politics and several big businesses. Needless to say, they have a lot of power, so he's used to getting his way. Guess that's what made him such a dick."

"Do you know why he's so angry with Amy?"

Becca sighed. "He blames her for what happened," she said carefully. "Not her fiancé's death as much as the demise of the band. He thinks she ruined his career, but in reality, he'd already been doing that himself by being verbally abusive, irritable, and unreliable. Half the time he didn't show up to rehearsals, and if he did, he was so drunk he could barely play. And when Nathan gets drunk, he gets angrier. The guy has rage problems." She speared more salad. "He's a bit of a narcissist. Gets it from his father, who's the same way, or so I hear from the women who have dated him. He never accepts responsibility for his actions, but always looks to blame someone else."

"Sounds like a great guy."

Becca's eyes turned frigid. "He's an asshole. I'll never forgive him for what he did to Amy."

"She has a restraining order on him, right?"

Becca nodded. "Supposedly, he's been behaving." She frowned. "Until now."

"I wonder what made him decide to bother her all of a sudden."

"That was probably because he couldn't find her until now." She promptly snapped her mouth shut.

Oh, no, you don't. She couldn't dangle that carrot in front of him and not expect him to go for it. "What do you mean?"

"I...I shouldn't have said anything."

"But you did." *And needless to say, I'm not letting this go.*

Becca tapped her foot, staring at what was left of her salad. She took a deep breath. "After her fiancé died, Amy wanted to forget. To start over. Part of it was her therapist's idea. She changed her name, changed her whole identity. She literally vanished."

"So, Nathan didn't know who to look for." The fact he could have been trying to hunt her down this whole time bothered him. What's more, why did Amy feel the need to go to all that trouble? What was Becca not telling him?

Just when he was about to ask, Becca sighed deeply. "Ames has been through so much." She stared at all the pictures on the wall. "She really just needs to find someone nice to take care of her, to love her the way she deserves to be loved. A person can only stand so much hatred before it warps them."

Wasn't that the stone-cold truth? He looked again at the wall. "You and Amy must be really close. You have a lot of pictures of her."

Becca stared at the wall awhile before she answered. "She's my family." She smiled.

"You don't have anyone else? Grandparents? Aunts, uncles?"

She shrugged. "My mom's family disowned her when she married my dad. They said he was no good for her. He didn't come from a very nice background. Both of them were only children." She clucked her tongue. "So, no. There's no one else. My mom died, and my dad's not around either. It's just me and my little brother." She looked at the wall again; her eyes softened. "And Amy."

"I'm sorry to hear about your parents," he said gently.

"Don't be. Even when Mom was alive and Dad was out of jail, they were never around. Mom was too busy with her painting career, which was starting to take off. She got really popular right before she was killed in a skiing accident, leaving me a bunch of money. So it worked out, I guess."

Scott didn't know what to say. Who said shit like, *"My mom dying worked out, I guess"*?

He stared at the picture of her family. They looked happy, normal even.

So why weren't there more pictures of them?

Becca cleared her throat as she stood and stepped in his line of vision, her arms crossed. She made a point of glancing at her watch. "I'm sorry to be a drag, but I have to kick you out soon. My lunch break's almost over, and I have to be getting back to the office. Traffic is a bitch during lunch hour."

"Tell me about it." He rose and went toward the door. "And don't worry about it. I appreciate you having me over at all."

Becca followed him to the door and opened it for him. He paused on the threshold. "Look, I know you're her best friend, and you feel obligated to keep her secret. I get that it's not yours to tell. But I'm telling you, I'm falling in love with this woman, and I want to do anything I can to protect her. So, if you know anything at all that will help me help her, please tell me."

Becca pressed her lips together as she studied him. "You're not joking, are you?"

"No," he said firmly.

She scrutinized him a few seconds longer. With a resigned sigh, she said, "January 14th, 2013. Michael Lewis." She shrugged. "There. Now I won't be lying to Amy when I tell her I didn't tell you what happened."

"Thank you." Scott nodded. "You have no idea how much I appreciate you helping me."

Becca smiled sadly. "I think I kind of do."

He didn't linger after that. Becca had to get back to work, and so did he. Parting ways, he walked toward his car, deep in thought.

Something nagged him at the back of his head. *Michael Lewis, Michael Lewis. Why does that name sound so familiar?*

He turned the corner, not really paying attention to where he was going. A teenager in a Metallica hoodie slammed into him. His hood fell back, exposing dyed black hair and a swollen eye of nearly the same color. His lips were uneven, probably due to the fierce cut that parted his bottom lip down the middle.

"Hey, why don't you—" The teen stopped abruptly and stared at Scott's face. His eyes slowly widened as he took in the small lion head symbol tattooed right below Scott's left ear. "Oh my God, it's really you! You're Scott the Lion Meyers!"

Scott's gasp gave it away. No one had called him that in years; it was a name he'd purposely avoided in order for it to be forgotten.

The teen looked like a kid at Christmas. He smiled so widely that the cut on his lip broke open. "Man, you're like a legend around the circuit. You're the whole reason I got into fighting, man, like, my frickin' inspiration!"

Scott tensed. "If I'm your inspiration, then you need

some serious help, kid."

"No, really, you're my hero. You're a motherfucking badass! No one was able to beat you. Oh my God, wait until Ghost hears about this. He's been saying how he's going to get you back in the circuit—"

Scott grabbed hold of the kid's shirt and slammed him up against the side of the building. "If you breathe a word of my name to Ghost, I'll hunt you down. Do you understand me?"

The kid still stared at him like he was a god. "Oh, man. No one is going to believe me." He reached into his hoodie pocket, pulled out a phone, and held it up to Scott's face. Scott grabbed it just as the flash went off.

"Hey!" the kid said indignantly.

"Where is it, where is it," Scott muttered. He quickly skimmed through the photos. The picture was blurry, but he wasn't taking any chances. Deleting it, he tossed the phone back to the kid.

"What the frick, man!" the boy yelled, examining his phone. "What's your problem?"

"Forget you ever saw me," Scott growled as he walked past him as quickly as he could. "And get the hell out of the circuit!" he called over his shoulder.

He didn't look back to see whether the kid followed him. His agitation, not to mention paranoia that Ghost was going to pop out of a shadow and grab him, made him anxious.

It wasn't as if he had any reason to be. He didn't fight for money anymore. He'd survived the circuit, had clawed his way out of that shadowy world of deceit through sweat and blood. Sure, he could probably have paid off his debt faster by fighting, but that would only tangle him up further with Ghost.

In the circuit, you never worked for yourself. You were always another cog in Ghost's money-making machine.

No, Scott was through with that shit for good. No way in hell would he be dragged into that drug-hazed hell again.

He couldn't do that to Amy. He wouldn't.

He knew if he had any chance at holding on to her, he had to become the kind of man she deserved.

Walk the line. Play it straight.

And pray to God nothing else happened to screw things up.

EIGHTEEN

A S PREDICTED, SCOTT didn't see much of Amy for the rest of the week. As the gala approached, she withdrew into her "artist cave." There was no telling how many brain cells she'd killed from inhaling paint fumes.

Every night, she came over and talked about her work. Scott let her, not having the heart or the time to do any more digging on the significance of January 14, 2013 or Michael Lewis. She'd rarely been completely happy these past few weeks, so he didn't want to do anything to kill it. He enjoyed the sparkle to her eyes and the fire in her voice as she chattered endlessly about the various techniques she'd employed in each piece, showing him painting after exquisite painting in her apartment.

There was no mention of Nathan or anything else related to what had happened to her. Scott was so thankful to have things back to normal, not to see fear in her eyes when she looked at him, that he'd dropped the subject of her attacker altogether, though he hadn't stopped keeping an eye out for the creep. Crazy stalkers aside, Amy seemed stressed out enough as it was, what with the impending gala.

Not that she had anything to worry about. At the event, everyone bragged about her work. It was held at the downtown art museum, a massive three-story structure filled with every kind of artwork imaginable. The main exhibit, which rotated visiting artists every month, was completely booked for her. Her mom had helped arrange the venue; apparently, she knew the curator.

Scott felt a little underdressed among the high-fashion elite who attended.

Amy catered to high-class clientele with her modern, and slightly tragic, pieces. Scott knew she got the bulk of her income off her prints, but she did pricey commissions, too. Overall, she was doing very well, and was starting to make a name for herself after a rather lengthy hiatus.

He didn't need to ask to know why she had stopped painting. His sweet Amy was stronger than she realized. It hurt him to know what she'd lost, which made her comeback all the more miraculous. Once darkness like that touched people's lives, they sometimes couldn't dig their way back to the light.

His chest swelled with pride as he watched her chat up the large crowd that had attended the gala. She looked beautiful, wearing a lavender gown that complemented her fair skin and hair. Her eyes sparkled with happiness, and her smile was the brightest he'd seen in a while.

The punch bowl, appropriately labeled since it could knock the breath from you it was so stout, had become his best friend throughout the night. Nothing helped him tolerate a crowd of rich snobs like cheap spiked Kool-Aid.

He sipped his glass as he looked around, body slightly tensed from being on the alert for any prowlers—aka Nathan.

Soft lips pressed against his cheek, and he grinned as Amy threaded her arms through his. "Enjoying yourself?"

"Oh, yeah. Lots."

She snorted. "Very convincing."

"Hey, as long as you're having fun, I'd tolerate anything for you."

Amy's eyes sparkled with mischief. "Including buying tampons for me, if I really needed them?"

"You want regular, super, or shark bait?"

She laughed and shoved him. The warmth and admiration shining in her eyes as she gazed at him made his heart flutter. Had it ever done that with Erika? Hell, had it ever done that with anyone?

"There you are!"

They both turned as Becca, wearing a sleek black gown and diamond jewelry, waltzed over to them and wrapped Amy up in a big hug. "I'm so proud of you," she gushed, rubbing her back as they embraced. "Your mother would be, too, if she could come."

Amy smiled as they parted. "Thanks, Becca. It means the world to me you came."

"Of course." Becca touched her arm and squeezed. Her eyes, glowing with admiration, flitted over to Scott and immediately cooled. The corners of her mouth seemed to tighten. "Scott," she said with a curt nod.

His brows rose. "Hi, Becca," he said warily.

She looked at him from head to toe, as if sizing him up, and then she turned her back to him and engaged Amy in conversation.

What the hell? Having pursued plenty of women, he could tell when a woman didn't like him. And with Becca, it was written all over her face. Or rather, in the way she clearly cut him out of the conversation with her body language.

Was it something he said at her apartment? Was she angry with him for prying for details about Amy's past?

He heard Becca say, "You have to show me your paintings!" right before she looped her arm through Amy's and tugged her away. If that wasn't a "fuck you" to him, he didn't know what was. She might as well have extended the middle finger.

Odd.

After he knocked back the rest of his punch, he opted for water instead, wanting to sober up before the drive after the gala. They had less than an hour left before the museum closed, but it didn't look as though the crowd was thinning. If anything, the room seemed more packed.

All the better for Amy. He didn't know shit about art, but he figured the more people present, the more money she could make.

His eyes followed Amy and Becca throughout the room. Becca never took her eyes off Amy, laughing and smiling at anything she said. The way she waved her hands, he could just imagine the praise rolling off her tongue.

His lips pursed as he casually switched positions in the room, affording him a better view of the pair. They were just about to move on to the next painting when Becca stopped Amy and smoothed out a wrinkle that had gotten snagged on the zipper in the back of Amy's gown.

Amy thanked her, standing still so Becca could fix the fabric. Once freed, her hand lingered at the small of Amy's back.

Almost like a lover's would.

Scott stared at Becca. The adoring gazes, the thick praise, the casual caresses...

He retraced his steps in his mind from earlier in the week, remembering the wall of framed photographs in Becca's apartment. Most of the photos had been of Amy, which he'd thought strange, but now...

"Oh *shit*," he breathed.

Amy's best friend was in love with her.

The chilled gazes thrown his way suddenly made sense, though it was a one-eighty from how she'd acted when he was at her place. She'd at least been friendly to him. Plus, didn't Amy say Becca had always dated men, though she'd never really settled down with any? Maybe Becca was uncomfortable with her feelings for Amy and wasn't ready to spill how she'd felt yet until she'd figured things out. He had a few gay and lesbian friends. Some of them had great parents who encouraged them to be themselves, while others not so much. Their parents either scorned them or tried forcing their will on them, telling them how to feel about their sexuality.

What kind of mother had Becca had? Had she been abused? Is that why she only had one family photo and had made that strange comment about it "working out" that her mother had died?

He suddenly felt sorry for Becca, despite her curt demeanor toward him. Shitty parenting was something he could relate to.

Sighing in resignation, he tore his eyes off his Amy

and continued to watch the doors and survey the crowd for Nathan. He kept constant vigil the remainder of the last hour, but the guy never showed. Not even the tingling sensation of being watched bothered him.

Before long, the museum started to close. They had to usher people out because they wanted to chat up Amy, including Becca. She gave Amy one last hug before she left, not bothering to cast Scott even a cursory glance.

He watched her go with a sad smile. *Sorry, sweetheart, but I think you're fighting a losing battle.* Far as he knew, Amy didn't go for women, or at least, she hadn't said as much. Not that he'd minded if she did. He didn't care what her sexual preferences were. All that mattered was that she was in his life now, and he had no intentions of disappointing her.

Amy at last thanked the curator and staff before they left. She seemed pleased. "I'm beat," Amy said as they walked to his car. She had her head leaning against his shoulder, with her arm draped through his.

"I bet. Rock star. Who knew you were so famous?"

She winced.

His eyes immediately narrowed in concern. "Did I say something wrong?"

She quickly shook her head and smiled, but he could tell it was to hide what was bothering her. "No. You're perfect."

"Speaking of perfect," he said as they got in his car. "I have a surprise for you."

She raised a brow as she buckled her seat belt. "Oh?"

He nodded. "I have a confession to make—we're not going home."

She blinked. "We're not?"

"Nope. We're going on a weekend getaway." He looped his fingers through hers and kissed the back of her hand. "Just the two of us."

Her eyes warmed for a few seconds before they turned glum again. "That sounds wonderful...but what about Nathan?"

"Already ahead of you. Trust me, where we're going, he won't be able to find us."

Amy softly smiled but didn't say anything.

She didn't believe him. Of course she didn't, and he couldn't blame her. If he'd been stalked by someone, going so far as to change his name and whole identity, and they *still* found him, then he'd be a little skeptical as well.

He started to drive off, determined to be optimistic. "I promise you, Amy. I'll protect you, no matter what."

She reached over and squeezed his leg. A rush of blood went straight to his sex, making it throb.

Down, boy.

They drove in comfortable silence and switched to a rental car on their way out of town. It was all part of the "avoid Nathan" plan.

Now, let's just hope this works.

Scott was pleased as hell when they drove up to their hotel about a half hour later. Run by an eighty-year-old couple who hadn't discovered online marketing yet, primarily only locals knew of it. Built in the Tudor style, it was an oversized two-story cottage with white walls and brown trim. The property was surrounded by wildflowers and trees, and the highway they'd taken to get here was a good mile off the dirt path that led to the hotel.

"Wow," Amy said as they parked and got out. "This place is beautiful. I've never even heard of it."

"Most people haven't, not unless you're from around here." He wriggled his brows. "Thus, its appeal." As far as he knew, Nathan wasn't from here. Scott hadn't noticed anyone tailing them, so he felt pretty good about this.

Their dinner reservations were at eight. After a delay with getting their room, they'd quickly changed into more casual wear and squeezed through the door just before their table was given up.

He'd gotten lucky in booking the room and dinner at the last second. Just because the place was remote and not on the Web didn't mean it wasn't popular with the locals.

The interior of the restaurant was classy, with vaulted ceilings, iron chandeliers dripping in real candles and flowers, and dark wooden tables, chairs, and floors to match the beams that striped the ceiling.

Scott noticed Amy looking over her shoulder and clinging to him as the waitress showed them to their private table in the corner of the main dining room. His heart squeezed. Not that he minded the clinging part, but damn, he could kill that asshole Nathan.

He took her hand and squeezed. That alone seemed to relieve some of her tension.

Once they were seated, he let her become acclimated before he spoke. He hadn't had a chance to talk to her much on the drive over, considering she'd fallen asleep almost right away. "You like it?"

"Yeah. It's gorgeous, like being in a fairy tale." She sipped her ice water and smiled at him. "I can't believe you packed my suitcase for me and boarded Braveheart."

"Wait 'til you see what underwear I packed. I really enjoyed that, by the way."

She nudged him with her knee from under the table; her elbow brushed his. They were seated right next to each other. "I bet you did. Creeper."

He shrugged. "What can I say? I'm a guy."

There weren't that many people in there at that hour, so they were able to put their orders in right away.

"So, what made you want to be a painter?" He leaned on the table and crossed his arms. He wanted to get her mind off Nathan, to have her feel some semblance of normalcy.

"My mom was a painter, self-taught." She idly stirred the ice around her glass. "She was always teaching me while growing up. And not just that, but sculpting, inking, even a little bit of comic book work. She became a big success later, having started her own online art gallery, where people could sell their work and get paid monthly royalties, with her taking a small commission, and she made a killing." She smiled sadly. "Taught me everything I know about being gainfully self-employed."

"You miss her," Scott commented quietly.

She nodded and bit her lip, as if debating on telling him something. A moment later, she looked away, and his shoulders released.

Scott waited a beat before he spoke. "Where's your dad, if I may ask?"

"In New York. He and my mom divorced when I was a kid."

"I'm sorry."

She smiled. "Me, too. They did seem really happy together, and then they just kind of grew apart. They didn't really have much in common, to be honest." She wrinkled her nose. "Things didn't start going downhill until Mom's anxiety attacks started. I think she stressed Dad out too much. He's a lawyer, so he was stressed out enough as is."

He smiled softly.

"What about you?" she asked. "What do your folks do?"

A deluge of memories flooded his mind: his father slurring as he hit his mother, the rage rolling off him as he hit Scott... Scott smiled sadly. "My father is a professional fighter, and my mom is a housewife."

"Oh, that's neat! I want to know who your dad is, though I probably won't recognize the name. I don't keep up with boxing."

"It's not boxing, actually. It's mixed martial arts."

"Wow. Sounds intense."

"It is. I was one, too—a fighter, that is—at one point in time." He smiled tightly. "Similar to your mom, my dad taught me everything I know about fighting," he said bitterly.

"That explains the calluses," she said with a small smile.

"Almost."

"Almost?"

A couple laughed as they walked by. The girl had on an elegant gold dress with a glittering brooch in the shape of a lion head.

The blood drained from his face.

Ghost is looking for you. He's been trying to get you back in the circuit.

The smile faded from her face. "You must have done

a lot of fighting to earn those." Her eyes settled on his knuckles and stayed there.

A lump formed in his throat. "I"—*thump thump, thump thump*—"got into a lot of fights when I was with Erika."

Pussy.

Amy leaned forward, waiting patiently for him to continue. She smiled at him in encouragement, which only made him feel more like a douche for lying to her.

Well, not lying exactly, just not telling the whole truth. It was for her own good. Or was it because he was so damned scared that if she knew the whole story, she'd leave his ass?

He shrugged. "Not much to tell, to be honest. I used to be pretty reckless and a bit of a thrill seeker." Not to mention inheriting his father's rage issues, but he'd worked through those. Mostly. He still drank like a fish, but hey, at least it was only a few beers a day and not a whole case.

Progress was progress.

"Anyway, I ended up meeting this girl named Erika. We fell in love—er, well, I fell in love, and she'd found a breathing ATM. I denied she was using me for a long time—until she left me high and dry with a mountain of debt to pay off."

He looked away, hoping she wouldn't see the lie written on his face.

She reached over and squeezed his hand, sympathy in her eyes. "I'm sorry."

He smiled and shook his head. "Don't be. Her leaving me was the best thing that could have happened to me. If she hadn't, I wouldn't have gotten my act together, and I never would have met you."

Amy flushed, and his sex throbbed again. He loved that color on her, especially on her naked body beneath a sheen of sweat.

A sultry look darkened her eyes. "I don't like it when you're glum."

His interest immediately perked. "Me, either."

"Well, I know something to cheer you up." She leaned in. "I'm not wearing a bra."

He grinned, his sex aching even more. It had been hard ever since she'd walked into his apartment and he'd noticed her nipples. "I noticed."

"Or any underwear."

He blinked. "Didn't you put some on when we changed?"

She shook her head, eyes on him the whole time. "Nope."

Dear God.

Praise the Lord there was a tablecloth, or she would have just flashed everyone in the restaurant as she slowly hiked up her black skirt and guided his hand between her legs. His fingers grazed the sweet curls that surrounded her sex. Taking her direction, he guided himself deeper.

Her breath caught as he touched her, gently and smoothly caressing her lips until her honey started to coat his hand. She widened her legs to allow him deeper access. Her breaths came faster now. She pretended to be studying the menu as he sank his index and ring fingers into her. He would have done more if the angle hadn't been so damnably awkward.

She slouched a little. There, that was better. He managed to go a bit farther. She bit down a gasp, slightly rocking her sex against his hand.

He leaned in and brushed her ear with his lips. "I'm so hard for you right now."

Beneath the table, she reached over and grasped him. "I know."

He growled low. "I want to strip you naked and kiss every inch of you until you moan."

"I'd like that."

He leaned in farther, pressed his fingers a bit deeper. "Then I'd like to bury myself in you and feel you come around me."

She whimpered.

The waitress stopped by, a bright smile on her face, completely oblivious of what was happening beneath the tablecloth. "Hello, again! I just wanted to let you know your dinner will be out shortly."

Amy discreetly straightened her skirt, Scott removing his hand as she did, and stood. She smiled apologetically at the waitress. "I'm so sorry to do this, but I'm afraid I'm feeling a bit ill. Is there any way to have dinner sent up to our room?"

Scott followed her lead, also standing, and casually wiped his hand on a napkin before he stuck it in his pocket. "Yeah, I'm so sorry to do this. I'll be more than happy to pay for room service."

"Oh, um, that's all right! I'll talk to the kitchen staff."

The waitress scurried away after Scott gave her their room number, and he and Amy made a dash for the door. They giggled the whole way. "I feel like a teenager again. I can't believe I did that. Guess the adrenaline rush from the gala still hasn't worn off, and it's making me bolder."

"I don't mind." He kissed the back of her hand. "Believe me."

They clutched hands as they walked through the foyer of the inn. A few people mingled about, checking in and out at the front desk a few feet away.

A sign caught Scott's attention. "Oh, a Jacuzzi. There's a place we haven't had sex before."

"We can add it to the list." Amy gave him a mischievous smile.

It was a running joke that they kept a list of all the places where they'd had sex. They'd already covered all the basics, so they had to get creative.

She frowned. "I didn't bring a bathing suit. I don't own one, so I know you didn't pack one."

"Who said anything about wearing clothes?"

She grinned. "Good point."

He couldn't stop the stupid grin that spread across his face. More eager than ever, they had started toward the steps when a gravelly voice stopped him cold.

"Well, I'll be damned. Miracles do happen."

NINETEEN

SCOTT STOPPED SO suddenly he almost ripped Amy's arm off. Her gaze swept the man in front of them, instantly on her guard.

She didn't recognize him. He was tall, with broad shoulders and a clean black suit. His white hair was slicked back with gel, and a scarlet handkerchief was doubled over in his pocket. He looked sophisticated.

And mean as hell.

He didn't look at Scott as if he was happy to see him. Rather, he looked at him as if he were something to possess, a mere object.

Her fists clenched.

Two large men flanked the mobster-looking guy. Each of them wore tight black T-shirts that showed off their impressive arm muscles, making a clear statement. In other words, "think twice before approaching this guy."

Scott's mouth pressed into a firm line. He discreetly positioned himself in front of Amy and raised his chin.

"What do you want, Ghost?"

Ghost? What kind of a nickname was that?

Amy stood quietly and listened. Whoever this "Ghost" was, Scott was not happy to see him.

Ghost smiled, flashing bleached-white teeth. "I'm here on business. Imagine my delight when I walked in and saw none other than the Lion himself."

Huh? The Lion? "What's he talking about, Scott?" Amy said quietly.

"Sssh." He didn't even look over his shoulder at her. "Stay out of this. And stay out of sight."

Hurt briefly flashed through her. Then Ghost chuckled, and she was more than happy to obey Scott.

But rather than inch behind him, she stayed put. "I'm not hiding."

"Amy," Scott started to push her behind him, "don't argue about this, please."

"Oh, don't bother hiding your lady friend." Ghost leaned his head so as to get a better look at her. "I've already taken notice. Such lovely coloring."

"Stop looking at her," Scott growled.

Amy blinked, drawing still as the tension in the air thickened between the two men.

Ghost smiled broadly. "I didn't know looking was not allowed. My apologies." He gave a low bow. "Hopefully, she'll be better for you than the last one was."

Last one? One of what? A girlfriend?

Did...did he mean Erika? If so, how did Ghost know her?

She glanced at Scott. *Just what kind of secrets have you been keeping from me? What do you not want me to know?*

Ghost glanced at his watch. "My, my, how these things happen at the most inopportune of times. I have somewhere else to be. You're welcome to join me." He grinned. "We can discuss that debt you owe."

"There's nothing to discuss," Scott said. "I've made my payments on time."

Ghost still smiled. "That wasn't an invitation."

The two bodyguards stepped forward, standing on either side of Amy and Scott with their arms crossed.

Amy's heart leapt to her throat, and she gripped Scott's arm.

Scott narrowed his eyes at the men, seeming to be debating whether he could take them on.

Amy squeezed his bicep and dug her nails into his muscle. "Don't. Let's just see what he wants."

"You should listen to your lady friend," Ghost said in a singsong voice. "I'm quite cordial. I just want to talk."

Scott snorted. "Right. Like I believe that."

Ghost pressed his lips together. "Fair enough. How about this? Come with me, and I promise no harm will come to your lady friend." He made a sympathetic face. "I would hate to have to resort to using her as leverage."

"Bastard!" Scott took a step forward. One of Ghost's lackeys was on him in a flash, gripping him by the arm to hold him at bay.

Ghost shrugged. "What can I say? One way or another, I always get what I want."

If looks could kill, Ghost wouldn't have any flesh left on his face. Scott bared his teeth at him. "Yeah." He jerked his arm free of the man's grip. "I get the picture." He put an arm around Amy and pulled her to him.

She pretended not to be scared out of her mind. After

all, it was what she did best for the media—pretend.

Amy stayed close to Scott as they followed Ghost through the foyer and down a set of stairs. The walkway they treaded now was made of stone, inlaid with bits of rainbow-colored shells that glittered in the low lamp light; it looked like some sort of path to a wine cellar. The ceiling was covered in decorative white tiles, broken up into three-foot sections by dark beams of wood. The walls were gray stone, contrasting with the warmer sand-colored rocks they walked along. Iron lanterns lit with small flame-shaped bulbs hung from the walls, interspersed between iron flower baskets dripping peonies. The lanterns cast a warm orange glow, making their shadows dance as they walked.

Where were they going? Most importantly, what would happen to them when they got there? Nerves set butterflies whirling in her stomach. And when she got nervous, a switch that controlled her mouth flipped. "Why do they call you Ghost?" Amy blurted. "I know it's not your real name."

"And what if it is?" he asked in a teasing tone.

Amy pressed her lips together, finding it incredibly difficult not to duck her head to this intimidating man.

He chuckled softly and faced forward again. "Whenever people on the run from me see me, they look like they've seen a ghost. All the color drains from their faces. Some have even pissed their pants."

He sounded proud to scare the shit out of people.

Prick.

Scott squeezed her hand, almost painfully so. She squeezed back, letting him know she didn't need him to display bone-crushing force to send the message. She got it—talking to Ghost was off-limits.

She didn't need to be told twice he was dangerous. The man exuded danger, as though something bad were going to happen by just looking at him.

They went through a large, worn wooden door. About ten feet ahead stood a larger door; this one looked as if it was made of steel or iron. Muffled voices slipped through the crack at the bottom.

One of Ghost's men opened it. Noise—men and women shouting and cheering—blasted them.

Amy looked around, wide-eyed, as they followed Ghost and his men along the outskirts of the large crowd gathered around the raised ring. Two fighters, both very large, muscular men, went at it in the middle. From the looks of it, the fight had been going on for a while; their noses and eyes were swollen or bleeding. Sweat coated their magnificent, scarred bodies, shining under the yellow lighting that barely lit the room. It smelled of beer and body odor, like onions.

Amy squinted. Was that...*barbed wire* being used as a fence around the ring?

"Where the hell are we?" Amy said to Scott discreetly.

"The circuit," Scott said darkly.

"Circuit?"

"I'll explain later." He squeezed her hand.

In other words, shut your mouth.

Amy promptly zipped her lips, her eyes riveted on the arena. One fighter got a jab in on the other, nearly knocking his head off his shoulders. The crowd's arms went up, flinging beer everywhere as they cheered, swore, and shouted.

On the opposite side of the room was a red door. Ghost went in, followed by one of his men, and then Amy and Scott.

The other man closed the door behind them and stood in front of the exit, arms crossed and eyes glued to them.

The room was small, with a simple wooden desk, a leather chair, and two metal folding chairs on the other side of the desk. Some filing cabinets stood along one wall.

Ghost took a seat in the leather chair. "Please, sit."

They both reluctantly sat down across from Ghost, though Scott remained near the edge of his seat. "How did you convince the owners to let you fight here?" Scott said evenly.

Ghost raised an amused brow. "Probably because the owner is sitting right in front of you."

"What did you do to get this place? Threaten to break the owners' kneecaps? Have their children and their grandchildren strangled in their sleep?"

Ghost laughed. "Nothing so dramatic as that, I assure you. I simply offered them enough money and then some to retire with. They didn't have much in terms of savings, and were looking to sell. They just never found the right deal." He flashed those sparkling white teeth. "Until now. Even you have to admit it's the perfect venue."

"I see." Scott's jaw ticked. He sat back and crossed his arms. "All right, we're here. What do you want?"

Ghost chuckled and smiled as he leaned back in his chair and steepled his long fingers. "You never were one to beat around the bush. Very well. I need the rest of the money owed me by the end of the month."

"*The end of the month?*" Scott spat. "You know I won't have it."

"Oh, I think you will," Ghost said pleasantly, casting a pointed glance in Amy's direction.

Scott's lips pressed together in a thin line. "We had an agreement."

Ghost shrugged. "I changed my mind. We've suffered a few...setbacks recently, a few bad investments, if you will, that didn't pan out. So, I need the cash sooner. Besides, you've had over a year."

"I've made all my payments on time," Scott fumed.

"And I appreciate that," Ghost said with another oily smile. "Which is why I'm giving you 'til the end of the month instead of demanding it now." His eyes sparkled with cunning. "There is, of course, another way you can repay me."

"Forget it. I already know what you're going to ask."

"You haven't even heard the deal yet," Ghost said mockingly. "Fight for me. Just for a month, and I'll forgive all your debt."

"So you can get me back in the ring? So you can *own* me?"

"Oh, Scott. You poor, naive boy. You really thought you were free from me this whole time? I still own you. Just because I loosened the leash a little doesn't mean I removed the collar."

The two men came behind Amy and Scott. Amy tensed and shifted her weight to the balls of her feet, ready to run.

Ghost held up his hand. "Easy, boys. No violence tonight. The Lion is, after all, on a date, and I would hate to be the asshole who ruined it for him."

The Lion? Amy made a what-the-hell face at Scott, but he minutely shook his head.

Ghost waved his hand. "You may go. Oh, but first, here's my card."

"I won't be needing it. And I'm not giving you my number," Scott said.

Ghost simply grinned. "No need. I'll find you if you try to go back on our agreement. And I insist you take my card," he added with a hint of steel.

Scott stared at it for a long while before he finally snatched it from Ghost's hand.

"One month," Ghost said. "Or I may have to look into other means of persuasion." His eyes roved Amy from head to toe, and she trembled.

Scott pulled her to him. "Go to hell!" he barked, spitting on Ghost's desk.

Ghost laughed as Scott yanked Amy out the door and into the crowd.

"What was that all about? Who are these people?" Amy yelled over the noise as Scott dragged her back toward the tunnel.

"I'll explain later." His face was covered in worry, and her stomach flipped.

What had she gotten into now?

About ten feet away from the door, people began to scream. Flashlights and people dressed in black body armor raided the room.

"Shit!" Scott swerved back around, running in the opposite direction as people began to stampede.

"What? What is it?" Amy frantically tried to look over her shoulder.

"Pigs."

Cops? Why the hell were the cops here?

Her heart skipped a beat as ice-cold fear washed over her.

Cops. Media. Michael. Blood. Oh God, so much blood...

A brief shake broke the memory that had been about to suck her in whole. "Amy! Stay with me! Come on, baby, run!"

They rounded a corner, and Amy could see where Scott was headed. It looked like a storage room, with a window up high.

"Gah!"

Amy was nearly jerked backward and would have been if Scott hadn't let go when he did.

He spun on his heel, driving a fist into the face of the cop who held him. The man swore, grabbing his walkie-talkie and shouting something into it.

Backup.

Scott started forward again. Amy was frozen in place, having no clue what to do, when two more cops came up from behind Scott and grabbed him before he got two feet.

"Run, Amy!" Scott bellowed.

She shook her head, inching toward the storage room.

"Run!" Scott shouted. He fought against the cops, a deadly, practiced dance only a pro fighter would know.

She stood mesmerized, watching him fight, when a cop slipped through and stalked toward her. Amy gasped and backed away clumsily from the cop's outstretched hand. Something tackled him from behind, and he went down to the ground hard, Scott on top of him.

"Get your pretty little ass out of here, now!" Scott said. "I'll be right behind you!"

Amy blinked and snapped back to her senses. "Promise?"

"Promise!" he yelled, grappling with the cop.

Amy's heart lurched. After one last glance at Scott, she turned and ran as hard as she could for the window.

The breaths coming in and out of her lungs seemed sharper, making it harder to breathe. It probably had something to do with the fact her heart was about to beat out of her chest as she entered the room and slammed the door shut behind her, locking it. For good measure, she pushed an empty filing cabinet in front of it, having to dig her heels in and grit her teeth to do so.

The whole room appeared to be filled with discarded furniture. Moonlight shone through the window, providing just enough light to see by. The chain of an overhead light slapped her in the face, making her shriek, but she didn't dare pull it. No way was she going to risk giving away her location, just in case the gathering cops outside hadn't noticed the ground-level window yet.

A dresser stood in front of the window, just high enough she should be able to pull herself up, open it, and get the hell out of here. Finding a nightstand to climb up on, she hoisted herself up onto the dresser and found the latch for the window. It was rusty, refusing to open at first.

Come on, come on.

A large crash threatened to nearly splinter the door behind her, and she clamped down a scream. From the sounds of the grunts and cries of pain that followed, Scott was still fighting.

Tears pricked her eyes. What the hell was she doing? She should be helping him.

By doing what? Screaming at them? She knew self-defense, but she'd be useless with more than one guy. Besides, the cops were probably all trained for this sort of scenario. They would take her down no matter what.

Frantic, she jiggled and pressed against the window until the latch finally screeched loose and the window fell open a few inches. She managed to cram her arms through and then used her body weight to pry it open the rest of the way before she squeezed her body through.

The smell of damp soil met her nose as she crawled through the mud, scraping her legs against the metal frame of the window. In the front of the cottage, just beyond the wall to the right, she could hear policemen yelling orders and the squeal of tires as more cop cars pulled into the driveway.

She scrambled into some bushes as a pair of cops ran by, yelling into their walkie-talkies about a crazy man taking on ten cops downstairs.

She knew that crazy man had to be Scott.

Please, please be okay.

Reining in her growing panic, she forced down a few deep breaths before she poked her head out of the bushes. The woods lay to the left, about fifty feet away. If she stuck to the shadows and bolted as quickly as she could…

Gravel crunched beneath boots to her right as more cops approached.

Realizing her opportunity to escape was slipping away, she said a prayer and darted from the shadows of the bushes.

"Hey!" called out a voice behind her. "Freeze!"

She didn't. "Freeze" meant possibly going to prison and revealing her true name to more policemen. From past experiences, she knew someone would eventually tip a reporter for a quick buck, and her new start in life would be compromised completely.

And she wasn't ready to back down yet, to give in to that fate. She wanted her old life back.

But in order to get it, she needed to run right now, to get as far away as she possibly could.

Which was why she didn't stop long enough to look over her shoulder until she was well into the woods.

TWENTY

AMY'S FISTS PUMPED, the cool late-night air chapping her throat and making her lungs hurt.

Scott's command echoed in her head, fueling her heavy strides.

Run, Amy.

When she reached the woods, she'd immediately hid until she was certain the cop who'd yelled at her wasn't going to give chase.

He hadn't, thinking she was probably just a partygoer and not worth the trouble. Besides, they had a whole basement full of fighters to contain. She caught the name Ghost being shouted between them more than once, too. Whatever he was, he wasn't very popular with the police.

Ducking behind some shrubs, she crouched and watched the chaos unfold, trying to catch her breath. Gravel spewed beneath tires as more cops pulled into the parking lot, surrounding the building and corralling people as they rushed out.

It was déjà vu. People cussed as they were slammed up against cars, and shouts filled the air; the red-and-blue glow of the police lights reflected off all the handcuffs being whipped out.

Amy watched the events unfold from the safety of the forest, so tired she could barely think of what she needed to do. She bit her lip to keep from gasping when Scott appeared from the front of the building, escorted by two police officers. They had his hands behind his back as they walked him to one of the waiting cars. His eyes searched the wildflower field and trees.

Looking for me.

Her muscles tensed and strained, desperate to go to him, but she rooted herself to the spot. Her breath caught as they shoved him down into the car, and the siren started up before they wheeled out of the lot.

She watched the car disappear down the driveway. Once it was gone, she crept away from the noise and into the forest.

Stepping over branches and holes, she dug her cell phone out of her purse until she found some reception. The second she had two bars, she speed-dialed Becca. The phone was pressed so closely to her ear that her cartilage started to hurt.

"Come on, Becca," she prayed. "Come on, pick up. Pick up."

The rings cut in and out with dead air, eventually giving her chunks of Becca's voice mail greeting.

"Dammit." Amy walked around some more, holding the phone up while her eyes were glued to the bars.

She gasped as three bars lit up for a split second, only to die back to nothing when she took the next step. "Shit.

Fuck. Damn." A slew of curse words flew out of her mouth as she pranced around, trying to retrace her steps. "Shit, son of a—ah! Stay! STAY!"

Immediately, she dialed Becca's number.

This time it didn't break up so badly.

"Come on," Amy breathed into the phone. "Come on, come on, come on, come—"

"Hello?"

"Becca!" Amy shrieked, gripping the phone.

Becca yawned. "Ames? What's going on? What's happened?"

Amy couldn't hold it together anymore. She started to cry.

Becca was silent. "Amy, what the hell happened?"

Amy spewed out the basics in barely intelligible sobs. "Scott wanted to surprise me with a dinner date after the gala, and...and...we met someone from his past. Someone not very nice."

"What do you mean?"

"I mean, I don't know, some kind of mobster!"

"Shit," Becca hissed.

"Anyway, some cops showed up." She swallowed as her voice caught. The dry night air seemed to have absorbed all the moisture from her mouth, making it hard to talk. "I think they took Scott to jail, with everybody else they caught," Amy finished. "I need to get there, please. He got me out of there before I got caught. I have to try to help him."

"But, Amy, won't that mean...your identity...the press—"

"I don't care! I have to help him! I can't hide if it means Scott gets in trouble!"

"Please, what kind of trouble is he going to get into?"

Amy froze. "Why aren't you supporting me on this?"

Becca sighed dramatically, an edge to her voice. "I'm just saying, they'll probably post his bail, he'll pay it, and be fine. That'll be that."

A thought occurred to Amy, and she pressed her lips together. "He...might not be able to afford bail."

"What do you mean?"

"I mean"—Amy sighed—"he works three jobs to pay off this mountain of debt his bitch of an ex-girlfriend left him." How much had he dished out for this hotel? The prices on the menu hadn't been cheap. And judging from their encounter downstairs, it sounded like every dollar Scott had belonged to Ghost.

"Oh, come on, Amy," Becca drawled. "That sounds like a load of bullshit if I ever heard it."

"What are you talking about? He's my friend!"

"So am I! I've known you longer! I know when I smell a rat! How long have you known this guy, huh? He's probably trying to take advantage of you!"

Doubt seeped into her heart. "He's not. I know he's telling the truth."

Becca snorted. "Right, because you're obviously great at judging when a guy is lying to you."

That felt like a slap across the face.

Becca growled a sigh. "I'm sorry, Amy. I don't mean to be a bitch. I've just barely had any sleep this week, and my head is pounding."

Amy forced herself to take a deep breath and count to ten. "I know," she said calmly. Being Becca's friend also meant dealing with her mood swings. She was irritable a lot due to chronic migraines. Amy honestly felt sorry for her; Becca had had them since she was a kid.

Becca took a deep breath and let it out slowly. Amy heard the creak of a mattress in the background. "I'm coming over to your apartment right now, don't worry."

"Actually," Amy bit her lip, "I'm not at my apartment."

Becca went silent. "Then where are you?"

Half an hour and a mile hike later, Becca pulled up to mile marker 51 along the highway, and Amy wearily climbed inside her car. Thank God for GPS and 4G; otherwise, Amy might have stumbled around in the woods all night searching for the nearest busy road.

"Thanks," Amy breathed, shutting the door. "I would have been royally screwed if—"

"What the hell were you thinking?" Becca screamed.

Amy startled and stared.

"Nathan just *attacked* you in public, he's still at large and could *attack* again, and you frickin' run off with your boyfriend to some secluded cabin in the woods bullshit? Frick, Amy!"

Years of anger and frustration surged through her. "I just wanted to move on past all this shit and live a normal, happy life!"

"I'm not saying you can't do that, but you can't be stupid about it!"

Amy blinked.

Becca rubbed her eyes, her shoulders deflating. Her eyes were bloodshot, as if she'd been crying. Then again, they usually were after she'd had a migraine, because it meant she hadn't slept much.

Becca leaned her head back against the seat and closed her eyes. Charged silence filled the car. "I'm sorry,

Ames. I'm being a total bitch, but I can't help it. I worry about you. A lot. You know you're family to me." She reached out and squeezed Amy's hand, hard.

"I know," Amy said cautiously, trying to pull her hand back, but Becca wouldn't let go. If anything, her grip got tighter.

Amy looked down. "Becca, you're hurting me," she said quietly.

Becca blinked a few times. "What? Oh, sorry," she mumbled, quickly withdrawing her hand.

"It's okay." Amy studied her friend with confusion. "You all right? You seem exhausted."

Becca shrugged. "Zach ran away from home again. I've been out half the night looking for him."

"Oh Jesus." Amy's voice softened. "Did you ever find him?"

Becca nodded. "He was over at a friend's, getting high." Tears formed in her eyes, and she sniffled. "I don't know why I try sometimes."

"Oh, come here." Amy hugged her, letting Becca rest her head on her shoulder as she shuddered. Amy rubbed her back. "It'll be okay. I swear it will be."

Becca took a few calming breaths and nodded before she sat up. She wiped at her eyes and smiled. "I'm sorry. Wow, I'm a mess."

"S'kay. Both of us are."

"Which is why we're perfect for each other." Becca smiled.

Amy smiled back. "Two peas in a pod," she said lamely.

A beat of silence passed before Becca said, "What do you say we get out of here and go grab some breakfast?"

Amy searched for a response. "But I have to go help Scott."

"Oh, Jesus Christ, not this shit again." Becca gripped the wheel, scowling. "He's just using you, Amy. You should let whatever is going to happen to him happen, and dump him."

"What the hell? What is wrong with you?"

"What's wrong with you? You're going to let him use you the same way Michael did? You're going to let that asshole treat you that way?"

"Stop calling him that!"

Becca shook her head and looked forward. "Fine." She jerked the key, and the engine revved. Snapping the gearshift into drive, she floored it, and they shot off down the road; the back tires spun for a few seconds. "Go help him. See if you get your heart broken again."

Amy deflated. "I don't want to argue with you." She wanted things to go back to being the way they were between them, before the fighting. "You're my best friend."

You're my only friend. Please don't leave me alone.

Becca softened and smiled a moment before her gaze turned serious. "By the way, I got one of my friends in the police department to look into why Nathan's parole officer has been ignoring your calls. Turns out he's banging her and paying off her house."

Amy's jaw dropped. She sat there, stunned, staring at the road as Becca slowed to a reasonable speed. "Son of a bitch."

"I know, right? Doesn't really surprise me, though. You know Nathan. He's a Hawke. They can buy their way out of anything."

Wasn't that the truth? Except, apparently, they

couldn't buy him a new career. He wanted Amy's blood to pay for that.

She shivered. "Thanks for looking into it for me. At least I know now what's going on." Though she had no idea what the hell she was going to do about it.

"No problem." Becca smiled. It was too tight. "That's what friends are for."

Amy gave her a smile back, unsure why Becca still seemed so tense.

"Now, let's go rescue Prince Charming," she said sourly.

Oh. That's why.

Whatever. She was too tired to argue anymore.

Amy sank into the seat, crossed her arms, and stared out the window as heavy silence filled the car.

He'd lied.

Well, not exactly. He just hadn't told the whole truth. That didn't qualify as a lie, then, did it?

Scott sat on the mattress in his cell and stared out through the bars at his fellow inmates. Most of them were fighters who looked beaten half to hell, with scars they'd be sporting for the rest of their lives. The worst ones had gone to the ER, where the medical staff was probably trying to put them together again like broken dolls.

Silly, stupid kids. Reckless kids.

Scott wanted to scream at them to turn around, to stop putting money in Ghost's pockets before it was too late. But he already knew once you set foot in the ring, once you signed your name on the dotted line, you'd essentially sold your soul to the devil.

Once a loan shark had you in its clutches, they would never let you go until you repaid the debt.

It had been a miracle Scott could find steady employment after he got out of the circuit. His case worker had had a hell of a time getting him work, considering Ghost's underground reputation and the fact no one wanted to hire anyone even remotely associated with him, but after much praying, he'd found a job. Good behavior led to more jobs, and he had finally started clawing his way out of the debt Erika had dumped on him.

Now, all that hard work was shot to hell. One of the conditions of him keeping his jobs—and staying on parole—was keeping out of jail. Once his bosses and parole officer found out...

He was so screwed.

The click of high heels approached as a door opened.

"Now here's a familiar sight."

All the air left him in such a rush, you'd think he'd been punched.

Shooting up out of his seat as though he'd seen a ghost, he gripped the bars of the cell and stared at the skinny bleached-blonde in front of him.

"Erika?"

TWENTY-ONE

H E WAS IN Hell. He had to be, because Satan herself stood right in front of him.

Erika wasn't what he remembered. If anything, she looked worse. The orange of her spray-on tan did a poor job of covering up all the bruises on her arms, left from her love affair with needles and various drugs. Her hair was too bright, too fake a shade of blonde. She'd always loved that color.

Consequently, as the reality of how poisonous Erika was sunk in, Scott began to loathe the sunny shade.

Except on Amy. Everything was perfect about his Amy.

Erika had grown skinnier. It looked as if her skin hung on her gangly form; he could see the hollow of her bones through the shadows that fell across her skin.

Calling her sickly would be paying her a compliment—calling her a corpse was more appropriate.

"My God," he whispered. "What have they done to you?"

She fidgeted and smoothed out a wrinkle in her dress. "You're looking well," she said brightly, with a wide smile. Despite her other..."modifications," it looked as though Ghost's money hadn't gone far enough to repair her teeth while she'd worked for him. They were yellowed, some broken off or rotten completely from years spent locked in a drug haze. It made him sad just to look at her. She, like so many other girls and boys, could have been so much more.

If Ghost hadn't sunk his claws into them.

Scott continued to stare at her, trying to squelch the rising pity he felt.

Erika bit her lip and looked away. "I picked out this dress just for you," she said in her raspy voice. Chain-smoking since she was twelve had been responsible for her eroded vocal cords. "I know you like violet."

"What are you doing here?" He struggled to keep his voice calm. He needed to punch something.

No. No more violence. You gave that up, remember? Yes, he needed to deal with his stress in another way. So he grabbed the bars and squeezed hard, leaning forward to peer at her.

Erika smiled, her eyes hopeful. "I came here to get you out."

His gaze narrowed. "In exchange for what?"

"Does everything have to have a price?"

"In our world it does." He pressed his lips together in a thin line.

Scott was lucky he'd even gotten bail. After spending the first few hours being ruthlessly interrogated and thrown back in his cell, he didn't think the police had believed his story. Of how he'd been in the wrong place at the wrong time, had only wanted to take his girlfriend out for a nice weekend out of town. Of how two thugs, and Ghost himself, had threatened them if they didn't come downstairs. Now, Scott may have fudged the part about mistaking the police officers for more thugs when he'd punched a few of them in the face. After all, Ghost owned most of the police station.

The detectives who questioned him had brought up Scott's past with Ghost. Scott had also pointed out he'd had a crystal-clear record since he'd made parole. The detectives hadn't said a word after that, and shortly afterward, Scott was escorted back to his cell and informed of what his bail would be. It was…odd. He was still waiting for the catch.

Erika finally sighed and crossed her arms. "I came to bail you out because I wanted to."

"With what money?" he almost asked. "You don't have to," he said instead, in an attempt to be polite, or at least civil.

She shrugged. "It's already done."

Sure enough, footsteps approached. Scott stepped back from the bars as the officer who'd put him in here, an older gentleman in his fifties, unlocked the door and pulled it back. "Lucky day, kid. Guess you owe this young lady a date or something."

She beamed at him.

Did Scott mention he wanted to punch something? He almost told the man to just leave him in here, that he'd make his own bail, but he needed to find Amy and make sure she was all right. He couldn't leave her alone with that creep Nathan on the loose. "Not likely," he said brusquely as he brushed past a frowning officer and a frozen Erika.

She skittered after him on her six-inch heels as he barreled toward the exit. Damn, his car was still at the inn. He'd have to hail a cab. Quickly collecting his personal effects, he checked his wallet.

"Son of a bitch." Where several ones, tens, twenties, and a one-hundred-dollar bill had been remained a few torn Washingtons.

Crooked pigs.

"Something wrong?" Erika leaned over his shoulder.

He slammed his billfold shut. Somehow, her seeing his wallet, something so personal that had been with him since high school, only pissed him off more. It felt like an invasion of privacy. "Everything," he growled, bursting through the exit. The door banged into the side of the building and made the glass sing. Some people leapt out of his way as he passed. Wise move.

The sky was starting to lighten. It had to be close to six a.m. Traffic had started to pick up with the early-morning rush hour, and pedestrians walked along the sidewalk, hustling to whatever glass-and-steel high-rise they worked in.

He'd have to ride the bus over a few blocks and walk the rest of the way. The police station was downtown, about fifty blocks from where he lived.

His long stride was purposeful as he stalked toward the bus stop.

The irritating *click-clack* of heels followed him. "Aren't you going to thank me?" Erika said, annoyed.

"Ha, thank you? Don't you mean 'thank Ghost'?"

She stopped and gave an exasperated sigh. "I wanted to repay you."

"Well, you didn't!" Scott whirled around. People stared at them as they passed. Let them. He was past his boiling point, a slow simmer that had started the moment he'd laid eyes on the woman who'd nearly ruined him. "You think anything good comes from cutting deals with that thief? Huh? You think he won't want something in return?"

Tears gathered at the rims of her eyes. "I only wanted to help you the way you've helped me, baby."

"Don't call me that." There was enough venom in his voice to rival a snake's. "Don't you ever fucking call me that again, you hear?"

A sob escaped her lips. People glared at him. He nearly rolled his eyes. Of course they'd take her side. They didn't even know him. Poor, helpless Erika.

Biggest mistake of his life.

Feeling himself on the verge of a complete meltdown, he turned and ran his hands over his face. *One, two, three, four...* Once he got to ten, he took a deep breath, let it out slowly, and turned back to face her.

She watched him with her head ducked and her shoulders rolled in, like a scolded puppy. That innocent act might have sucked him in once, but not now. Not after he knew better.

Still...he felt a bit like an ass. "I'm sorry," he said gruffly. "I'm sure you tried to do the right thing, but it was with the wrong method. Ghost will think I owe him even more now."

"You don't have to owe him anything." She clung to his arm and gazed hopefully into his eyes. He resisted the urge to shrivel his lip and step back. "We can leave right now, never come back."

Restraining his anger, he peeled her hands off. "Erika, don't."

"Please!" She gripped him even harder and dug her nails in. "Please don't walk away from me again, don't leave me all alone." She shook her head as her voice broke. "I couldn't live through it."

"Yet you survived somehow," he said dryly.

"Only because I kept dreaming of the day when we would be together again." She cupped his face with her hands, eyes shining. "I've missed you so much, baby."

Before he could blink, she planted her mouth firmly over his.

"I still think this is a horrible idea," Becca said tiredly as they turned on to the street where the police station was. The sun had started to peek over the horizon. It felt as if Amy hadn't slept for ages. Emotional and physical fatigue were probably to blame for that.

Speaking of which…this topic was getting really old. Amy grated her teeth. "I know. You've said that at least fifty times."

"Because I keep hoping what I'm saying is going to sink in." Becca parked along the curb. They got out into the brisk early-morning air and walked along the sidewalk. The police station was just around the corner.

Amy kept her pace quick, partly from her desire to get this over with so she could leave Becca and her obstinate opinions behind and partly from her desire to get Scott out.

Deep down, she knew Becca had a point. Illegal fighting rings? Blood money? Scary mobster-like bosses who basically threatened her life? Any other girl with common sense would have pounced on the opportunity to run for the hills and leave Scott to his fate.

But not her.

Since meeting him, she'd felt more alive. More like her old self, a part of her she never thought she'd see again. It felt comfortable and right being with him, even if it was wrong on so many other levels.

Nothing else had done that in years. Not therapy, money, shopping, or meaningless blind dates.

She literally owed Scott her life. Finally, for the first time in two years, she felt as if she was actively participating in her own life and not just going through the motions.

She felt *alive*.

Her heart pounded as they rounded the corner. The police building was in view now; the American flag waved jovially in the breeze on the pole out front, along with the state's and city's flags.

They were close to the steps when a lip-locked couple caught her eye—and drew her to a complete stop.

Becca nearly slammed into her. "Hey, what's wrong?" She looked up; a small gasp escaped her lips. "*Oh.*"

Oh was right.

Amy stared, wide-eyed and open-mouthed, at Scott.

Who was apparently too busy sucking tongue with blondie to notice her.

She didn't know how long she stared. It felt like an eternity, as if all the sound of the things happening around her vanished, leaving her with tunnel vision of the couple directly in front of her.

Becca grabbed her arm and gently tugged. "Come on, Amy," she said quietly, "you don't need to watch this. Let's go."

Amy couldn't move. She felt her heart break. Her chest hurt. She couldn't breathe, and her knees shook.

Becca stepped in front of her and placed her hands on her shoulders. "Amy, please. Come on."

She knew she should go. Hell, she sure wanted to. But still, her eyes wouldn't budge, and neither would her legs.

Then something amazing happened that made Amy gasp and lean forward.

Scott broke the kiss and shoved the woman away. "What's wrong with you?" he said. "I don't feel that way about you anymore!"

Amy listened intently, holding her breath because she was afraid if she so much as breathed, she'd miss a word of what they were saying.

The woman's eyes were starry as she gazed adoringly at Scott. "But didn't it feel good, baby?" Her eyes dropped to his lips, and she leaned in again. "You taste amazing. Always did."

Planting his hands on her shoulders, he firmly held her back. "Look, I don't know what Ghost promised you in exchange for helping him get to me, but I'm not part of some package deal. You can't win me over with money."

She trailed a finger down her breasts. "I have other things that might interest you."

"No," he said firmly.

The girl was on the verge of speaking again when she looked up and spied Amy and Becca. "What are you looking at?"

Scott turned around. All the blood drained from his face when he saw Amy. They stared at each other for a pregnant second. "Amy, I can explain—"

"It's okay." She held up a hand to stop him. She stepped closer, smiling. "I heard everything. It seems you were forced?" She looked at the girl.

The girl sneered and glared at Amy. "I didn't force anything on him. He begged me to kiss him."

"That's not true," Scott growled. "Erika, you should leave."

Erika? Amy racked her brain. Where had she heard that name before?

Realization sank in. "You're the woman whose debt he took on."

Erika blinked. Her heavily glossed lip rolled up to her nose. "Excuse me? Just who the hell are you?"

Scott gave Amy a questioning look. There was a wariness to his eyes that made her heart squeeze, like a puppy waiting to be scolded.

Stepping up to him, Amy took his hand and looked Erika in the eyes. "I'm his girlfriend."

"Girlfriend?" Erika shrieked. Her eyes did a full-body take on Amy, sliding from her head to her toes and back again. "You're not even that pretty! Plus, you're fat!"

"Erika!" Scott snapped. "Not everyone has the same limited definition of beauty as you."

Erika's face turned red. She crushed her bony hands into fists. "Is she another stray? Another 'damsel in distress'?"

Scott hesitated.

Erika smiled. "I know your type. You like to try to rehabilitate people and then release them back into the wild. He'll do the same to you, honey." She pointed at Amy. "It's just a matter of time. He'll leave you, mark my words."

"That's enough," Scott said with quiet fury. His jaw ticked, and tension radiated off him. Amy could tell he was walking along a very tightrope of patience that was about to snap.

A hand touched Amy's shoulder. "Come on, Amy," Becca said softly. "You don't need this right now."

Damn straight she didn't. Wasn't getting away from drama the whole point of starting over? And here she was, right smack in the middle of another soap opera.

Maybe some people were just screwed like that.

Amy remained rooted to the spot, unwilling to leave Scott's side.

"It's okay." He turned his back to Erika with a warning glance. "I'll handle her and then come get you."

"Why can't I come with you?"

"I...need to take care of something."

She raised a brow, not liking the guarded look in his eyes. Much as she wanted him not to keep secrets from her, she couldn't blame him. It wasn't time to have that conversation yet. Because if she expected him to spill his heart, to reveal all his monsters, then she'd have to return in kind.

And that was going to hurt like hell.

So instead, she smiled. "Okay. Call me when you're ready."

"I will." He smiled back, giving her hand a squeeze before he let her walk away.

Becca eagerly tugged her along. "Nice ex," she commented dryly.

Amy made no comment. She was too busy thinking about how she was going to tell Scott the truth about Michael.

About exactly how he'd died, and how it had all been her fault.

TWENTY-TWO

BECCA'S PLACE HADN'T changed. At least, not to Amy's memory. Which was a little fuzzy, considering she hadn't been over in a while. Becca was always tied up with her little brother or work. The girl definitely led a busy life.

Amy walked around the living room and looked around as Becca made them breakfast in the kitchen. A man's leather jacket lay draped over the top of a chair. Did Becca already have a new boy toy? She hadn't mentioned it. Then again, Becca changed men the way some girls changed outfits. Sometimes, she went through two or three a day.

Amy continued her casual lope around the living room, coming to a wall stacked with shelves of pictures. Actually, something had changed. There were more pictures.

And, she noted, most of them seemed to be of her.

She stopped to stare. Slowly, her eyes ran over the

frames from wall to wall, noting how many were of her.

A chill tingled its way through her, and her muscles tensed. Without really meaning to, she glanced at the door. Was it locked?

It felt silly thinking about running. Becca would have no reason to harm her.

"Here we go!"

Amy jumped and looked behind her, where Becca stood in the kitchen entrance with a tray of cookies and milk.

Becca gave her a weird look and grinned. "Little jumpy there, Ames?" She walked over and placed the tray on the coffee table.

Amy nervously laughed and ran a hand through her hair. "Yeah, I guess." She frowned. "I don't think that will ever go away."

Becca remained silent for a beat. She pressed her lips together, as if thinking about something. Grabbing a cookie and a small glass of milk, she brought it over to Amy. "Here." She handed the warm, gooey palmful of chocolatey goodness to her. "I know I said I'd make us breakfast, but I changed my mind. I remembered the other day how much you love chocolate chip cookies, so I made a batch. I thought they might cheer you up more than bacon and eggs."

"Thank you," Amy said absentmindedly, staring at the cookie as it warmed her hand. "But *you* hate chocolate chip cookies. You said they're 'too fattening.'"

"Yeah." She shrugged and looked away. "Doesn't mean I can't make 'em for you when you come over." Becca stared at her, seemingly waiting for something.

Smiling tensely, Amy took a bite of the cookie. It was

fresh-from-the-oven gooey. "Hmmm…" she said as she chewed. "This is amazing."

Becca's shoulders relaxed. "I know, right? Mom left me some kickass recipes."

Amy nodded and glanced back at the wall. "You don't seem to have many pictures of your mother," she said carefully, gesturing with the napkin at the sole picture of her whole family. "I mean, I know you two didn't exactly get along, but I, well, I thought I remembered you having more pictures."

Becca shifted her weight as she stared at the picture of her family with an unreadable expression. "I did. My brother broke them."

"Oh." Amy bit her lip. She knew Becca carried a lot of anger and resentment over their mother's neglect and other grievances, but Zach seemed to harbor borderline rage, from what Becca had told her. The kid had problems. "I'm sorry I brought it up. It can't have been easy, what you guys went through."

Becca shrugged and steeled her gaze. "Abuse happens to kids every day. It just means we're part of the statistic."

Amy's heart sank. *Way to go, Ames. Make her feel like shit. Oh, by the way, Becca, why do you have so many pictures of me?* The question burned on her tongue, daring her to ask, but she couldn't bring herself to needle Becca further. Amy went and picked up another cookie, sensing it would make Becca feel better, and opted to change the subject. "I still can't wrap my head around the fact Scott was a street fighter and involved with a loan shark."

"Yeah, that's pretty wild." Becca sounded anything but surprised as she came over and sat down on the sofa.

Amy sat down beside her, chewing pensively. "I

mean," she said between chews, "you think you know someone…" She sighed. "I should have known it was too good to be true. I'm never that lucky, and things are never that easy for me, not even falling in love."

Becca gave her a sympathetic smile and rubbed her arm. "Don't give up, Amy. Maybe it was never meant to work out with him."

And that is so not what I want to hear right now. Amy's jaw tensed, and she leaned forward. As predicted, Becca dropped her hand and sat back.

Amy downed the rest of her milk and set the glass back on the tray. "I have to try to work this out with Scott," she said with quiet determination. "This is the first time I've felt something for someone in years. I think that's worth fighting for, because it means I'm not as broken as I thought I was. I'm getting stronger." She looked at Becca and held her gaze. "And I'd like your support on this. But I just want you to know I'm not giving up on him, with or without your consent. I hope you understand."

"I do understand," Becca cooed, leaning forward. She brushed the hair away from Amy's face; Amy flinched. "You want somebody in your life, and you need that. I just don't want to see you get hurt again. You've been through so much." Becca ran a strand of Amy's hair through her fingers, letting the ends curl around her fingertips.

Amy scooted away, pulling her hair free as she cleared her throat.

Becca's hand remained in the air. It clenched before it lowered to her side. Becca closed her eyes, took a deep breath, and let it out. "I think you need to leave Scott."

Amy shook her head. "He deserves the benefit of the doubt. He's never tried to hurt me."

"Yet!" Becca shot out of her seat. "Look at the company he keeps! Did you see that girl? Did you not hear what she said? Scott is bad news, Ames. He's only trying to lure you in so he can have his way with you, land you in a hot mess with that loan shark, and then ditch you."

"I'm not giving up on him!" Amy yelled back, standing.

"Amy, did you ever stop to consider that this isn't about you giving up on him as much as it's about you not wanting to be alone?"

Amy blinked. "What?"

Becca sighed in exasperation and threw her hands up. "You were always so lonely in college. You didn't have many friends. Actually, I think I might have been your only friend. You always acted like it didn't bother you, that you couldn't afford any distractions of any kind. And though you never voiced that loneliness out loud, I could see it in your eyes. I could see the longing when you looked at a group of girls giggling as they went to a party, or the envy that would come over your face when you saw a happy couple holding hands. It tortured you, because you felt like that could never be you."

Amy felt about an inch tall. Was Becca right? Was she really so desperate for companionship that she'd accept anyone in her life, even if they were toxic for her? "That's not true," she said weakly.

"Isn't it, though?" Becca took a step forward, and then another. Amy stood her ground and stared Becca in the eyes.

"You have too good a heart to let someone rip it out again," Becca said sadly. "And I won't let that happen, no matter what."

Amy held her gaze. "And I appreciate that." Her voice was barely audible because her throat had grown so tight. "But it's not your choice to make."

A coldness settled in Becca's eyes, making them seem to darken. Nodding curtly, she turned and picked up the tray. "Get out."

Amy blinked. "What?"

"I said get out!" Becca snarled. She whirled on her and slung milk onto the wooden floor. "Go, run to your dark prince! Just don't you dare come crying to me when he uses you up and tosses you aside! Then, maybe you'll wish you'd listened to me!"

"What's the matter with you?" Amy's brows slanted. "Becca, this isn't like you."

Becca blinked, as if startled. All the anger drained from her face. "Oh God. I'm sorry, Amy. I didn't mean it, really. It's just..." The tray trembled in her hands.

Amy rushed over and took it from her. "Hey, easy. It's okay." She searched Becca's face. She seemed... frightened. "Is everything all right? You've been acting ...'off' lately."

"Yeah," Becca said breathlessly, smiling too widely. "Yeah, everything's fine. I just haven't been getting enough sleep because of my job and Zach."

Amy studied her as her inner lie detector went off. *What are you hiding, Becca?* "You know you can come to me if something's wrong," she said gently.

"Yeah." Becca's voice sounded small. "I know. Thanks." She took the tray back, her hands much steadier this time. "Here, you don't have to take this. I'm fine, really. Go on. Go to Scott."

Amy slowly backed toward the door. "You promise

you're okay?"

Becca nodded a few times. "Yeah. Everything's fine. I'm just stressed. Call me if you need me, okay?"

Amy's doubt softened, and she smiled. "I will."

Becca didn't wait to see her out. She turned and disappeared into the kitchen, at which point Amy saw herself out. As she walked down the sidewalk, she glanced back at the town house. Her gut wasn't usually wrong about these things. Having a perfectionist for a mother, you learned to tell people's moods pretty quickly through some sixth sense.

Something was wrong with Becca.

Should she turn around and try to help? Let her sort it out? Then again, maybe everything was fine. She did have a lot of stress. The no-sleeping thing was pretty common knowledge by now. The girl chugged espressos as if they were going to stop making them. Though she tried to hide it with makeup, dark circles forever lurked beneath her bloodshot eyes.

Amy was probably freaking out over nothing. But the touching and all those pictures and the cookies…

Becca's just trying to make you feel better, she tried to convince herself, without much luck. She'd have to be an idiot to believe that.

Then a thought hit her, and she stopped dead in the middle of the sidewalk. Could Becca like her? Like, *like her* like her? The thought was ludicrous. Not once had Amy ever seen Becca with a woman. She dated regularly, and by dated, she meant screwed around for fun.

Screwed *boys.*

Nah, she told herself as she kept walking. Becca couldn't possibly be bisexual. That thought was way out in left field.

And if Amy were totally, one-hundred-percent honest with herself, she'd admit the only reason she thought that was because she didn't want to think about the alternative.

That her best friend could be in love with her.

Which meant, because she was in no way attracted to girls, that Amy was doomed to lose her best friend.

TWENTY-THREE

S COTT GLANCED BEHIND his shoulder. Good Lord, if he ground his teeth any harder, he'd grind them down to the gums.

They'd gotten off the bus a few minutes ago. Erika had taken off her shoes about two blocks back, after nearly falling. The sudden absence of clacking heels made him nearly dizzy with relief—until he saw she was still padding along silently behind him, like a lost puppy.

"Don't you have other lives to ruin?" he asked over his shoulder.

She stopped in the middle of the sidewalk. "Stop it!" she screeched. Her little hands balled up into fists and shook. Her mascara had run, leaving oily trails down her sunken cheeks.

Scott finally whirled around. "Stop what? Telling the truth? Ruining lives is what you do, Erika. You latch onto people and drain them of everything. Money, happiness, sanity."

"That's not true." She trembled.

"Oh? What do you think your ex, Jason, would say about that? Or your sister Rachel, or that poor old couple who tried taking you in, only to have you drain them of their life savings?"

Erika stared at him, mouth hanging open in shock.

"Don't look so surprised," Scott said with a bitter smile. "I did some digging into your past, once I finally started listening to my friends' advice. They said you were a leech. Turns out they were right. Word gets around."

Fresh tears leaked from her eyes. "I never meant to hurt anyone."

Scott pursed his lips. His heart had hardened to her a long time ago.

At least, that's what he told himself as he forced himself to turn around and keep walking. "Save it. I've heard it before."

"That doesn't make it less true," she insisted.

He growled a sigh, not bothering to hide his annoyance. "I told you I'll deal with Ghost, so you don't have any reason to hang around. Go home, or wherever you came from."

"I can't."

The answer was tiny, but it rang loud in Scott's ears. He stopped and turned to look at her. "What do you mean 'you can't'?"

Erika swallowed and ducked her head as if expecting a scolding. "Ghost told me not to come back until I had the money you owed him, plus what he loaned me to get you out—or when I had you."

"What?"

"Gh-Ghost said not to—"

"No, I heard you the first time." Scott pinched the bridge of his nose. This was a disaster, as in, he was royally fucked if he didn't think of something fast. He knew Ghost. He would make good on his word to hurt Amy should Scott not give him what he wanted and when he wanted it.

Shit.

He paced for a bit, trying to think. "How did you get tangled up with Ghost? The whole purpose of me taking on your debt was so you could get away from him."

Erika deliberated. "I was free of him. Or, at least, I thought I was. I don't think anyone is ever truly free of Ghost."

"Isn't that the truth," Scott said darkly. "Go on."

She took a deep breath. "About a week ago, he found me and coerced me into getting you to come back to the circuit. He needs you to fight for him."

"Why? Why is he so desperate all of a sudden for money? He's swimming in the stuff."

"I don't know. It wasn't my place to ask."

"And you haven't heard anything?"

"No."

Odd. If there was one thing you could count on in the underground circuit, it was gossip. Someone had to have some dirt on Ghost, some idea of what these "bad investments" were he'd spoken of back at the inn. If Scott could figure out what was driving him, then maybe he could stop him for good.

And keep him from hurting Amy.

Scott felt restless. He gestured toward the next street. "Let's talk while we walk. I need to get my car back, in case Amy calls."

"You mean your girlfriend?" Erika sneered as she fell into place beside him.

"That's none of your business, got it? You stay the hell away from her."

Erika glared at the sidewalk, her lips pressed into a firm pout.

Scott inwardly shook his head. How had he not seen how childish she was? Perhaps the old adage was true, that "love really was blind."

"So, Ghost loaned you the money to get me out," he said flatly. His pace quickened, mostly from his agitation. "You do realize how incredibly stupid that was? Now I owe him even more money."

"Hey! Don't be a dick. I was only trying to help you."

"You were trying to help yourself," he growled as they crossed the street over to the next block. Only six more to go. "Admit it—the only reason you wanted to get back with me was so you could have another host to feed off of."

"That's not true! I'm doing just fine by myself. I don't need anyone's charity."

Scott shook his head. "No, you're not fine. You're still sick, Erika."

"No, I'm not," she spat back.

"Erika, look at you." He stopped. He waved his hand in front of her body. "You're skin and bones. Your arms are covered in bruises. You look like death warmed over."

"Well, gee, now I remember how charming you were when you kicked me out and onto the street," she sneered, a hand on her bony hip.

His chest tightened. "You left me no choice. I tried helping you. You wouldn't go to your support groups. You refused to get a mentor. You refused help of any kind, except if it came in a bottle, a syringe, or a cock."

"Hey, you make me sound like some strung-out whore! Well, I'm not, pal! I've had jobs. I've worked for my money."

"Yeah? And how's that gone? Last time I heard you were broke—again. And you got evicted for avoiding rent—*again*."

"I've…just had a string of bad luck."

"Does that bad luck include being caught lifting from the register or hitting up patrons for extra cash on your breaks?"

She blinked. "I'm—how did—?"

"Word gets around," he said bitterly, walking again. This conversation was starting to drain him.

Her eyes lit up as she trotted beside him. "So you've been checking up on me?"

He was silent a minute. "Yes. I guess I have."

"So you do care about me," she breathed. "I knew it!" She gave a little squeal. You'd think she was a teenager who'd just had the star quarterback ask her to prom.

He swallowed hard, took a deep breath, and let it out slowly. "It makes me sad, seeing you like this. You never saw your potential, but I did. You could be so much more than you allow yourself to be."

Her eyes jerked to his, searching.

She didn't say another word the rest of the way to his apartment.

"Swanky place." She looked around as they climbed the stairs.

Bless her heart. If she thought this shit-hole was swanky, he could only imagine where she'd lived. "It's all right. Do you have somewhere you can go?"

She shook her head. "No. Ghost told me not to come back without you or the cash, and I was crashing a friend's."

"And let me guess: they kicked you out?"

She nodded quietly.

Typical. Scott ran a hand through his hair. It'd be a miracle if he didn't end up pulling it all out by the time this was all said and done. "I might have an empty apartment you can crash. It's one of the apartments we keep to show potential tenants, so you can't stay there long." He took his key ring out and let himself into his apartment.

Erika stared at everything. The thought of her in his living space made his skin crawl. He had to get her out of here, fast. Going into his bathroom, he opened up his "extras" drawer and retrieved common items he always kept extras of in stock, just so he wouldn't be without them: shampoo, conditioner, deodorant, toothbrush, toothpaste, and a comb.

He walked back out to the living room. "I'm going to get the place set up and make sure everything is fine. I'll only be gone a minute. Stay here and don't touch anything."

"Wait." Erika glanced at the clock on his wall. "It's almost eight."

"So?"

"So Ghost told me he needed an answer by then."

"Jesus, Erika. Why didn't you tell me that sooner?"

"I don't know! I guess I forgot!" She hugged herself. "Stop yelling at me!"

He threw his head back. *Just shoot me.* "Well, I don't have an answer right now."

A buzzing emanated from Erika's purse. Fishing through it, she produced her cell phone. It looked like a prepaid phone. The calling number was blocked. "Well, you need to come up with one now, because I think this is Ghost calling."

He went cold all over.

When he didn't move to take the phone, Erika pressed it into his chest, nearly dropping it. "Are you an idiot? Don't make Ghost have to call twice!"

Ah hell, she was right. Swallowing, he lifted the phone to his ear. "You have some nerve."

"Oh, now is that any way to treat someone who just bailed you out of jail?" came Ghost's cultured voice. "I would at least expect a thank-you."

"Thanks."

"You sound appreciative as ever," Ghost drawled. "Did she explain my terms to you?"

"No," he ground out, casting a glare at Erika.

"Of course she didn't. Then again, I didn't expect much from that bumbling idiot."

"Get to the point."

"Ah, there's the Lion I remember! So demanding, as to be expected of the king of the jungle. Very well. Look, I know our reunion was a bit rough, and I wanted to patch things over by helping you out."

"You never help anyone out, not without a price."

"True," Ghost purred. "But you already know my price, which is to pay me what is owed of Erika's debts. Except, of course, you must also now pay me back the bond money."

"Or come be your slave and get the shit beat out of me again in the ring so you'll forgive all debt."

"That's really the gist of it. Oh, but don't forget about how lovely Amy plays into all of this. We wouldn't want to get her tangled up in my web, would we?"

"She already is. And don't you dare come after her, or I'll—"

"Or you'll what?"

Truth was, he couldn't do shit. He literally had nothing, and Ghost had a freaking empire of thugs at his disposal. His pockets ran deep.

But perhaps not as deep as he'd thought...

"Why are you doing this?" Scott asked.

"Hmmm?"

"Why are you so desperate to get me back? Why do you need the money so badly?"

"I told you. I've had a few bad investments of late, and I need to bounce back quickly."

"Why? What happened to that pile of money you were sitting on?"

Silence met him.

"Unless," Scott said slowly, fishing for information, "that big pile of money has run out, and you fell in deep with some people worse than you?"

Ghost cleared his throat. "It's none of your concern. Leave the business to me, as I have always left the fighting to you. You have until noon to make your decision."

"And if I refuse?"

"Then I guess I'll be talking to Amy next."

The call ended abruptly. Ghost's threat echoed through Scott's head.

With a lump in his throat the size of Texas, he handed the phone back to Erika. "I'll be right back," he said, his voice raspy. "Stay here."

Thoughts racing faster than ever, he left and quickly went to the unoccupied apartment.

He needed to come up with a plan—and fast.

Erika couldn't believe it. If someone had told her a month ago that she'd be standing in Scott's apartment, talking to him, she'd have laughed and told them they were high.

Being here reminded her so much of what she loved about him. His rebel streak hadn't died; that much was evident in the beer cans that littered the coffee table and the spiky rock-and-roll memorabilia that decorated most of the room.

Glancing at the front door, she tiptoed down the hallway to his bedroom. She had no idea why she was tiptoeing, considering she was alone, but she felt the need to be discreet. If he came in, she'd pretend she'd been looking for the bathroom, which wouldn't be a total lie. She needed to pee and wash off her feet. They felt icky from walking along the sidewalks.

She let her eyes sweep over his bedroom. Her gaze rested on his bed. It had the same old wooden headboard; it even wore the same threadbare sheets. She remembered spending many nights tangled up in those sheets and his arms. She'd missed those nights. Still did.

Had he meant what he'd said about believing in her? Her chest tightened. No one had ever told her that before, except him. Not her family, who'd only cut her down with scathing remarks that she wasn't pretty enough, smart enough, or ambitious enough to be of any use to them.

Not her friends, who always stabbed her in the back.

Not the men who were only interested in sex and then left her.

No, Scott was different. He was so much better than all of them.

And within her grasp...

An Eric Clapton song blared from the living room. Heart leaping to her throat, she thought maybe he'd come back and had turned on the radio or something. Only, she discovered as she padded back out to the living room, it wasn't Scott.

It was his phone.

He must have been so rattled by Ghost that he'd left it when he'd set his things down.

Curious, she picked it up and peered at the display.

A low growl went up her throat. It was that Amy woman.

So, she thought she could steal Scott away from her so easily, huh?

Like hell.

Erika hit the Talk button and pressed the phone to her ear. "What the hell do you want?"

TWENTY-FOUR

I F ERIKA HAD slapped her, Amy wouldn't have been more surprised.

She stood there, stunned. A car honked at her. She had stopped walking in the middle of crossing the street.

Waving to the driver, she hurried along. He sped past, yelling, "Watch what you're doing, crazy bitch!"

And this is why my faith in humanity has yet to be restored.

"Hello?" called Erika from the phone. "Did you hear me?"

"Yes," Amy snapped. "I heard you."

"Well?"

"Well what?"

She sighed loudly, as if having to repeat herself was too much of an inconvenience. "What the hell do you want?"

Oh no, she didn't. "First of all, I want to know what

213

you're doing with Scott's phone."

"He left it behind," she said flippantly. "I'm at his apartment."

"His *apartment*?"

She heard a door open in the background. "Hey, is that my phone?" Scott said.

"Um…" Erika said nervously.

"Son of a—give me that!"

Wrestling ensued. Scott must have won, because a few seconds later, he said, "Amy?"

"Hi," she said tersely.

"It's not what it seems."

She sighed. "You keep saying that."

"I know, I know. I don't know why this random shit keeps happening to me."

"Tell me about it," she ground out.

Erika whined in the background about not having any toilet paper. *Ugh. How on earth did he stand her long enough to actually date her?* She was like a bratty little kid trying to get his attention.

"Can it! Check the closet!" he yelled. "Sorry, Amy. I promise I'll explain everything when I see you. You need me to come pick you up?"

"Uh…" Suddenly, given these new, surprising circumstances, she wasn't so sure that was a good idea.

"Amy, please," Scott said, his voice gentle. "There is nothing going on between Erika and me. You have nothing to worry about. Now, tell me where you are."

She pressed her lips together. "Okay—but on one condition."

"Name it."

"You tell me the truth, Scott Johnathan Meyers. All

of it, without a detail left out." She took a deep breath. *Might as well take the plunge.* "And I'll do the same for you."

It took him a fraction of a second to answer. "Deal."

Scott was one lucky son of a bitch.

Thank God Amy had agreed to do anything with him, given that little stunt Erika had pulled. After he tugged her ass into the spare apartment with some food and any other necessities, he'd locked her in, gone down the street to an ATM, and then hailed a cab to pick up Amy. She didn't say much as the cab driver drove them to the wood-surrounded inn to pick up the rental car so he could actually get his car back. She sat on the opposite side of the backseat, arms folded, facing away from him. Her eyes scanned the woods.

He couldn't stop looking at her; how the sun brought out hints of gold in her hair, or how the silky material of her shirt pulled at her breasts. He wanted to strip it off her and make love, to show her how he really felt. But that would have to wait.

First, he had a lot to account for.

After he paid the cab driver and got in the rental car, he drove them out to his favorite spot in the countryside. Shadow Lake was remote, plus it wasn't exactly a lake. More like a pond, he supposed, but hell if he cared. Surrounded by a green meadow with dainty purple and white wildflowers, it was one of his favorite places to think.

"So is this the part where you tell me I know too

much and now you have to kill me?" Amy gave him a teasing smile as he put the rental car into park beside the lake.

He chuckled and relaxed a bit. Maybe she wasn't too pissed at him.

Yet.

"Nah. I'd never hurt you. Not intentionally, anyway," he added with a grimace. "Though I guess I've already done that." He turned to her and took her hands, looking her in the eyes. "I know there aren't enough ways to say it, but I'm so sorry for pulling you into this. It was the last thing I wanted. I knew you were too good for me the moment I saw you, but I couldn't stay away from you. You drew me in, like a magnet." He brushed some of that sunshine-yellow hair away from her face, reveling in its softness. He smiled sadly. "I guess what they say is true—opposites do attract."

She raised a brow. "Opposites? We're pretty similar."

"No, we're not," he said softly. "You're a much better person than I am. My soul has been washed with darkness and blood, and I'm afraid it's going to stain yours."

"Oh, don't be ridiculous." She took his hands and covered them in her own. "I've seen how good you are. I *know* how honest, kind, and caring a person you are." She pressed her lips together.

He braced himself. *Here comes the "but."* He sat back with a sigh. "Go ahead and ask. I know you've got to be dying to."

Her eyes shone with understanding. And a bit of apprehension, though he could tell she was trying to hide it.

His stomach twisted into knots. *You knew this was coming. Are you honestly surprised she's reacting this*

216

way? I'd be afraid of you, too.

Amy stared thoughtfully at her lap. "I had a whole list, and now I can't remember a single question."

Scott smiled tightly. "I know the feeling." He needed some answers, too. Starting with what happened to Michael Lewis, and why she was so afraid to talk about her past.

She finally looked at him. "How did you meet Ghost?"

Scott paused, thinking. "I frequented a lot of bars in my younger years. Thanks to my temper, I also tended to get into a lot of fights. One night, Ghost was there with some of his men, and he saw me fight. That's when he approached me."

"And made you an offer you couldn't refuse?"

"Something to that effect," he said grimly. "He said 'I'd have riches beyond my wildest dreams. I'd have girls, fame, fortune—everything a man could want.'" He chuckled darkly. "It still amazes me to this day, how stupid and naive I was. I thought I was 'street smart.' But no, I was swimming in the kiddie pool. I thought Ghost was a god. At one point, I'd dare say I thought of him as a father figure. It wasn't until I met Erika and everything went down with her that I got a slap in the face and woke up to what kind of man Ghost was, and I found out exactly what he thought of me—as his property."

"So that's how you met Erika," Amy murmured. "Through Ghost."

Scott nodded. "We met after one of my fights." He shifted in the leather seat, mumbling the next part and looking away briefly. "Ghost, as promised, usually brought women—or 'fans,' as he called them—up to my room after a fight. One night, it happened to be Erika."

Amy's lips only tightened slightly, pinching at the corners of her mouth. "And the rest is history."

"More or less. She was as reckless as I was. I thought I'd found a soul mate, that I knew what real love was. Then I found out Ghost had been bribing her with drugs to seduce me, to ensure I stayed in the circuit." He sighed hard and leaned back in the seat. "One day, Ghost decided that he had been generous enough, and that she had to pay back the cost of the drugs. Out of the blue, all up front, not a penny spared. Erika, naturally, didn't have a dime to her name, but Ghost didn't care. He only sees people as objects to be exploited for his personal gain. He knew Erika had a drug addiction she couldn't control. So he funded it in order to use her to reel me in tighter."

"What would happen if she didn't pay?"

Scott's mouth formed a thin line. "Then he said he'd find other ways of using her to earn back the money."

"Oh my God," Amy breathed. Her face went white, as if she was going to be sick. "So you stepped in to defend her."

"Just like Ghost knew I would. He knew I cared for Erika and would do anything for her. She was so frightened of him that she left me after I'd practically signed my soul over to him."

"Bitch," Amy spat, eyes glittering with anger.

"I can think of a few other words, but that about sums her up."

Amy took a deep breath and let it out. "Okay, so how much is left of the debt?"

Scott inwardly winced. "About five hundred thousand."

"Five hundred thousand?" Amy screeched.

"That's low, compared to what it used to be," Scott said grimly.

Amy's eyes nearly popped out of her head. "How high was it?"

"You don't want to know."

Amy stared at the dashboard as she processed all this. "Did you know the circuit was going to be at the inn?"

The question took him by surprise. "What? No! If I did, I never would have taken you there."

Amy searched his face. Sadness settled in her features. "I saw the look in your eyes when you gazed at the ring. You longed for it. You wanted to fight."

"Amy"—he took her hands and looked into her eyes —"I'm not going to lie that I enjoyed fighting. It's always been a part of my life, and I think, in a small way, it always will be. Fighting is in my blood. But I don't want it. I'm not going to suddenly snap like some seventy-year-old pro wrestler trying to relive the glory days. I've found something I want a hell of a lot more than fighting, and I'm looking right at her."

Amy stared back at him. "I can't bear to lose you," she whispered, shaking her head. "I can't go through that again."

"And you won't." He cupped her cheek in his hand. "I promise. I'll never leave your side."

The uncertainty and fear in her eyes briefly vanished as she touched his hand and leaned into him. She closed her eyes, a slight, contented smile on her mouth.

His eyes lowered to her lips, and all thoughts of asking about Michael Lewis vanished. Hunger built in him as he leaned forward and kissed her. She opened her mouth eagerly, her tongue slipping out to slide along his.

He needed to be with her, to feel her in his arms and know she was real. Mostly, he just wanted to hold on to her and never let go—at a time when he felt the rest of his life was falling apart.

He reached up and slipped his hand beneath her bra to cup her breast; the hard nub of her nipple caressed his palm as he pressed her against the door. Her answering moan only made him harder.

His phone vibrated in his pocket. With all brain function essentially shut off, he promptly ignored it—for the first four times.

About the fifth time it buzzed, Amy broke the kiss and said breathlessly, "Shouldn't you get that? It might be important."

"I'd rather finish taking your shirt off." He eyed her full breasts.

She demurely pulled her shirt back down and ran her fingers through her mussed hair. "I would, too, but what if something's wrong?"

"When is nothing ever wrong with Erika? Because I can almost bet money that's who it is." Sure enough, he had about a bajillion texts from her.

Are you coming home?

Ghost wants you to call him. Soon.

It'll be noon in an hour. Where r u?

Irritated, he texted back. *Give me Ghost's number.*

Can't, she replied two seconds later. *I don't know it.*

Of course she didn't. Ghost couldn't make himself too accessible.

Fine. I'll be there. Stall him if he calls early.

"I'm guessing whatever it is, it isn't good." Amy

studied him.

"Yeah. Ghost is supposed to call Erika's phone at noon, and I need to be there to give him my answer."

Her brows furrowed. "You saw Ghost again?"

He quickly relayed to her how Erika had come to bail him out and about Ghost's subsequent offer/threat. "It wouldn't surprise me if the bust was staged, too, in order to get me arrested so he could bail me out and I'd owe him a favor. I know for a fact Ghost owns the chief of police, along with most of the cops, at that station."

"He can't do this!" Amy slammed her dainty fist on the dash. "I won't let him get away with hurting you!"

"It's you he'll hurt if I don't comply." Scott gripped her shoulders. "And I can't let that happen."

"And like I said, I can't lose you! It'll crush me." Her body slumped. She looked a bit crushed already.

Scott's chest tightened. "If there were any other way …"

Amy's eyes snapped up. "Run away with me."

His mouth lifted up on one side. "It's sweet of you, but I can't."

"I'm serious, Scott. Run away with me. I'm an artist. I practically have a portable job. I don't make much, but I can support us for a while until you find work. And it's not like I have other reasons to stay rooted in this city."

He smiled sadly. "I wish it were that simple."

"It can be. Just be with me."

God, how much he wanted to. He took a deep breath. "If he hurt you—"

She placed a finger to his lips. "Ssssh. No more 'ifs.' Let's worry about the present. I'm here for you, and I'm not going anywhere. We'll get through this, together. Just

221

don't give in to him. Okay?" She squeezed his hand.

Staring at her then, it struck him just how much he'd grown to care for her. Was this what love felt like? Real, honest-to-God love? It was so…fragile. It scared him.

Suddenly, for the first time with any woman, he could see himself going further. A ring, a house or apartment, children…

They could be happy. *He* could be happy.

Leaning forward, he placed a gentle kiss on her lips. "Okay."

She smiled back and then buckled her seat belt and settled into the seat as he started the engine and drove off.

As they drove along the highway, he stared at the road, lost in his own thoughts.

Amy wanted things to be simple. He could do simple; that's not what he had a hard time grasping.

Because things had been real black-and-white for a while now, starting with the night Ghost first threatened Amy's life.

The risk was too great. He couldn't leave Amy's life to chance.

Which was why he hoped she'd understand and forgive him for what he was about to do.

Amy had never been so grateful to see her apartment. It felt strange, coming home and actually looking forward to it. Dreading a stranger standing in the shadows or seeing fresh blood on the floor were what usually played out in her mind, but not this time. Today, there was a surety to her steps, a sense that everything was going to be all right.

As soon as they had gotten inside the building, Scott had told her Erika had been blowing up his phone, claiming it was an emergency. Amy had rolled her eyes, but she didn't want to give him a hard time. He was under enough stress as it was. Besides, she was convinced from the revulsion on his face earlier that he was in no way still attracted to Erika. Strangely enough, she wasn't worried about him cheating on her.

Okay, maybe a little. That kind of burn was hard to get rid of. It left scars on not only your heart, but also your self-esteem.

She had kissed Scott at Erika's door and said, "Good luck" before she ducked into her apartment for a quick change of clothes and to freshen up. Part of her longed for a nap, but there was way too much nervous energy running in her body. She'd never be able to sleep, not with everything that was going on.

It was chilly inside her apartment. Apparently, she'd left the AC running full-blast.

She hummed to herself as she walked across the room to turn the AC down. It was ridiculous to feel so cheery in a time like this, but she was hopeful. So damned hopeful, it hurt.

Things had to work out. There was a sense of rightness with Scott she'd never once felt with Michael, and at the time, she'd thought he'd hung the moon.

There was no way anything this perfect between two people couldn't have a fighting chance, if they worked together and just tried.

It took some effort, but she finally managed to twist the AC knob to OFF. As the fan died down, she could barely make out the squeak of wood behind her.

She immediately knew where it was, which was why it didn't strike her as strange. There was a loose floorboard near the kitchen countertop.

Directly behind where she stood.

As realization struck too late, her heart leapt as the air heated behind her back, contrasting with the cool blade that pressed against her throat.

TWENTY-FIVE

AMY COULDN'T BREATHE. It seemed every shallow breath she took, the blade dug that much deeper.

"Na…than," she gasped. Her heart beat so wildly that it caused her pulse to thrum almost painfully in her neck and head. The taste of fear coated her throat, sucking the moisture out.

"Hello again," came that dark voice from beside her ear. His free hand snaked around her waist, taking its time in feeling her curves. "I'd forgotten how soft you were, how plush. You always were a chubster, but hey, I'm not complaining. I've fucked some bigger girls." He squeezed her sides. "Feels just like a cushion."

She strangled a whimper, not wanting to give him the satisfaction of seeing her afraid. She refused to give this monster another piece of her.

He buried his nose in her hair and inhaled deeply. "Ah, Amy. You always smelled like lavender and vanilla.

I've never forgotten that scent."

Amy racked her mind. It was hard to talk with the blade pressed against her throat. "Were you the one who broke in here and took my lotion?"

He paused. "The hell you talking about?"

"Don't lie to me, you sick son of a bitch." Her anger made her eyes sting. "You've been stalking me."

"Lovingly keeping an eye on you for Michael is more like it."

"Yeah, right. You never gave a damn about Michael."

"Don't say that!" he bellowed. She jumped and squeezed her eyes shut. "Michael was like a brother to me! And you took him away!"

"Nathan—"

With a disgusted grunt, he twirled her around and forced her down onto the couch. She immediately scanned for things she could use as a weapon, but all she had lying around were a few paintbrushes and some empty paint cans.

She glared at him as he towered over her, that smug smirk stretched over his lips. "How did you get in here?" she demanded.

"I know a little bird." Nathan crouched next to her. He placed the tip of the knife on her knee and scraped it up her thigh. She shivered, hugging herself, her eyes trained on the blade that he could plunge into her at any moment.

"What do you want?" she whispered, trembling.

"Justice," he said simply, dragging the blade point back the other way on her leg. "Retribution. Whatever they call it." The blade stopped, and those cruel eyes lifted to hers. "Revenge."

"I didn't do anything wrong," she said, surprised by

the strength in her voice.

"Of course not. Perfect, sweet little Amy. A god-damned saint in everyone's eyes. Oh, how I've waited to see you fall." He leaned forward. By instinct, she started to lean backward and then stopped herself. Though fear gripped her mind and body, some defiant part of her wanted to fight, to show him he would not claim her.

His face stopped about an inch from hers, their eyes level. Once again, the blade pressed against her throat. "What was it like, walking in and seeing his blood all over the floor?" he said softly. "You can't tell me that you didn't feel guilty. After all, you're the reason he got into this mess."

Her mind started to sink back into the memory of that horrible night.

"No," she breathed, closing her eyes.

When she opened them, she wasn't in her apartment anymore—she was in Michael's.

The memory was always in stark clarity. Somehow, going through a traumatic experience made you remember all the details. The chill of the room, for example, from him always leaving the windows open in the dead of winter.

And how her mind was still reeling from her and Michael's fight earlier.

Becca had told her to trust her gut. God, how much she wished she had. She knew there was something going on between Michael and Roxanne. "He wouldn't do that to me," she'd argued, both with herself and with Becca. "He knows how that would make me feel. He wouldn't hurt me like that."

But he had. And it'd broken her heart when he'd admitted it, the night before their wedding.

He'd said he'd made a mistake, that he'd been drunk when he'd slept with Roxanne. That the singer didn't mean anything to him, and he only loved Amy and wanted to spend his life with her.

Michael had a past filled with rumors of womanizing, so his unfaithfulness shouldn't have come as a surprise.

But it did, and it had hurt like hell. She'd always hoped to be "the one" who'd make him change his ways, the one woman he'd want to be faithful to. Now, she saw it was a concept that belonged in a Disney movie, not real life. Not *her* life.

Her throat was raw from screaming at him in their argument over the phone, right after he'd confessed and she'd fled his apartment, and her eyes had been filled with so many tears that she'd barely been able to see the road while she was driving.

"Please, Amy," he'd begged on the phone, his voice raspy. "Come back. Let me talk to you in person. There's something…there's more…"

"More," she'd choked out. "What more can be left to say after you just confessed to fucking Roxanne?"

"I… Just come back. Please? Please, babe?"

Why the hell did she say yes? She must be a masochist, because she knew the moment she saw him, the knife he'd buried in her heart with his confession would only cut deeper.

The gated apartment complex was quiet, but it usually was on a Monday night. After she let herself inside the

locked-entry building, she took the elevator up to his condo on the top floor.

Michael had done well for himself. Thanks to the
band's chart-topping success, he'd been able to dig himself
out of nearly living on the streets to taking up residence in
one of the ritziest places in town. She was proud of him.

Her heart squeezed as the elevator climbed. The air
seemed to be getting thinner, and she grabbed hold of the
cold metal railing for support. Could she really do this?
Would she ever be able to face Michael again after what
he'd admitted?

No. No, she'd never be ready. Which was why if she
didn't do this now, she knew good and well she never
would.

The elevator dinged, and a second later the doors
opened. Her heart jumped into her throat. With a deep
breath, she took one step and then another, until she stood
in front of his door.

Her feet felt like lead. She stared at the key in her
hand, poised above the keyhole.

Should she knock? God, that sounded so weird. She
hadn't knocked on his door in ages. And he had told her to
just come in.

Tha-thump, tha-thump, tha-thump...

All she could hear was her heartbeat as it thrummed
violently in her chest.

Just do it, she thought.

Holding her breath, she put the key into the keyhole
and twisted. The door opened into darkness; the light from
the hall spilled onto the hardwood floor in a yellow rec-
tangle.

Maybe he's gone out. A heads-up would have been

appreciated, but hey, she had no choice but to wait for him now.

Feeling along the wall, she found the light switch and flipped it.

"Damn," she said when no lights came on. It wasn't a power outage, considering the lights in the hall were on, so maybe a breaker had flipped. The breaker box was in the back of the condo.

Not wanting to leave the door open, she closed and locked it and carefully made her way through the apartment, using her cell phone as a makeshift flashlight.

Not that she really needed one. She knew the place by heart. After all, she'd lived here for the past six months. Laughing, snuggling, dancing, being the happiest she'd ever been.

Then her whole world, her whole concept of love, had been torn apart at the seams, leaving her feeling broken and hurt inside.

"Michael?" she called, just to be sure.

No answer. Definitely not home.

The breaker box wasn't far, a short walk down the hall, in the laundry room. Just past the kitchen, her boot hit something slick. Being the middle of the hallway, there was nothing to grab onto. Flailing her arms for balance, she couldn't correct herself in time and went down with a yelp. The phone shot out of her grip, flinging forward when she opened both hands to catch her fall.

Her palms slammed into the floor and splashed in whatever liquid had been spilled on it as her phone slid down the hall and into an open room.

Her nose wrinkled in disgust; she slowly stood and wiped the gooey substance onto her jeans. It was...*warm*.

What was it? Some kind of syrup? It smelled weird, and the air had a faint metallic tinge to it.

An alarm went off in her brain, telling her something wasn't right. With a hand on the wall for support, she carefully walked down the hall to retrieve her phone. The dim blue glow from its screen highlighted the contours of the objects around it. The sink base, the toilet, the rug, the—

Every muscle in her body froze as a chill cut through her. Eyes wide, she gazed at the slumped figure beside the tub. A tremor started in her knees, working its way up her legs as she whispered, "M-Michael?"

There was no sound, except her barely controlled breathing.

Feeling as if she were about to swallow her heart, she stepped forward to retrieve her phone. It rested just inside the bathroom, a few inches from familiar sneakers.

Those are Michael's favorites. He'd gotten them when he was sixteen. Though they were beat to shit, he swore they still fit and refused to part with them. They'd "been through stuff together," he'd said.

"Michael?" she whispered again, desperation in her voice.

With a trembling hand, she grabbed her phone. Her hand was so clammy, she nearly dropped it. Holding her breath, she lifted the phone and shone the light on the figure's face.

Michael's lifeless eyes stared back at her, his head tilted back and his throat split wide open.

A scream started, but she couldn't give it enough air to ring. Shock, terror, and horror rushed through her as she stumbled out of the bathroom and back down the hall, her eyes fixed on the dark figure of her very dead fiancé.

Her brain wouldn't work. It refused to process the grisly scene before her. The smell in the air became that much more pronounced; she nearly gagged at the metallic taste of the blood that coated her throat and tongue.

Oh God. That's Michael's...Michael's...

She turned and vomited on the floor, retching until her stomach didn't have anything left to chuck up.

Straightening, she stumbled toward a phone and then stupidly realized she had one in her hand.

She was barely able to think straight enough to dial 9-1-1. The phone rang on the other end what felt like a bazillion times. The third time an automated voice told her they were experiencing high call volume and someone would be with her shortly, she screamed at the phone and into the poor dispatcher's ear who just picked up.

"Help! My boyfriend, no, my-my fiancé is dead! He's dead!"

"Calm down, miss. Who's dead?"

"My boyfriend—dammit, why do I keep saying that?!" She closed her eyes and took a deep breath. "My fiancé is dead, in the bathroom."

"Are you sure?"

"HIS THROAT'S CUT! OF COURSE I'M SURE!"

"I'm going to need you to calm down, miss."

Hearing that seemed to make her hysteria worse, because it reminded her why she was in this state of mind in the first place. "I...I can't...Michael..." She started to cry. Her legs gave out, and she grabbed hold of the marble countertop just as she stumbled into the kitchen. She couldn't catch her weight in time, and her knees slammed to the floor. It hurt, or at least, she knew it should hurt. But she couldn't feel it. She couldn't feel anything.

"Hello? Miss?"

"I'm here," she whispered.

"Is there anyone else there?"

Oh God. Coming onto her knees, she peered over the counter. "I-I don't think so."

"Just to be safe, I need you to exit and get to a safe place until I send help over. Can you do that for me?"

"Y-Yes."

She dragged herself to her feet. The toe of her shoe caught something; a metallic *zing* sang as a bloodied knife skidded across the floor.

Her heart stopped.

"Miss? Can you hear me?"

Her voice got smaller. "I...I think I just found the murder weapon."

Furiously typing fingers *ratta-tap-tapped* in her ear. "Don't touch it. I need you to get out, now. Where are you?"

She barely remembered the address, something she knew by heart, but she sputtered it to the lady.

"Your name?" the dispatcher said, followed by more typing.

"Julia-Julia Gray."

"Run, Julia. I need you to run."

That felt impossible, given the jelly-like feeling of her legs. She obeyed anyway, hauling ass as quickly as she could toward the front door. She'd just cleared the living room when the door cracked open, and Nathan's face popped in.

Her heart dropped into her stomach. "Oh God," she breathed.

"Miss Gray?" called the dispatcher from the phone at

her side. "Can you hear me?"

"He's here." Terror froze her into place as Nathan opened the door wider.

His gaze found hers, his eyes widening and slipping from her head to her toes. She knew what he saw.

A girl covered in her fiancé's blood.

He swallowed hard.

Then his eyes, cold as stone, lifted to hers, and she knew without a doubt that she would be next.

The metal of the knife against her throat had warmed, thanks to being pressed against her skin. Amy barely thought about it. She was locked inside the memory, reliving the terror of facing down Nathan on her own all over again.

He'd been reciting her story to her verbatim, just like how she'd told the police.

"I thought you'd done it," he whispered. Anger made his voice razor-sharp. "You were covered in blood; you looked like a wild woman. But before I could find out, the police stormed the room and you started screaming about me being a murderer." His eyes hardened. "You framed me for Michael's death."

She blinked. "I—what?"

"Don't play dumb with me!" He dug the knife into her throat. A sharp pain said it'd finally broken skin. "You planted my knife there. I'd left it at his place, back when we used to hang out. You knew we were both into collecting knives, and how pissed I was about you breaking up the band. It was the perfect way to get rid of me for good."

"I—that's ludicrous! I would never do something like that!"

"Oh, my dear, sweet Amy. Many people have said the exact same thing until they, too, destroyed someone's life." He paused; his eyes dipped to the knife.

Her heart stopped. Oh God. He was going to cut her throat, right here, just like he had Michael's. She probably wouldn't even get in a scream, to alert someone he was in the building. Scott would never know how she truly felt about him.

In that life-or-death moment, she realized one important thing.

She was in love with Scott.

Abruptly, as if changing his mind, Nathan grunted and withdrew the knife.

Amy gasped as he stood, and she clutched at her throat. The skin felt chafed, and a dribble of blood smeared across her hand.

"I need to settle things once and for all, Amy." Nathan flipped the knife closed and tucked it away in his pants pocket.

"Then why didn't you kill me?" she rasped, glaring at him.

He smiled. "Don't give me any ideas. Besides, this isn't the right place. It's too obvious. If you're going to kill someone, you need to make them disappear. Which is exactly what you're going to do." He walked forward and bent down so his face was in hers. "You're going to meet me at the boathouse by the Mermaid Marina tomorrow night at nine p.m. Come alone, and don't call the cops." He started to walk away but paused to look over his shoulder. "Oh, and if you tell Scott, I'll kill him. Remember, Amy." He pointed to his eyes and then to her. "I'm always watching."

Without another word, he turned and let himself out.

Amy sat there, staring at the floor.

What the hell was she going to do? Nathan had demanded she sacrifice herself, or he'd kill Scott.

Nausea swarmed in her stomach. The memory hadn't worn off. Under the threat of death, all she could see when she closed her eyes was Michael's throat slit. Only it wasn't Michael anymore.

It was Scott.

"Oh God."

She bolted for the bathroom and collapsed in front of the toilet just in time to spill her guts. She didn't vomit up much, considering she hadn't eaten anything except a cookie this morning.

Someone banged on the door. A moment later, she heard it creak open. "Amy? Why's the door unlocked?"

Shit. "I'm back here," she rasped as she flushed the toilet.

Footsteps approached, and Scott's voice floated down the hallway. "Sorry it took so long," he said. "I'm starting to know what parenting is like."

She ran a wet rag over her mouth and then pressed it to her throat to hide the cut as Scott came in the doorway.

His brows instantly furrowed. "Jesus, Amy, you look pale. You okay?"

"Yeah," she said as casually as she could. "I'm fine. Just ate something that didn't agree with me. How's it going with Erika?" she asked suddenly to veer the conversation off in the other direction.

"Um, fine." Scott sighed. He shifted his feet, not looking at her.

"Everything okay?" she asked.

He gulped, took a deep breath, let it out. "Yeah," he finally said after a beat of silence. "Yeah, everything's fine. Or, at least, it will be."

Then why do you look so sad? Before she could ask the question, bile pressed up her throat. She forced it back down. "Ugh, I wish I could stop hurling."

"Here." He started forward. "I'll hold your hair."

"It's okay." She waved him off. "I'll be fine. I just need a moment." She winced at the pressing headache building in her temples. "And maybe a nap, some water, and an aspirin."

"That sounds good. I'll go get you—"

"No, no! It's okay, really. I'm fine. I can handle it." She smiled and stood. "I'm feeling better already."

He gave her a concerned look but didn't press the issue. "You want to give it maybe an hour or two and then come over to my place?"

She smiled. "Sounds like a plan."

He kissed her forehead. After much convincing that she would be all right, she finally got him to leave.

Without him there hovering, she felt as if she could breathe and think.

But that still didn't mean she had a damned clue as to how the hell they were going to get out of this.

TWENTY-SIX

H E WAS GOING to tell her. Really, he was.

The second they got in, he said he was going to check on Erika. She had, after all, been blowing up his phone, though Scott hadn't exactly specified why. Amy frowned but didn't question him. He was surprised the guilt in his eyes didn't give his plan away.

Hey, Amy, I'm going to, um, kind of tell Ghost I'll fight for him again so he doesn't kill us both. Cool?

God, he felt like such a douchebag. Here he was, promising her earlier that everything would be okay, when he had no idea how this would all pan out.

He was a liar. A fucking, no-good liar.

All the same, he'd put on his big-boy pants and headed over to her place afterward to confess. His throat had dried up when he'd seen her sick. He didn't want to put any more stress on her.

At her insistence, he'd finally walked away and back to his apartment, like a chicken. It was just as well she'd shooed him away, because the second Scott stepped back into his place, his phone rang.

"Stubborn woman," he muttered as he pulled his phone out.

He closed his eyes when he saw the caller ID. *Shit.* Just what he needed. He must be doomed to not get any peace today for a power nap.

Knowing he'd just keep calling back, Scott braced himself and answered, "Hey, Mack."

"Cut the civilities, Scott," Mack barked.

Typical Mack. Polite to a fault.

Scott heard the creak of a chair against the background noise of the police station. He imagined Mack leaning back and running his free hand over his face. "You're in deep shit," Mack said.

"You think I don't know that?" Scott said irritably. This no-sleeping shit was making him cranky as hell.

"You know what this means."

"Yeah." He sighed. "I'll be down in twenty."

All right, maybe in twenty-five, because that's about the time Scott sat down across from his parole officer. The police station was the last place he wanted to be, but considering the circumstances, it couldn't be helped.

Mack, dressed in his pressed black uniform, was about Scott's age but looked significantly older due to a variety of chronic stress in his life. Divorce, bankruptcy, and a slew of surgeries to repair an inherited back problem will suck the life—and money—out of a man.

Mack glared at him, big arms crossed over his chest.

Scott *almost* flinched. "You can quit trying to set my hair on fire with that look. I know how badly I fucked up."

"'Fucked up' doesn't begin to cover it. Dammit,

Scott, do you realize how hard it was for me to find you work the first time you landed yourself in trouble with Ghost? No one wants to hire one of his lackeys."

"I'm not one of his lackeys," Scott growled. "I was just in the wrong place at the wrong time."

"That's the understatement of the year." Mack blew out a breath. Remorse settled in his deep-brown eyes. "You know I have to report this to your bosses. It's part of your contract."

Scott felt as if he'd swallowed gravel. "Yeah. I know." Mack didn't have to spell out the rest. It'd hit Scott while he was in prison before Erika showed.

Bye-bye jobs, bye-bye money, and bye-bye any slim chance I had at paying Ghost back without having to fight. I am royally screwed. He couldn't be any farther down shit river if he had a motorboat.

Thank God his piece-of-shit car was paid for. He'd bought it used so he wouldn't owe on it for long. That's how it was with everything he had—used. Cheap. Afford-able.

"You haven't been making any deals with Ghost, have you?" Mack said quietly, leaning in.

"What? Hell no!" It was another lie, but at least it had been true until about an hour ago. "That asshole has ruined my life enough. I'm still trying to get out of the last mess he landed me in."

"How's that going? You still owe?"

Scott nodded.

"How much?"

"A lot," he said tersely.

"Shit." Mack balled a fist and slammed it on his desk. His keyboard and pencil holder rattled. "Wish I could bust

that son of a bitch. He's so deep in the pockets of my com-
rades I couldn't touch him."

It was a sore point with both him and Scott. It proved
how easy it was to buy power and protection. People's
moral compass tended to break when enough money was
involved. Everyone had at least one problem, usually
more, that could be fixed with money.

Mack's eyes lifted to Scott's. "But you might be able
to do something about it."

Scott blinked. "What?"

Mack pulled his chair closer and lowered his voice.
"The feds have been sniffing around for Ghost."

"Feds? Why the hell do they care about a fighting
ringmaster?"

"Dunno." He glanced around, and his voice became a
whisper. "But it's gotta be pretty big to get their attention.
Word has it he's gotten into abducting girls and selling
them into prostitution."

"Prosti…" Ghost's words from their earlier conversation drifted back. What he'd threatened to do with Erika,
another lifetime ago…

"That son of a bitch," Scott spat. Horror consumed
him. If Scott didn't comply, Ghost wasn't planning to kill
Amy. No, what he had in mind was much, much worse.

And much more profitable.

Why the hell hadn't it crossed his mind sooner? He
felt slow, but he blamed the mind fog brought on by his
exhaustion.

"Now it all makes sense," Scott breathed, stitching
the pieces together. "I've heard on the news about girls
being rescued in the surrounding states as feds shut down
prostitution hubs. But I had no idea Ghost was involved. I

mean, I've heard rumors, but I didn't think he'd be that stupid—or that desperate."

So that's what "bad investments" meant. "Jesus," he breathed, feeling sick when he thought about what Ghost had planned to do with Amy if Scott hadn't met his demands.

Scott's eyes narrowed in thought, backtracking to something that had been nagging him since this morning. He looked at Mack. "Hey, were you the one who got me bail earlier?"

Mack shrugged. "The detectives who questioned you earlier called me soon as they saw I was your parole officer. They explained what you'd told me, and I confirmed it. I really do believe you were just in the wrong place at the wrong time. You haven't even had a parking ticket since you've been out."

Scott heaved a sigh of relief. "Thanks, man."

"Don't thank me just yet. I think, after digging through your record, those detectives tipped off the feds you were previously involved with Ghost." He leaned forward. "Listen, the feds asked me if you could get them close to Ghost. I know you're trying to forget about him, but maybe, considering the circumstances, this will interest you."

Scott paused, letting this bit of information stew in his brain a bit. "Let me guess: *the feds* were actually the ones who so generously got me bail, all so I could help them. And if I don't comply, I get thrown back in the slammer."

Mack stared back at him, silent, his mouth pressed in a hard line.

Amy's sweet face flashed in his mind. Scott's foot began to tap. "They'd put him away for good? And drop all charges against me, if I help?" he said.

"I know they'd lock him up for life, if they can," Mack said. "And I can talk to them about your charges vanishing. They need an inside guy, and Ghost's prized pony is as good as it gets. I think they'll cave to that demand."

A chance to be rid of Ghost for good and clear his name of all the debt? Scott barely had to think about it.

A deadly look flashed in his eyes. "What do I have to do?"

It was a miracle Scott made it back to his apartment without wrecking, he was so distracted.

The weight of the burden Mack had laid on his shoulders haunted him from the police station all the way back to his apartment.

He was going to act as a lure for Ghost and lead the feds right to him. The plan was to catch him in the act of doing something illegal, probably fighting—because that's what he was acquiring Scott for—and then once they booked him and dragged his sorry ass to trial, they would pile on all the evidence they had against him. But he had to catch him in the act of doing some bad shit, and that scared the hell out of him. What the hell was he thinking? He must have a death wish. If he wasn't in deep before, he sure as hell was now.

He paused at Amy's door. Though he desperately wanted to tell her about the deal with the feds, to share the burden with someone, he also knew it wasn't her problem.

She already had so much worry on her plate. He remembered how sick she had looked earlier. Guilt swarmed him.

You're nothing but trouble.

If he were a decent man, he'd walk away from her and let her get on with her life. But he wasn't decent, and he sure as hell wasn't about to let a woman like Amy slip through his fingers, though he might not have a choice by the time this was all through.

Once inside his apartment, he paced until he was sure the carpet was about to wear out before he headed to the fridge for a beer. He popped the cap and took a long, healthy swig. It was mostly froth, but it still tasted damn good. At one point in his life, he'd drunk like a fish. Though he told himself he would quit a thousand times, he never could quite put the bottle down and walk away. Beer was as much a friend to him as a poison.

The first bottle was empty in one minute flat. He was about to go for a second when someone rapped sharply at his door.

"Shit, what now?" he muttered, wiping froth off his upper lip as he walked to the door. No one was there, but a folded piece of paper had fallen to the floor when he opened the door. He knew what it was before even picking it up.

His boss was not only firing him—he was evicting him. Mack must have called him shortly after Scott left. Guess living at his previous place of employment would make things awkward. Or maybe the owner was afraid Scott would go nuts and set the building on fire, like that one guy he'd evicted six months ago.

Taking another swig, he closed the door and tossed the letter on the coffee table with resignation. There was no fighting it. Mack had made it clear what would happen if he got in trouble with the law again, and he'd blown it. All to save Amy, a sacrifice he'd gladly make again and again.

His butt had just hit the couch when another knock came.

"Damn." He stood when the knocking became louder. Did they want him out right now? The only reason he bothered getting up at all was because he was afraid the loud pounding would wake Amy.

"Hold on a frickin' second—" He opened the door.

Scott froze and stared. "How the hell did you find me?"

TWENTY-SEVEN

BECCA AWOKE WITH a groan. The meds to make her headaches go away always left her brain feeling foggy, but it was a small price to pay to ease the pain. The room was blurry at first, until she blinked a few times to clear her vision.

Her cheek was smashed against the bathroom floor.

Not again. Had she been drinking too much? Sometimes, when the headache pills weren't enough, she'd drink herself into oblivion. Or combine it with nighttime cold medicine, anything to knock her out quicker. Sure, she knew it could kill her. In the back of her mind, she kind of hoped it would. Yet here she was, time and time again, perfectly fine except for brain fog and some minor aches and pains.

The smell of lemon-scented cleaner invaded her nostrils as she sniffled and slowly sat up. Gripping the towel rack, she pulled herself up and peered at her reflection. The pink outline of the tiny tiles was imprinted on her face. She must have been there for a while. A patchwork of red nerves crawled across her eyes, and her lips looked thin and pale.

There was nothing unusual. Normally at this point, she'd start piling on the makeup to unzombify herself, but today she didn't care. She didn't have anything to do because she'd taken the day off, craving a much-needed "mental health" day.

The stress of her job, and looking after her little brother, was definitely getting the better of her. God, could she really go on like this for forty-something more years? Some days it took an act of God just to get her out of bed. She was so tired all the time, as if she never got enough rest. Which was crazy, considering she made sure she slept at least eight hours every night.

Turning her eyes away from her reflection with a disgusted grunt, she padded out of the bathroom and down the hall into her bedroom for a fresh change of clothes. Her hair was still partially damp from the shower she'd taken after Amy had left.

That's right. She'd driven to the woods to pick up Amy, had brought her here for cookies. What had happened after that?

Memories pushed through the fog and trickled into her brain.

She'd been cleaning the bathroom when her headache started. Going for the pills, like she always did, she'd washed it down with—cough syrup? Vodka? Hell if she knew. She remembered being scared out of her mind, of the tray rattling in her hands after she'd snapped at Amy. The fear had rocked her to her core, had driven her to get rid of it and to forget by any means necessary. Usually, that involved cleaning. Brainless busy work always took her mind off things. What happened after she started cleaning was a mystery, but somehow she'd ended up on the bathroom floor.

As she tried to recall the hours before now, she rummaged through her closet; her eyes sifted through the hangers of shirts, skirts, and pants.

A frown formed, deepening as she looked. "What the …?" She pulled out a blouse with pink polka dots. When had she bought this? It wasn't like anything she would normally wear.

Putting it back on the rack, she kept looking. Actually, there were a lot of things here she didn't recognize. Brightly colored leather pants, sky-high heels she'd never in her life wear, glittery, tight tank tops that would be more appropriate in a lady of the night's wardrobe. The hangers screeched along the rack faster and faster as she scanned. Her breathing quickened.

Finally, she made herself stop and turn around. She squeezed her eyes shut. "It's nothing. You've just been so tired lately and so busy that you're…not remembering a single damn thing you've bought. Shit, that sounds bizarre."

Was she really so tired she was forgetting things? She used to live to shop for clothes, and she was picky about what she bought. Surely, she would remember making these fashion blunders.

A dull, familiar ache started at the base of her skull, and she whimpered. "Not again," she whispered, already going for the pill bottle she kept on her nightstand.

Her toe caught something, and she nearly went down. When she looked around her feet, she saw a pair of sneakers below her, along with a gigantic hoodie, pants that were way too big for her, and a baseball cap.

She stared. Where had *those* come from? They looked …looked…*masculine*.

She racked her brain, starting to feel herself coming unglued. No man had been over here since Eric, her gay coworker, had binge-watched *American Horror Story* with her on Netflix.

"Hello?" she called, trembling slightly as she walked farther out into her townhome. No one answered. Not satisfied, she checked every room, even the closets. No one was there but her.

She ran her hands through her hair, clutching strands and trying not to hyperventilate. What the hell was going on? Where did all those clothes that weren't hers come from?

She stood in her living room. Her fearful eyes lifted to the pictures situated so lovingly along her shelves.

"Amy," she breathed.

Diving for her purse, which she'd left on the coffee table, along with a pair of aviator sunglasses she didn't recognize, she sped-dialed Amy's number. Her voicemail picked up. Dammit, she must have her phone turned off. She tried again and again and again. Still no answer. Her voicemail picked up again, but Becca bit her lip. There was no need to freak Amy out, not when she had enough problems on her plate.

Becca looked around and hugged herself, suddenly not feeling safe in her own apartment. But where could she go? She didn't necessarily want to be in a crowd, so strip malls, movie theaters, and coffee shops were out of the question.

She checked her phone. Dammit, why hadn't Amy called her back yet?

Her head throbbed, and she gritted her teeth against the mounting pain.

Pills. She needed her pills.

She started up the stairs, when she heard someone test the back door to see whether it was locked. Keys jingled, and a moment later the door opened.

She frowned in concern. "Zach?"

The brown-haired boy was tall and thin, clad in a baggy hoodie, torn pants, and high-top sneakers. He froze when he heard her voice and slowly turned around to face her. His face was white, his eyes fearful.

A little gasp escaped her lips as she rushed toward him. "What's wrong? Where have you been?"

His eyebrows furrowed. "You know where I was. You found me at Jaden's house."

"I did? When?"

"Last night. Remember?"

Last night? She remembered picking up Amy. Before that…before that…nothing but darkness and murky memories she couldn't access.

What had she been doing? Why couldn't she remember?

She spotted a fresh bruise on his cheek and reached to cup his face, but he flinched and avoided her. "Why don't you remember?" He gazed at her with wariness. "You've been forgetting things a lot lately."

"I know," she said tiredly. "It's my headache medication. I think my dosage might be too strong or something."

He rolled his eyes. "Keep telling yourself that." Before she could respond, he rushed past her and headed toward his room. It often remained vacant because he was never home anymore. She followed him and paused in the doorway as he dug through his dresser for fresh clothes, which he placed into the duffel bag on his shoulder.

She watched him silently from the door. "Zach, why do you always try to run away? Isn't this place good enough for you?"

He paused. "It was," he said quietly and then finished packing. Re-situating the strap on his shoulder, he brushed past her and headed back downstairs toward the door he'd come through.

She followed at his heels. "Will you at least tell me what I've done wrong? Is it me?" When he didn't answer, she reached for him. The second her fingers touched his arm, he thrashed as if he'd been burned, whirled around, and stared wide-eyed at her with the same fear as before.

She stared back in horror and confusion. "Jesus, Zach, what's the matter?"

Her brother searched her face; tears formed in his eyes. "Just leave me alone," he choked out before he rushed out the door and slammed it behind him.

"Zach!" She started after him, when her head gave a violent throb. Her body veered toward the wall as a gasp was torn from her throat and stars burst before her eyes. Dizziness and nausea set in, as they always did with her migraines. Swearing, she stared a moment longer at the back door before she forced herself up the stairs.

Just get your pills. Your pills make everything better.

She was halfway up the stairs when the doorbell rang, followed by persistent knocking. Thanks to the migraine, it sounded as if a gong was going off inside her head.

Maybe they'll go away, she thought, waiting.

No such luck. The doorbell buzzed again, and she winced.

"Coming!" she called, hoping it would make them stop ringing the doorbell.

Her head hurt so much, she completely forgot to check the peephole to see who was at her door. When she opened it, she wished she had. "What are you doing here?" she breathed, staring in horror.

Nathan stood there, hands tucked in his jeans pockets and an easy smile on his handsome face. He gave her a funny look and walked past her.

"Hey!" she said. "You can't come in here!"

Another "what the hell?" look. "You told me to come by, like, last night, remember?"

"I...I did *what*?"

It was as though a switch had been flipped inside her brain, triggered by his words and the very sound of his voice. Sucking in a tight breath as her brain literally switched gears, she squeezed her eyes shut. It felt as if her internal wiring were being reprogrammed, but it only lasted a split second. When she opened her eyes, she felt like a brand-new her.

A very dangerous her.

Smiling seductively, she said in a lower voice, "Sorry, I forgot. Long day." She sat on the chair and crossed her legs. "So, how'd it go?"

Nathan eyed her another long second but didn't comment on her strange behavior. "I did what you asked." He reached into his pocket and tossed the knife on the coffee table. "Now, I believe you owe me."

Her eyes flicked to the knife. "Not so fast. How do I know you actually followed through?"

He shrugged. "Call her. She's pretty freaked."

Good. Aroused by the power she held over this man, to command him to do her bidding, she stood and sauntered over to him. She placed a nail on his chest and dragged it up over his lips, leaving a faint scratch mark. "You always were obedient. Did you also leave the anonymous tip at that gossip magazine?"

"Yeah." He grinned as he wrapped his arms around her waist. He frowned. "You sure this will work?"

"Relax, lover. It won't be long before we draw her closer. When the press comes knocking on her door, who do you think she'll run to?"

He inclined his head to her.

"Exactly. Her best friend—her *only* friend."

It was brilliant timing on her part, convincing Amy to move so far from her family. Things were tense enough with them back home, considering her mother's nerves and inability to handle stressful situations. There was already a rift forming between Amy and her family. It was all she had left, since she'd stopped talking to most of her friends out of embarrassment over what happened and a refusal to answer difficult questions. Her silence was a "way for her to forget and move on." That had been Becca's idea, too, ditching the rest of her friends. All she'd had to remove was Amy's family, and she would be completely dependent on her. Convincing her to move so far away to complete her ostracizing was simple enough. She almost snorted. "Amy 2.0" indeed.

Nathan's eyes glimmered in anticipation. "And when you draw her in…"

"I'll hand her over to you, just like we planned."

Her cell phone chirped. It was Amy calling her back, finally.

Becca winked at Nathan. "One second, lover. I've gotta take this." Pitching her voice higher, she answered cheerily, "Ames, hi!"

"Hey." Amy sounded a bit frazzled. "Um, sorry it took me so long to call. I saw you called a bunch—"

"You know what, it's okay." Becca smiled at Nathan. "It's totally no big deal, and I've got it all taken care of now."

"Oh. Okay. Um, if you're sure…"

"Yeah," Becca sang. "But thanks for calling me back! Sorry to worry you! Gotta go!"

She killed the call as Amy was saying goodbye and then tossed the phone onto the sofa.

Reaching down, she grasped the hem of her T-shirt and slowly pulled it over her head to expose her bare breasts. Nathan hungrily took her in.

"As you were saying"—she shimmied out of her sweatpants—"I believe I owe you my gratitude."

Nathan didn't wait. He seized her and crushed her to him as their lips met.

Becca kissed him back, forcing her tongue past his lips and into his mouth. He growled, picking her up and tossing her onto the sofa. Nathan ravished her, kissing her throat, her breasts, her stomach.

He was far too distracted to notice Becca's hand had found the knife, lying so close by on the coffee table. Flipping it open, she rammed the point into Nathan's back.

He gasped, rearing up, his eyes wide and terrified as they searched her face. "What are you doing?" he rasped.

She smiled. "Making sure you never hurt my Amy again."

Jerking the knife out, she buried it to the hilt in his throat.

TWENTY-EIGHT

SCOTT COULDN'T BELIEVE what he was seeing. It was like the Ghost of Fights Past had come to haunt him.

Jeremy hadn't changed much in the year and a half since Scott had last seen him. He looked a little more scarred, maybe. His knuckles were covered in thick calluses from countless nights spent beating the living hell out of people in the ring. The Lynyrd Skynyrd T-shirt he wore fit small on purpose; it showed off just how ripped he was—and how deadly.

Add to that the fact he was over seven feet tall, and you had one scary son of a bitch. He wasn't called the Destroyer for nothing. Many men's faces, limbs, and, in one case that haunted Jeremy to this day, lives had been destroyed. Scott believed him. The shock on Jeremy's face when he realized his opponent would never get back up again was evidence it had been an accident. Jeremy might have been good at kicking ass, but he wasn't a killer.

All the same, Scott was thankful Jeremy fought under the same employer and he never had to face him in the ring. He'd look a whole lot more fucked up today than he did if he ever had to face Jeremy.

Jeremy raised one of his thick black brows. His father was straight-off-the-boat Italian, and Jeremy had inherited the olive skin and curly black hair of his old man.

"You gonna stare at me all day or invite me in, asshole?" Jeremy asked with a slight smirk.

Scott shook his head. "Sorry, man." He stepped forward and embraced Jeremy in a tight man-hug. "Just shocked to see you, that's all. I thought you'd gone dark after that fight with Mickey."

The deep regret and pain of killing the legendary fighter flashed in Jeremy's eyes briefly as Scott let him in and shut the door. "Yeah," he said quietly, looking around. "I did."

"As in, not anymore?" He went to grab two beers, figuring they could both use an icebreaker.

"Thanks, man." Jeremy took the beer and sat on the couch when Scott gestured. Scott sat back in his recliner and popped the cap off his bottle before he took a healthy swig. Jeremy looked troubled. Scott had seen a lot of troubled people in his life, so he'd learned to recognize it fairly easily. They carried a heaviness about them that was missing from happy people.

He waited for Jeremy to speak on his own; the both of them sipped on their beers in silence. "Ghost sent me," Jeremy finally said, forcing his gaze to Scott's.

"Shit. I figured as much. You're not back in the ring, are you?"

Jeremy's silence was answer enough.

Scott's brows furrowed. "What happened? When did he approach you? How did he find you?"

Jeremy chuckled, a broken, brittle sound. "Where do I start? You know once Ghost lets you go, or says he is, anyway, that he's lying. 'Just because he loosens the leash doesn't mean he's taking off the collar.'"

A chill ran through Scott. Ghost had said exactly the same thing to him back at the inn. Swallowing hard, he waited for Jeremy to continue.

Jeremy leaned forward. The half-empty beer bottle dangled from his fingers. His gaze grew distant, saddened. For the first time Scott could remember, the insurmountable man looked…broken.

"I knew he was having me followed about two months into 'disappearing.' I'd catch guys watching me in the park, a restaurant, on the bus, everywhere, always pretending to be fellow pedestrians. Then Ghost himself showed.

"I had just picked my little girl up from preschool." His voice trembled, making Scott tense. He didn't blink—hell, he didn't even breathe—as he listened. "The doorbell rang. Figuring it was my wife with the groceries, I answered it. There stood Ghost instead, flanked by two goons. I couldn't refuse him. I had to let him in. You know Ghost isn't the type of man to stop trying to get to you simply because a door is slammed in his face. So I let him in. He said he just wanted to talk, to catch up, but I knew better. There's always a motive with Ghost—and there was. He'd come for me, to get me back in the ring. Said he'd had some business ventures go sour and needed me to help him out." He chuckled darkly. "'Help.' Like I had a choice.

"When I refused, he didn't take it so well. Said he'd find a way to make me change my mind. People always had things that could be used for leverage." His face paled, and his voice lowered to a haunted whisper. "I saw him glance at my daughter, and I knew exactly what kind of leverage he intended to use. I wasn't about to give him that chance. After he left, I packed a bag as quickly as I could, with all the things me, my wife, and my kid would need, and we hightailed it out of there.

"Sharon dialed me just as I was about to call her, and I told her the plan. We never went back. For six whole months, we bounced around from state to state, changing our names, changing our occupations, staying in extended-stay hotels. It sucked. My dream was to save up enough money to buy our way out of the country and into a brand-new life, free of Ghost, but that was wishful thinking. One night, the night before we were about to move again, I needed to make a grocery store run. I called Sharon to tell her where we were heading, but she never picked up. I didn't think anything of it, at first. When she was out and about, my wife never really answered her phone. Too damn busy, she said. But as the night went on, and I never heard from her, I grew worried. We lived out in the boon-docks. More privacy. Since Sharon wasn't returning my calls, I decided to stop somewhere closer to town in case I needed to go back for her. I'd just filled up the tank with gas and stepped into the gas station to get my little girl some water. I was gone maybe thirty seconds. When I got back in the car, one of Ghost's thugs was in the backseat, with a gun pointed at my little girl's head." He formed a gun with his thumb and forefinger and pointed it at his temple.

"He told me to drive." His voice got lower and lower, evaporating into a whisper, those deadened eyes staring at nothing. "We went back to the cabin, where Sharon was tied up in the living room. It took me a second to recognize her; they'd beaten her to a pulp. Ghost said I needed to be taught a lesson. He made me choose—my wife or my kid. My wife looked at me with understanding and nodded. Before I could do anything to stop it, they killed her. Right in front of me and my little girl. All because I tried to get away from Ghost. Because I told him no." His hand shook, threatening to drop the bottle.

Scott's mouth was pressed in a hard, thin line, his eyes grave as Jeremy looked at him.

"Do you understand where I'm going with this?" Jeremy rasped.

"Yeah." Scott glanced at the wall, where he knew Amy was sleeping just on the other side. "I think I do. And I've already told Ghost yes. I'll fight for him."

"Wise move." Jeremy nodded and finished off his beer before he set it on the coffee table with a thud. A moment of heavy silence passed before he finally stood and walked toward the door. "You don't need me then, to bore you with more of my sad tales."

Scott noticed the glint of gold around Jeremy's ring finger. "I'm sorry," he said softly.

Jeremy froze as he ran his thumb along the ring. "You're a lot smarter than I was." He looked back with sadness in his eyes, as if it was the last time he'd ever see him again. "Take care, man." He started to open the door but paused. "A word of advice? Cut your lady friend loose."

Scott wasn't surprised he knew about Amy. Ghost

had probably informed him of the stakes. "Jeremy—"

"I'm serious." He held up a hand, stopping Scott from interrupting. "Think about it, man. You're gonna wreck this girl's life. If you really love her like I think you do, you'll let her go."

Then he left, leaving Scott sitting there with what felt like a block of ice in his chest.

After Becca hung up, Amy stared at her phone for a good long minute. Becca never hung up on her. Ever.

Has the whole damn world gone crazy?

After Nathan left, she couldn't go back to sleep. Hell, she'd grabbed a butcher knife and sat on her couch, facing the door, waiting for someone to break in, but it never happened.

Still, the knife had remained glued to her hand.

Eventually, her restlessness and anxiety had won out, and she'd begun to pace. Just what the hell was she going to do? Nathan had made a clear threat on Scott's life. But he hadn't on Becca's...

Nuh-uh. No way could she get her friend involved with that psychotic son of a bitch. She had to figure out a way to solve this problem on her own. She stopped in the middle of her living room, knife in hand as she thought.

The thing about running is that you eventually grow tired of it. She thought she wouldn't, that running was the safest thing she could possibly do. There was a certain comfort in it. Now that she had something worth fighting for—Scott, her life, her future—she found she was so damned exhausted. Not just physically, but mentally.

Did she really want to spend the rest of her life looking over her shoulder all the time? Did she always want to live in fear of Nathan finding her and finishing what he started? What if she had kids? Would she be terrified sending them to school every day, afraid Nathan would abduct them to get to her?

The more the wheels of her mind spun, the quicker her fear drained, replaced by burning anger.

Nathan had taken so much from her over the years: her freedom, her love, her happiness.

Thing is, she'd *let* him. Her therapist had said that she could only conquer her fears when she wasn't afraid of them anymore. Amy had thought that sounded like a load of BS at the time, and she'd never really understood it.

Until now.

Sometimes fear faded on its own as you grew braver. And other times, like right now, you could only overcome fear when another emotion took its place.

Anger.

"That cocky prick." Amy seethed, grabbing her phone and her purse. "I'll show him." She stomped to the door, not even really sure where she was going but knowing she couldn't sit here any longer. "He won't know what hit him."

She grabbed the knob, twisted, and flung the door open.

Her determination dried right up as her eyes widened.

A woman and a guy holding a camera stood right outside her door. The woman's fist was poised, as if she'd been about to knock. She was dressed sharply, with a pencil skirt and blouse, cute round-toed pumps, and super curly hair. Her makeup was camera-perfect. A lanyard hung around her neck, from which dangled a badge that read Channel 8 KHTV Correspondent.

A rock dropped to the pit of Amy's stomach. *No. No, no, how did they find me?*

The reporter blinked, recovering first. "Are you Miss Julia Gray?"

A chill shot straight to her core, rendering her speechless. Her feet turned to lead.

"Oh my God!" the reporter whispered to her cameraman. "It's her! It's actually her! We're live in five, four…"

TWENTY-NINE

"THREE, TWO, ONE." The reporter pasted on a smile. "I'm Camille Braxton, live here with KHTV. Thanks to an anonymous tip, we've just located longtime missing fiancée of rising rock star Michael Stone. If you recall, two years ago she disappeared after the brutal murder of her intended. Julia, can you please tell us how you're feeling now? What have you been doing?"

"I...I..."

A door opened, and a second later, a muscular arm slipped around Amy's shoulders. "I'm sorry, but did I hear you call her 'Julia'?" Scott's eyes narrowed on the reporter.

Her eyes roved Scott head to toe and then back up again, mouth agape. Blinking and shaking her head, she said, "Yes, that's correct."

"Well, you must be mistaken. Her name's not Julia. Now, if you'll please see yourselves out before I have to call security. This is a private building."

The reporter frowned. Scott stepped in front of Amy, crossing his arms, and gave the reporter a heavy look.

Face turning red, she whirled on her heel and snapped, "Come on, Simon! Stupid story is a bust. Crazy tippers, giving us false information…" She prattled like an insolent child the whole way down the stairs and out the door, her poor cameraman following behind.

Scott sighed and turned around. "You okay?"

"Yeah," Amy breathed. Her voice trembled a little. "Now I am, thanks to you. I just…she surprised me."

He raised a brow. "Care to explain what's going on? I thought I heard them call you the lead guitarist of Leviathan 5's fiancée."

A sinking sensation started in her gut. *No sense in hiding anymore. We're moving forward, remember?* Thing was, she didn't really want to keep the past bottled up inside anymore. She was tired of carrying the burden of her pain all by herself. And she trusted Scott. He cared about her; she knew it in her gut. She needed to be fair with him and get all her baggage out in the open like he'd done with her.

"Actually," she said, voice low, "it's not so crazy. Come inside. I'll explain everything."

Amy sat beside Scott on her couch, twisting the bottom of her shirt into knots as she thought about what to say.

They'd sat in silence for almost five minutes now, an untouched glass of white wine on the coffee table in front of her.

Scott waited patiently for her to talk.

Finally, she laughed, her stomach alight with butterflies. "I don't even know where to begin."

He touched her hand and squeezed gently, smiling.

That settled her nerves a bit, and she gave him a small smile back. She started with the first thing that popped into her head.

"Some of it you already know, but I'll go over it again anyway because I think it will... I don't know, help me tell the story. Put all the pieces together a bit better, so to speak." She cleared her throat. That wine was looking real tasty right about now. "I grew up in Upstate New York. Like I said during dinner, my dad is a lawyer and my mom is an artist. So is my sister. We're all 'artsy.' Anyway"—she tucked a strand of loose hair behind her ear—"their relationship ended in divorce. They never really got along. I can remember sitting up at night, listening to them arguing. He was always telling her to 'get a normal job,' since she worked at home as an artist. He never really got the whole freelancing thing. I think it made him nervous. He liked knowing exactly how much he was going to earn every month, exactly when that paycheck would come in, and exactly where every dollar was going. My mom tried a normal job for a few months and hated the rigidity. I think she grew to resent it after awhile." She smiled sadly. "It was a complete one-eighty from how they were when I was really little. They were so in love. Then he got promoted, making partner, and he turned into a totally different person."

"You ever talk to him?" Scott asked quietly.

Amy shrugged. "Sometimes. He sends a birthday card, and we talk at Christmas. But every time I said I was going to be in the neighborhood and was wondering if I could stop by, he always said he was busy."

Scott's jaw ticked. "Well, it's his loss then."

Amy didn't know how to respond to that. "I never really knew him that well. Sometimes, I don't think I ever will. I don't think he wants to," she said quietly. "He remarried and has a new family now." Clearing her throat in the heavy silence, she went on. "After they separated, my mom moved us to another neighborhood and enrolled us in a school for the arts. The change in her, and our household, was like night and day. She seemed so much happier, so much freer. Granted, being scatterbrained, she often forgot to pay the bills if we didn't remind her. There were some scary moments, but I can honestly say those were the happiest moments of my life up until then. Both my sister and I had shown a propensity for art. Our dad, fearing we would want to be artists like our mother, always discouraged it. He told us art was fine as a hobby but not as a profession. Mom wasn't like that, though. She encouraged everything we did, and we really grew under her wings. By the time I graduated high school, I knew with all my heart I wanted to be an artist. So I went to college for it when the time came. There, I met Michael."

"Michael Stone? *The* Michael Stone?"

"The one and the same. Though he was called Michael Lewis back then. 'Michael Stone' was suggested as a stage name by his record company because it sounded 'sexier.'" She laughed and shook her head. "I never let him live that one down. Neither did his bandmates. He did, um, some extracurricular activities that earned him the nickname of 'Michael Stoned.'"

Scott nodded, still looking a bit dazed. "Yeah. The media talked about that."

Amy winced.

Scott stilled, studying her. "What?"

A knot formed in her throat, which made it difficult to swallow. "Sorry." She shook her head, suddenly finding it difficult to put what she wanted to say into words. "It's just, well, I, um, kind of have a love-hate relationship with the media. And by that I mean mostly hate."

Understanding and sympathy shone in his eyes. "Understandable. They didn't take it easy on you."

"They never do. Not if it means getting a good story that will improve their sales or ratings." *Take a deep breath. Let it out.* She inhaled slowly and sighed. "Michael and I eventually got engaged. The lead singer of Leviathan 5, Roxanne Duncan, wasn't exactly thrilled about it. I mean, she was nice to my face, but I heard the gossip. About how she would be so much better suited to become the bride of a rock star, considering she was one herself. Michael was easily as popular as her in the fan polls, and they were both drop-dead gorgeous and super talented. It made sense. The prince and princess of rock." Amy stared at her hands, feeling small again, just as she had every time some gossip columnist made fun of her "drabness" next to Roxanne's perfect looks.

"I thought I'd seen looks exchanged between them. I mean, I knew she liked him. That much was obvious, and she wasn't very good at hiding it. But I guess some part of me was always in denial that he would betray me that way. But he did."

She hadn't realized she'd begun to cry until a big fat tear plopped onto her hand. Scott didn't move to hug her, as if sensing how breakable she was right now. Any further show of sympathy might push her over the edge. Steeling her heart, she forced herself to finish the story. "It happened during the band's first world tour. Somehow, the news Roxanne was pregnant with Michael's child—which turned out to be nothing more than a rumor—leaked onto a celebrity blog, and soon the whole Internet was buzzing with it. I was used to rumors, so I initially ignored it. It wasn't until I saw the photo of them kissing that I started to think maybe there really was something going on. It took a damn *Tweet* to shake up my denial." She laughed once and swatted at her eyes. "Of course, some part of me still thought it wasn't true, that it was yet another Michael fangirl-troll looking to pile on more Julia hate. Like, maybe the photo was Photoshopped. But when I met up with him the night they got back, when I saw the look on his face and the guilt in his eyes, I knew. It hadn't been a lie—our relationship had been."

She shuddered, remembering what happened next. "We got into a screaming match. I ran away, just like I always do when things get tough. He called me a million times, wanting to work things out. When I finally decided to go back over there that night, to face what had happened and see what the future held for us, I…I found him…"

"You don't have to say anything," Scott said quietly, touching her arm. "I know."

She smiled softly. "Nathan walked in as I was calling 9-1-1. His knife was there, covered in Michael's blood. They both collected knives. Nathan swore at his trial that he didn't do it, that he'd been set up. He said he'd given that knife to Michael as a birthday present, right before things went to shit for the band. He also had an alibi. Some girl he'd spent the night with corroborated his story. With no proof, and I'm sure a hefty sum from his family to pay off the judge, they had to let him go. They never caught the killer, and the case went cold."

"So Nathan's family bought his freedom—and paid to keep the officials quiet," Scott said tersely.

Amy licked her suddenly dry lips. "I'm pretty sure they did, and the court just looked the other way as they took their bribe. Nathan's father is pretty high up in politics. He was country club buddies with most of the judges, and several other prominent figures, in the community and around the country. You know, anyone who might come in handy someday. He knew freedom could be bought. With their wealth, no price is too steep."

"Jesus, Amy." Scott shook his head in disbelief. "I'm sorry. I'm so damned sorry."

"Don't be. You didn't have anything to do with it." She felt better. Drained, but somehow lighter for it. "And my name's not Amy. Well, it is. It's my middle name. My first name is Julia. Last name's Gray. I took on my mother's maiden name, Miles, when I changed my name and moved after school."

Scott stared at her with big, sad eyes. Taking her into a hug, he held her tight and caressed her hair. "What do you want me to call you?" he murmured.

"Hmmm..." She hugged her arms around him and buried her face into his chest. She inhaled the smell of him, trying to memorize it.

Who was she? When she'd taken her middle name, she'd vowed never to look back. "Julia" was tied with pain, suffering, and heartache. "Amy"…Amy's story was still being written.

She leaned back and gazed into his eyes. "Call me Amy. Because that's the name that led me to you."

Something unnamable danced in his eyes. Tilting his head, he whispered, "Amy. My sweet, beautiful Amy," before he kissed her tenderly.

She closed her eyes and leaned into the kiss; his tongue darted into her mouth to caress hers. She could feel her breasts begin to ache, a sure sign her nipples were tightening, as he gently leaned her back against the couch. She wrapped her legs around him, and he ground against her once. Though he wore jeans, she could feel him hardening for her. Pushing back, he sat up, a question in his eyes, the blue of which quickly deepened to something darker as she pulled her shirt off and tossed it onto the floor. His shirt followed. His adept fingers reached around as they kissed, unhooking her bra with ease. It loosened, and she impatiently tugged the straps off before she cast it aside.

His chest was hard, with a patch of dark, curly hair crowning his pectoral muscles. She leaned into him, sighing as his hair tickled her nipples. A shiver of want rolled through her as she rocked against him.

That sent him over the edge. Reaching up, he cupped the back of her head, inhaled a desperate breath, and pulled her mouth to his. Gone was the earlier tenderness, replaced by a desperation both of them seemed to feel.

As if this would be the last time they ever made love, when they'd finally bared all to each other.

That thought danced along the back of Amy's mind, taunting her and threatening to snatch away the one last remnant of happiness she had left. She fumbled at his jeans' button, starving to be closer, as close as two people could get. She needed to feel him, to know he was real and this all wasn't a dream she would wake up from.

As she freed the button, Scott scooped her up and carried her into her bedroom. Their kisses came hot and furious as they fell onto the bed. Scott kicked off his pants. Amy's skirt came next, only Scott took his time. He slowly peeled it off, along with her panties, looking over every inch of her as if to memorize the moment.

The lust that had lurked in his gaze the first time they'd met was replaced with something stronger as he gazed at her, something that made her heart skip and her breath catch.

As he slid out of his boxers, he prowled over her, brushing back the sweat-dampened hairs stuck to her face. "I want…" He swallowed hard, his voice rough and pain scrunching his features. "I want you to know that—"

"Sssh." She placed a finger to his lips. "Just kiss me."

He searched her eyes and then planted his mouth on hers at the same time he thrust.

She cried out in surprise, spreading her legs wider as he rose and thrust again, this time going deeper. Slowly, she stretched as he made love to her, settling into a rhythm of rapid breaths accented by the staccato of slapping skin. He held her to him, grabbing one leg of hers and hoisting it up to go deeper. His long, thick sex stroked her sweetest spot, shooting fireworks of pleasure through her body as she gasped and clawed at him.

They didn't speak. They didn't need to. Sometimes, words were not enough.

Except for three.

I love you.

She couldn't say it out loud, not to him. She'd said those words to Michael, and look where it had gotten him: to an early grave.

So she'd keep it bottled up inside, where it could never hurt the man she loved.

A tear rolled down her cheek as she climaxed, the bittersweetness of the moment accentuated by the fact she knew she was about to lose him.

Scott came soon thereafter, releasing himself with a final thrust and a deep, feral groan. Afterward, they lay there panting hard, listening to the sounds of their racing hearts.

Scott finally looked up—and frowned. He delicately brushed the tear from Amy's cheek. "What's wrong?"

I love you.

The words froze on her tongue. Instead, she smiled through her pain. "I'm just happy. So incredibly happy to have met you."

"Don't talk that way." Scott cradled her face and stroked her cheek with his thumb. "Don't you dare think this is the last time we'll meet, because I promise you it won't be. I'll keep coming back for you, even if I have to face hell itself. I...I..."

A knock came at the door. Well, more like a banging, as if a caveman wanted entrance.

Amy's eyes flashed to Scott's. "What if that's Nathan?"

"For his sake, I hope he's not that stupid," Scott growled, standing and tugging on his pants. Storming to the door, he grabbed the baseball bat Amy kept nearby, and peered through the peephole.

"Shit," he breathed.

"What?" Amy said, suddenly terrified as she leapt out of bed. Her foot caught on the sheet, and she nearly went down, but she grabbed the footboard and righted herself. She scrambled to get dressed. "Who is it?"

"Another unwelcome visitor." Scott held up a hand as she stepped into the living room. "Stay back. I got this."

Her brows furrowed in confusion, but she didn't argue. She trusted him, body and soul.

Stepping back into the shadows of the bedroom, she nodded once, and Scott took a deep breath.

With his whole body tensed, he opened the door.

Amy recognized the man immediately. It was one of Ghost's henchmen from the inn.

He didn't look too happy to be there. He scowled at Scott.

"Ghost wants you. Now."

THIRTY

"N OW?" SCOTT ASKED, perhaps a little sharper than he should have. After all, most smart men didn't bite off the heads of mobsters. "Couldn't you have just called?"

"Ghost wanted a little insurance." He lifted the flap of his coat to reveal a handgun strapped to his waist.

"Ghost said I had until tonight."

"It is night. Look out the window, genius."

Scott glanced over his shoulder. Hot damn. It was dusk. The sun was starting to set. His teeth ground together. "How did you know where I was?"

"Doesn't take a genius to guess you'd be at your girl's when you don't answer your door. And I know you're not stupid enough to ignore me."

Scott glanced at the bedroom, where Amy was hiding, and shifted his weight. It felt as though he'd swallowed a bunch of rocks. *Not yet. It's too soon.* He realized leaving her anytime would be too damned soon, regardless of if he had a day to prepare or a lifetime. "I don't have anything ready to go."

"Then get to packing. We're leaving in five minutes. Don't make Ghost wait." He paused. "Bring the girl."

"Amy's not going anywhere—"

"The other girl, jackass. The lanky blonde."

He turned and thudded down the stairwell. Once he was gone, Scott growled a sigh and let the door slam closed.

Amy came out as he walked toward her. "What's going on?" She glanced nervously at the door.

"Ghost is here." He glanced out the window. The meathead who'd summoned him knocked on the window of a pitch-black limo. It rolled down, and he said something to the man sitting in the back.

Ghost. Come to collect him already, to tighten the leash again.

Scott remembered his earlier conversation with Mack, his words drifting through his head.

"How far are you willing to go to protect that girl, Scott?"

"To hell and back," Scott murmured, thinking of what he'd promised Amy while they lay tangled in each other's arms only minutes before.

"Scott?"

Scott kissed her quickly. The fire of determination burned in his gut as he strode to the door. "Walk with me?"

She followed on his heels as they went into his apartment, and he pulled his duffel bag out of the bedroom closet. "What's going on, Scott?"

Guilt wrenched his gut. Steeling himself, he turned to

face Amy. He had to look at her eyes. He owed her that much for what he was about to say. "I made a deal with Ghost. I'm going to fight for him again."

Her eyes nearly popped out of her head as her jaw hit the floor. "What?" she screeched.

He held up both hands to calm her. "It's okay. I have a plan."

"A plan." She laughed in her nervous, high-pitched laugh. "What kind of plan could you possibly have for fighting that asshole? He's dangerous!"

"Which is why I'm going to put him away for good," Scott said earnestly, gripping her arms. Hell, the more he talked about it, the more he saw his future in Amy's eyes, and the more fired up he got about this suicide plan. "But I need your help."

She pursed her lips as she scrutinized him. "What do you need me to do?"

Reaching into his pants pocket, he produced a piece of paper with a phone number and a name scribbled on it. "My parole officer gave this to me earlier when I went down by the station to meet with him. I need you to call this number after I leave and tell Agent White I've left with Ghost. That's all."

"Agent White? What the hell's going on?"

"I can't tell you." He forced himself to look away so he could throw some stuff into the duffel bag. Ghost wasn't exactly known for his patience. "That way if Ghost has someone check in on you, and I guarantee he'll try, you can honestly say you don't know anything." Cramming his toiletries into the bag, he zipped it closed and hoisted it over his shoulder.

"Why can't you call this number?" Amy asked as he

walked to the door.

He glanced at his watch. Four minutes had passed. One more to go before Ghost sent someone in for him. "It's not part of the plan. I can't have that number available in case Ghost checks my phone."

He stopped in front of the door and turned around to face her. Before she could argue or he lost his nerve to leave her, he grabbed her by the arms and whispered, "Wait for me?"

She froze; fear and pain flashed in her eyes. Bottom lip trembling, she pressed her lips together, closed her eyes, and nodded. "Always," she whispered back.

Scott took her face in his hands and kissed her one last time, savoring her taste, her smell, the feel of her soft skin and hair beneath his fingers.

Amy clung to him; the tremble had worked its way into her arms.

God, if he didn't stop now, he'd never be able to let her go. Calling upon every ounce of control he had, he forced himself to break the kiss, giving her one last lingering look before he headed out the door and down the stairs.

She didn't follow him. About halfway down the stairs, he couldn't help it anymore and looked up.

There she was, standing in his doorway, looking as though the life had been sucked out of her. He felt hollow and cold inside, staring at his angel.

Don't think like that. This isn't the end. It's just a brief break while you settle an old score.

Giving her an encouraging smile that was as much for his benefit as hers, he kept walking. He made a quick detour on the way down to grab Erika and haul her downstairs with him.

The thug who had come to claim him met them at the car. After a thorough pat-down to make sure one of them wasn't secretly packing heat, the goon begrudgingly nodded. A second later, Scott heard the click of the car doors being unlocked. Goonface opened the door. Erika got in without hesitation, and Goonface glared at Scott as he waited for him to get in.

The inside of the car was dark, thanks to the super-tinted windows. Ghost sat there, smoking a cigar. He offered one to Scott as he reluctantly sat beside his old master, but Scott shook his head. Goonface shut the door and got in the front seat on the passenger's side, drawing a gun and aiming it at Scott before the driver sped away. "Don't try anything stupid," he said.

Scott raised a brow. It didn't surprise him, and it wasn't the first time he'd had a gun aimed at him.

The thug raised a hand. "Give me the bag. You, too, blondie."

Erika handed over her purse as if it were on fire. Fear flashed in her round eyes.

Scott handed his duffel bag over without batting a lash, making a point to look bored. "Be my guest, if digging through men's underwear is your thing."

The guy leered at him but dutifully searched the duffel bag's contents. He briefly took out Scott's cell and thumbed through it. "Looks clean." He placed everything back inside, except the phone. He handed that to Ghost, who pulled it apart to check for a bug before he stuck it inside his coat pocket after he'd taken the battery out.

"Wouldn't want someone tracking us via GPS, now would we?" he said congenially as Goonface searched

Erika's purse. "I'll determine when you can make calls, as part of our arrangement."

Scott's jaw gritted. "Okay, Mom."

Ghost chuckled and knocked off ash into the fancy glass ashtray at his side. "You haven't lost your fire. Oh, how I've missed it."

"Wish I could say the same," Scott said tersely.

Ghost only grinned wider. "I'm glad you haven't lost your old spark. You'll need it inside the ring."

Scott swallowed, though he couldn't deny a small ember of excitement glowed in his belly at the thought of getting back in the ring.

Over my dead body. Dammit, he'd made a promise to Amy.

And he was damn well going to keep it.

No more fighting. No more running, after tonight. No, after tonight, things were going to change, permanently.

Scott just hoped he lived long enough to see the outcome.

Watching Scott drive off felt like ripping out her own heart. The hopelessness that had been so pronounced at Michael's death, and at Nathan's trial when they'd let him walk free, almost took over. It always did, anytime her life threatened to fall apart. Once again, happiness was within her grasp, and it had slipped through her fingers.

More like it had been yanked—by Ghost, by Nathan, by Michael's anonymous killer.

Why was it whenever she touched something, it got

fucked up? Was she cursed?

The sudden biting urge to talk to her mom or sister gnawed at her, but she promptly shut it up. They already had enough on their plates, and besides, she couldn't risk Nathan somehow finding out and going after them. They were all the family she had left.

Deep in her heart, she knew letting Scott go was the best thing for his safety, even if it was into the hands of another monster. At least, in a twisted way, she could rest assured Scott would be somewhat safe with Ghost. He viewed his fighters as investments, and from the sound of it, Scott was a pretty big one. He'd protect him at any cost.

Yeah, good luck getting through the mob, Nathan, she thought with bitter satisfaction.

Rain pelted the glass as thunder boomed and shook the building. Thunderstorms were nerve-racking enough, but they were ten times worse at night. Though it was unlikely to happen in California, she had nightmares of a tornado ripping through town and lifting her up into the sky. The giant, bone-crushing wind tunnels had always freaked her out.

Braveheart whined from beneath her bed. His two golden eyes reflected the lightning, and he shrank further into the shadows, terrified.

You and me both, buddy.

Not in the mood for a freak-out session, she focused on performing the task Scott had left her with. Grabbing her phone, she punched in the number scrawled on the piece of paper. The agent was deep-voiced and brief. He said maybe ten words and then hung up after he took her name.

"Well, you're welcome," Amy muttered, staring at

the CALL ENDED message that flashed on her cell phone screen.

She paced afterward, nibbling on her lip as she wondered whether Scott was okay and what she was going to do about Nathan. She was supposed to meet him tonight. She needed a plan—now.

And it was nowhere to be found.

"Shit." She wrung her hair. "Okay, breathe." She took a breath and let it out. "Who do you know who you can talk to?" She couldn't go to the cops; Nathan's father probably knew someone who could cover up his son's tracks if Nathan caught wind of Amy's snitch and decided to make good on his threat. He could go after Becca, or her mom or sister...

She stopped.

The thought was ludicrous. And dangerous, potentially deadly. But it might be her only option, and frankly, she was running out of those.

Her heart ached as she walked to the bedroom. The smell of their lovemaking lingered in the air, along with Scott's pine scent. It assaulted her, teasing her that he was never coming back.

Don't think that way. He's coming back. And you have to make sure you're here when he does.

She didn't even dare turn on the bedroom light, for fear Ghost's men were watching the outside of the building. Using the light on her cell phone screen, she opened the bottom drawer of her dresser and removed a bundle of cloth.

The cloaked item wasn't light, but it was far from being unbearable. She rested the item on her bed, staring at it as her heart hammered in her chest.

She swallowed hard. Was she really going through with this? Could she do what needed to be done, when the time came, if she even made it that far?

Holding her breath and not blinking, she slowly reached down and lifted the flaps of cloth until the item beneath was exposed.

Her last resort stared up at her, its black frame more menacing, somehow, considering what she was about to do with it.

This weapon of destruction—this gun—could literally be the key to her salvation.

Right then and there, she made a promise to herself.

She would do it. If it came down to him or her, she would shoot Nathan.

And hell, she might even enjoy it a little.

THIRTY-ONE

ABOUT FIFTEEN MINUTES into the car ride to wherever the hell they were going, Scott wanted to kill Erika. He gave himself major points for lasting fifteen whole minutes. His patience must be improving.

"The hot water didn't work in the apartment." She glared at him. She sat with her arms crossed, pouting. "I couldn't even enjoy my shower. In fact, I almost didn't take one, and whose fault would that have been? Seriously, do you never answer your phone? What kind of landlord are you?"

"For starters, I'm not a landlord," Scott said evenly, shooting her a glare right back. "I'm just a building manager." He grimaced. "*Was* a building manager. And get over it, princess. People deal with random shit all the time. It's what grown-ups do."

"Are you calling me a baby?"

"Silence!" Ghost barked. "Both of you! You're quibbling like a couple of children, and I won't stand for it."

Erika's eyes widened, like a puppy that had just been scolded. Scott bit his tongue. Now wasn't the time to piss Ghost off. That would come later.

And he was going to fucking enjoy it.

Wait 'til you see what's coming, asshole.

Tempted by the ensuing silence, Scott leaned his head back against the plush leather and closed his eyes.

He could still see Amy clearly in his mind, gazing at him from his doorway as he left her. God, it killed him to have to abandon her. What if the press went after her again? What if that psycho Nathan paid her another visit, and he wasn't there to protect her? Granted, he'd asked Mack to watch over her for him, as a condition of him helping out the feds, but still… He didn't trust anyone to protect his Amy half as well as he could. More like he didn't trust anyone to care enough to protect her, especially not a police department infested with rotten cops. Mack swore he'd get someone clean, someone he trusted, but how could he know whether the guy or girl was secretly taking money from Ghost under the table?

Anxiety twisted his gut. His foot began to tap.

Ghost studied his foot; those oily, calculating eyes slinked up his whole body. "You look nervous."

Scott opened his eyes and popped his neck, playing it casual. "I'm in the car with you, aren't I?"

Ghost chuckled. A slow smile spread on his face. "You always were my favorite. You and I are a lot alike."

"I doubt that."

"No, we are, more than you think." Ghost poked his cigar at him. As soon as he'd finished the last one, he'd started on another. "Both of us have the drive, this competitive edge, to get ahead in life and get what we want, no matter what."

"You mean take what you want? Ruin people's lives? Nah, doesn't sound like me."

Ghost's eyes narrowed, but that arrogant smile, the smile of triumph Scott used to sport in the ring after a long, bloody fight, remained on his face. "You say that now, but we'll see how long that lasts."

Scott tensed. "Meaning?"

Ghost shrugged and glanced out his window, watching the buildings get larger and larger. They must be headed downtown, toward the business district. "You'll see soon enough."

If a man should fear hearing anything come out of that snake's mouth, it was those words.

Shit.

Ghost remained silent the rest of the drive there, leaving Scott to stew over what he was about to face. He knew it was useless trying to get details out of him before Ghost was ready to reveal them. He'd just be wasting his breath.

Erika didn't speak to him the rest of the way, though she kept glancing at him every few seconds with a mixture of hope and longing. He made a point of turning his body away from her, preferring to look outside instead.

It was fully dark out and had started to storm by the time they pulled up to a large domed building he recognized as one of the huge auditoriums where they held concerts. The parking lot was packed with a lot of fancy cars. Scott went on the alert, studying his surroundings as they parked and got out. Goonface—Trevor, he was called—flashed his gun at him as he took a position behind Scott. "Get any ideas and…"

"Yeah, yeah. I know." Scott sounded bored.

They didn't have far to walk, considering the driver had pulled right up to the door. It didn't surprise him Ghost was considered a VIP, allowed to park wherever the hell he pleased.

Security must have recognized Ghost, because they let him and his entourage through without question. Scott raised a brow, wondering what the hell they were doing here. Ghost normally didn't conduct his business in such a public place.

Ghost paused and turned to face Erika. He took out his billfold and handed her a one-hundred-dollar bill. "For your trouble. I'll be in touch should I need your services again."

Erika glanced at the money longingly and then at Scott.

Scott steeled his gaze, already knowing what she would do.

Her lips pressed together, Erika snatched the money and walked back out the door, never once glancing over her shoulder.

Scott watched her go with loathing. *Good riddance.*

The auditorium was fairly new, having just been renovated this past spring. Gleaming marble floors, thick red carpets, and state-of-the-art TVs and sound systems made up the inside. Black wallpaper featuring actual sheet music and lyrics from famous artists over the years covered the walls. The music notes had LED lights, alternating slowly through the full spectrum of the rainbow as they walked. "Private Event," along with tonight's date, flashed across the screen of a giant monitor that hung above the walkway. Inside the auditorium, from behind closed doors, Scott could hear a popular rock band jamming out to a background of cheers and whistles.

More signs and advertising indicated a charity concert for the children's hospital. He thought maybe they were going to go in, when they went through one of the staff-only doors and proceeded downstairs. It must have been where the props and other stage gear were kept. Curtains, costumes, sound equipment, and musical instruments sat in organized groups as they walked down hallway after hallway. The carpet here was black, as were the walls, with simple fluorescent lighting above to light the way.

A few people milled by who definitely didn't look like stage crew. The fancy dresses and tuxedos they wore glittered under the light as they caught sight of Scott and whispered excitedly to one another.

Scott raised a brow, watching them until they'd turned the corner. "Care to explain what's going on and what I'm doing here?"

"Soon enough." Ghost smiled at him.

Scott hated that smile—always had. It usually meant shit was about to get real.

They stopped at a room marked with a glittering golden star. A dry-erase board, presumably where one wrote a name, was pinned below the star.

Scott's jaw ticked. He didn't like the looks of this at all. Warning bells went off in his head, but what the hell was he going to do about them? Run and be shot?

Alec, Ghost's driver, opened the door for him. Scott followed him inside—and drew up short in the doorway. "What the hell?"

Jeremy stood there, dressed in his fighting gear. His face paled as he stared at Scott; a loaded second passed between them. He turned on Ghost. "No way, man. You said no friends."

"And as of right now, he isn't one. He's the enemy, the competition. Which you will eliminate, if you want to keep your little girl alive."

Scott quickly caught on. "Wait a minute. You want me to fight *him*? *Now*?"

"Don't look so surprised." Ghost leaned against the makeup counter and crossed his arms. "You knew you were coming here to fight. What did you expect?"

"Not to fight the Destroyer," Scott grit out, heart pumping fast. The temperature in the room seemed to double.

"Are you afraid?" Ghost's eyes glimmered.

"Hell yeah, I'm afraid," Scott said. "You've seen Jeremy fight. He didn't earn the nickname of 'the Destroyer' for nothing."

"Seriously, Ghost." Jeremy stepped forward. "Please. Choose someone else, anyone else."

"No," Ghost said firmly. His eyes turned glacial. "You will fight each other to the death, in approximately half an hour."

"Half...*half an hour*?" Scott's brain hurt, it sounded so crazy. "Do you realize I haven't had dinner yet, I'm exhausted because I've been awake nearly forty-eight hours, and I'm not warmed up? That it's been ages since I last fought?"

"You seemed to hold your own well enough against the police, back at that delightful little inn," Ghost said.

"That was different. Most of them aren't trained fighters, not like Jeremy."

Ghost simply stared back.

"Shit," Scott spat, pacing. Jeremy would kill him—

literally. "What if I refuse?" Scott said.

Ghost barely nodded. Trevor poked the barrel of his gun in the middle of Scott's back. "Then you're as good as dead anyway."

Scott weighed his options. There wasn't a good way out. He knew there wasn't. Death faced him on one side of the coin and on the other. He'd been screwed, just like he knew Ghost would do.

"How much money do you have riding on this fight?" Scott said bitterly. "How much are our lives worth?"

"Enough to pay off my debt and then some," Ghost said evenly.

Bastard was ice-cold, worse than Satan himself. He didn't give a damn about anyone or anything but himself.

The severity of the situation sank deeper in Scott's gut. Jeremy looked as distraught as he did. Apology shone in his friend's eyes, but Scott shook his head and smiled back.

They were in this together, had been forced into this horrible situation by a monster with an insatiable greed.

Ghost glanced at his watch and stood. "Jeremy, return to your room, please. Scott needs time to prepare." He flashed another smile. "Trevor will come get you when it's time. You'll find what you need in the closet."

Jeremy cast one last lingering look at Scott on the way out, and then he was alone.

Scott heaved a shaky breath and caught himself on the countertop as his knees shook.

He was so fucked.

THIRTY-TWO

AROUND SEVEN THIRTY P.M., about a half hour before visiting hours were over, Becca pulled up to Rose Hill Hospital. You'd never be able to guess it was a mental health facility from the outside. If anything, it resembled a nursing home. The outside was lined with pretty, well-kept rosebushes. The sidewalk had been freshly swept, and the building was painted in warm, welcoming shades of sand and orange.

The inside was homey. The walls featured the same warm-colored paint, with beautiful landscape photographs hanging in large frames along the walls. The front lobby had an area filled with red-cushioned chairs and a coffee table strewn with magazines.

A nurse sat behind a glass panel at the reception desk. She looked up from the chart she was scribbling on and smiled warmly. "Good to see you again, Becca. Your mother's been looking forward to seeing you."

A small trill of excitement went through Becca. She

smiled. "I never miss a visit," she said meekly, suddenly nervous. She loved seeing her mother, but the visits themselves... They could be hard. Unbearable, even.

It wasn't her mother's fault. She knew that and had accepted that fact a long time ago in her therapy sessions. No one was to blame but the disease itself.

The nurse asked her to have a seat. After checking in her things, because she wasn't allowed to bring anything back during visits, Becca went over to the waiting area and sat down in the most inconspicuous seat, right in the corner. Though the waiting area was empty, she adjusted her hat once more, making sure the bill was pulled low and her hair was tucked underneath the cap.

It was embarrassing, and, if she admitted it, even a bit ridiculous she had to hide her identity like this. The fact her mother was still alive was her most closely guarded secret. It was a lie she hadn't started telling until college.

Grade school had been torture. Kids ridiculed and terrorized her once her mother began displaying symptoms. Their taunts still haunted her nightmares: *Crazy. Psycho. Schizo.* She'd heard it all. Their hurtful words had battered her fragile self-esteem until her head hung so low, it was a miracle her chin didn't drag the ground. As if living with her mother didn't make life hard enough.

How many hot summer days had she gone out wearing long sleeves, all for the purpose of hiding the colorful array of bruises that coated her arms? How many excuses had she come up with to teachers about the cigarette butt burns on her body?

Eventually, the truth had come out. She'd thought things had been bad before, but she quickly learned things could always get worse.

And they did. Once the state learned of what was going on, they swooped in and took Becca and Zach away. It had been hell, living in foster homes, separated from her brother.

To comfort herself, she did the only thing she was good at—she studied. Hard.

Math, science: they made sense to her. People didn't. She didn't understand their cruelty, or her foster parents' indifference to her inner turmoil.

Didn't anyone care about her?

As she became older, family was something she craved more than anything. The intense desire to get her brother back was the fuel that kept her working hard on her grades, which allowed her to earn a full ride to college. Another wonderful thing about college was that she could start over. She'd changed her appearance, donning trendier clothes and sporting a different hair color from the sickly blond she'd grown up with. Contacts gave her a different eye color. Her mother also conveniently "died."

It was as though she'd been set free. Her mother's shadow had loomed over her for her entire life, and now she could finally be allowed to explore who she was without judgment.

No one recognized the daughter of the famous "mad artist" who had to be locked up when she nearly burned her house down, convinced it was wicked and needed to be purged of its evils.

If anything, her mother was the one who needed to be cleansed. The things she'd done…

Becca shook her head. Traveling back in time wasn't something she liked to make a habit of. Not just because her therapist didn't recommend it, but because of her own volition.

She frowned.

At least she could remember her childhood.

Lately, her memory had started to "deteriorate," for lack of a better word. Not only waking up in places she didn't remember going to sleep in, or finding items that didn't belong to her, but weird, inexplicable lapses in time. Maybe she couldn't remember what she did from three o'clock to five o'clock one day, or where she was or who she was with one evening. It was starting to scare her.

And the headaches...they had never been this painful. Her doctor said, "Our bodies adapt to medication over time, and the dosage has to be tweaked, or, sometimes, we have to switch to a different prescription entirely."

She swallowed hard. A familiar lump formed in her throat.

The lapse in time was the one factor that had kept her from seeking out the doctor.

Because Mom experienced the exact same thing before she was clinically diagnosed.

Footsteps startled her, and a door opened by the reception desk. A middle-aged brunette dressed in burgundy scrubs smiled. "Becca?"

Becca blinked, cleared her head, and stood. "Yes."

"Sorry for the wait. Follow me, please."

Becca fell into step just behind her as they navigated the pristine white halls of the hospital. Her heart thrummed wildly with a nervous jitter.

You could be here, someday. Trapped in these white walls, with no one to come visit you.

The thought of never seeing Amy or Zach again was unbearable.

No. No, I don't want to be alone. I can't. She'd been alone for so much of her life. She was tired of it.

The nurse stopped before the visiting area and frowned. "Are you all right, miss? You're pale."

"Yes, I'm fine." Becca's voice was breathy. A chill crept up her arms as she stared through the long, rectangular viewing window embedded in the door.

There sat her mother, staring despondently at the table. Her once-luminous skin looked dull and gray, and her golden hair had more white than she remembered. The curls were so unruly, it looked like a frizzy, tangled mess. Someone had tried to help her fix it; it was pulled halfway up in a pretty clip.

A nurse stood by the wall, watching her mom intently.

It was far too easy to picture herself there, with all hope gone from her eyes. The thought chilled her to the bone.

The nurse looked Becca over again; worry still danced in her eyes. "You ready?"

"Yes," she rasped, clearing her throat. "Yes," she repeated, stronger this time.

The nurse hesitated and pressed her lips together. She didn't say anything as she opened the door and motioned for Becca to enter.

Becca took a few hesitant steps into the room. Her mother never looked up as she slowly sat down. Every muscle in her body tensed. "Hello, Mother," she said quietly, feeling like a child. Her voice hitched up in pitch as she watched her mother with anxious eyes.

Her mother didn't look up, not at first. When her eyes did finally drag themselves up from the table to her daughter's face, Becca's breath caught. Her mother blinked slowly, her eyes squinting slightly. "Becca," her mother whispered after a beat.

Becca's eyes watered. "Mommy."

For a moment, the cloudiness in her mother's gaze faded, and her mother, her real mother, shone through. With tears brimming in her eyes, she smiled and reached over, grasping her daughter's hand.

Becca clung to that grip. The little girl inside her remembered the good times and yearned for them again. Her mother was not always dark and cruel. At one time, when Becca was barely old enough to walk, she had been every little girl's dream mother. She took her out for playtime at the playground, read stories to her before bed, and treated her to ice cream. Those were happy times.

Then the darkness descended.

The hospital bracelet around her mother's wrist glinted in the fluorescent lighting. At last, she let go of her hand and sat back, staring at Becca with a happy smile. "How's your brother doing?"

"He's fine," Becca rasped, unable to tell her the truth. That she was so royally fucking up as a guardian. Her mother had enough problems. Her already unstable psyche might not be able to handle it.

"And you?"

Becca nodded. "Well. Thank you," she said quietly.

Becca's mother seemed pleased. "Tell me, child, what adventures have you been up to lately?"

This was Becca's favorite part of the visit. Like an excited little girl, she rattled off recent happenings, highlighting only the good. The wider her mother smiled, the more exuberant she got.

The conversation quieted a little. "Seeing anyone?" Becca's mother asked.

Becca felt her cheeks heat, and she pulled at her cap. "No."

"Just haven't found anyone interesting?"

Becca pressed her lips together.

Maybe. I don't know. I'm still confused about how I feel.

She never expected to be in love with a woman. She wasn't even sure when those feelings had developed. They'd lurked quietly for a few years now, growing stronger and deeper with every moment she spent with Amy.

But would Amy ever feel the same way? Doubtful.

The realization she was in love with someone she could never have broke her heart a little more every time she thought it.

She shook her head; her shoulders slumped from sadness. "No, Mommy."

Her mother stared at the table. Her hands shook as she picked at her nails. The tremble lasted only a few seconds, but Becca's eyes snapped to them as if neon lights had gone off on her mother's fingers.

Her heart sped up. No. No, she'd been careful with her words, about not diving further into the topic of relationships, just as the nurse had requested a few visits ago. What triggered the change? What had she done wrong?

Her mother's head snapped up; her eyes darted back and forth frantically. Becca gasped as her mother seized her hand, her eyes pleading. "Where am I? What is this place? Did something happen to me?"

Becca's heart squeezed at the rising fear in her mother's voice. "You're in a mental hospital, Mommy," she said calmly. "You checked yourself in years ago."

"I—what? I would never have abandoned my children that way!"

"You didn't. The state took us away."

Her mother locked eyes with her, going still. There was no tremble this time, only a slow blink.

A sardonic smirk came over her mother's lips as she sat back, eyes glinting darkly. "You little slut. You think you can lie to me to my face? You're the one who put me here. How else would I get so crazy? You brats drove me nuts."

Becca steeled her heart. *She's not herself. You know she doesn't mean it.*

Her mother patted her jeans. There were no pockets on them, as required by hospital regulations. "Where the hell did I put my damned cigarettes?"

Becca squeezed her lips together.

Her mother stilled, glaring at her. "The hell you looking at?"

Becca's heart slammed against her chest. *Don't switch, don't switch, don't switch—*

The hand flew out across her face before she could draw breath. Her cheek sang from the burn.

The nurse ran forward, shouting something into a walkie-talkie. She seized Becca's mother before she could deliver another blow.

"You little whore!" her mother screamed. "You good-for-nothing brat! You took my cigarettes, didn't you? Didn't you?!"

"No, Mommy," Becca stammered.

The door flew open as two more nurses ran into the

room. Two now grappled with her mother, who'd begun to kick and scream and claw like a wild animal. Rage filled her eyes and voice, making it raw.

"I never wanted you!" she screamed. "You ruined my career! I never…wanted…"

She went limp in their arms, and her gaze clouded over. The third nurse removed a needle from her mother's arm.

A gentle hand landed on Becca's shoulder. It was the brunette who'd led her back here. She smiled in sympathy. "Time to go, sweetheart."

Becca followed her out, not really seeing or hearing anything around her. She'd gone numb inside.

I never wanted you!

She hadn't realized she'd been crying until the nurse went behind the reception counter, plucked a few tissues, and retrieved Becca's belongings.

"Thank you," Becca whispered, happily accepting them and dabbing at her face. The nurse handed her things to her. "I'm so sorry. I—I tried to be careful, watch what I said so it wouldn't trigger—"

"You have nothing to be sorry for. Sometimes, we think we have the triggers narrowed down. But when we think we have them figured out, they change. It varies from patient to patient." She grasped Becca's shoulder and smiled encouragingly. "Don't give up hope. We'll get there."

Becca smiled back and nodded. "Thank you."

She didn't tarry. She all but ran outside and got into her car.

Her whole body shook. The key clanked against the steering mount as she missed the keyhole over and over.

I never wanted you!

Memories of her mother screaming at her, beating her, assaulted her. The last of her control slipped away, and she crumpled over. Her face pressed against the steering wheel. Sobs shook her whole body.

Pathetic, a sarcastic voice said in her head. *You really are useless, aren't you?*

A tremble started in her hands, crawling through her body and into her toes.

The pain suddenly stopped. All of it. Not an ounce of mourning remained.

When she sat up, she felt much calmer. More in control, as if nothing could hurt her.

Flipping the mirror down, she wiped away the smeared mascara on her cheeks and got out her makeup bag.

Thirty seconds later, she had fresh makeup, complete with a new coat of red lipstick.

She looked over her face in the mirror and smacked her lips. "Didn't I tell you, little girl?" she said, her voice deeper than it was a moment before. "No one is ever going to hurt you again. I promise."

Starting the car, she glanced at the clock on the dash. It was almost eight p.m.

Driving off, she hummed a tune as she merged into traffic.

Soon, it would all be over. The moment she felt she'd waited her entire life for.

Just a little bit longer, and then you'll finally be mine ...Amy.

THIRTY-THREE

A MY DIDN'T KNOW how long she stared at the gun. It seemed to weigh more and more as time passed; the minutes became longer and longer.

The weight of her decision settled around her shoulders like a leaden cloak.

She was going to kill someone.

For some stupid reason, it had never dawned on her when she bought the gun that she could use it to kill. Simply having it made her feel safer. Yes, she obviously knew what guns were used for. Some part of her didn't want to acknowledge the real reason she'd bought the weapon. She was sick of death. Absolutely sick. But as her therapist had said, it was just another part of life. Natural. Normal.

So why was she so scared? Would she stall when it came time to pull the trigger?

Could she pull it?

Unable to hold it any longer, she put the gun away.

There were still two hours left before she had to face her fate. She should have been getting ready, should have been preparing herself, but she was restless. Pacing with nervous energy and the urge to paint, she'd finally caved and picked up a brush.

Painting always allowed her to think and calm down. And if she had any hope of not falling apart completely in front of Nathan, she needed to calm down and get her shit together. A blank canvas and an arsenal of colors were her best weapons against becoming a nervous wreck.

The paintbrush swept across the canvas in grand strokes. The bristles and somber colors poured all of her sadness, worry, frustration, and fear into the painting.

Scott still hadn't called. Not that she'd expected him to. He wasn't exactly in a position to chat at his leisure.

Tears stung her eyes.

Why was it when she found something good it always got taken away? Could she not have a damned moment of peace?

The strokes became angrier, scarring the dark forest landscape she'd painted with streaks of red. It hadn't even occurred to her she had dipped her brush into the red. The trees were beaten by a bloodied rain, making the atmosphere of the landscape heavier somehow.

Death. Pain. Sorrow. That's all she'd felt and known these past two years. And it looked as if it might be all she would ever know.

Tears poured down her cheeks, plopping into her paint vials and splattering against her jeans. She sat there, breathing hard, as her eyes roved over the canvas.

A raw calmness settled over her, as if her emotions had literally leaked out via her tears. She didn't feel empty, exactly. Just…lighter.

Swallowing, she dabbed her brush into the white and yellow paints and dabbed a small patch of sunlight onto the bruised cloud cover. Diluting the paint in her water container, she drew delicate beams to cascade down from the heavens, highlighting the beautiful greens of the forest below.

Satisfied, she sat back and stared.

A smile broke out on her face.

At first, she thought she may call the painting *Fear*. But now, she had a better name for it.

"*Hope*," she whispered.

Her foot had fallen asleep. The tingling sensation had escaped her notice, she'd been so enraptured with her work. After nearly falling onto her painting, she grasped the wall for support and waited for blood flow to return to her foot. Once the numbness subdued, she got in the shower and lingered under the hot water, inhaling deep breaths of steam. She wanted to stay longer but knew she shouldn't. She had somewhere to be soon. Reluctantly, she killed the water, toweled off, and got dressed. Feeling far better than she had earlier, she made herself a ham-and-cheese sandwich. Having your emotions thrown into a blender worked up an appetite.

Unfortunately, the damned sandwich wouldn't go past the lump in her throat.

It was nearly eight fifteen p.m. now.

Forty-five more minutes. The marina wasn't far, but she'd still need to leave within the next half hour if she hoped to be there by nine. What felt like forever earlier now felt as though she didn't have nearly enough time to prepare.

Nerves made her tummy tingle, threatening to pitch what little sandwich she ate back up her throat.

On the verge of giving up after she dry-heaved, she got up from the couch to toss the remainder of the sandwich, when her phone went off.

She nearly dropped the plate in her hurry to grab it.

Scott. Please, be Scott.

The sting of disappointment made her wince when she saw Becca's number on the screen. Jeez, was that bitchy? Being sad your best friend was calling? Sure, they'd had a fight recently, but Amy hadn't exactly been a peach to deal with after Michael's murder.

She briefly considered letting it go to voice mail. What if Becca needed something? What if it was important?

"Hello?" she answered.

"Guess what?" Becca sang. Amy heard heels clicking, and a car honked. Wherever she was, she was walking outside.

Amy smiled softly. "What?"

"This girl just got a promotion!"

"No shit?" Amy exclaimed. "Becca, that's awesome! You've worked really hard for it." With everything else going on, it had completely slipped Amy's mind her friend had been vying for a promotion at work recently.

"You bet your ass I have. And I'm ready to celebrate. Hope you're decent, bitch, because I'm coming for you."

"What? You're on your way over *here*?"

"Actually, I'm kind of already here."

"*What?*"

"Jeez, don't blow out my eardrum!"

"Sorry," Amy breathed. "It's just, now isn't a good

time."

"Really? Do you have important sex to get caught up on with Scott?"

Amy pressed her lips together. "He's not here," she said quietly.

"Perfect! Then what's the problem?"

Amy didn't know how to respond.

Becca sighed, exasperated. "Come on, Ames! Just one obligatory celebratory drink, and I'll let you off the hook. It's damn good wine, if I do say so myself. Better be, anyway. I paid two hundred dollars for this shit."

"Two hundred dollars, for a bottle of wine? Are you nuts?"

"No, just excited! And eager to par-tay! Now, let me in."

Amy bit her lip and at last sighed. "Fine. I'll be down in a sec."

Becca squealed, and the call ended.

Amy groaned, rubbing her temples to ease the throb that had begun there. Why, oh, why did Becca pick the most inopportune times to party?

It's okay. You've got half an hour before you have to leave. Just have a drink and say you have something else going on soon that you can't put off.

A drink did sound good, actually. She just had to go easy on it. Inebriation and guns didn't mix well.

After she let Becca in, Amy listened to her rattle off her new pay, duties, hours, and all the other perks that went along with her new position. "I was worried about 'Brown-Nosing Jake' getting it after last quarter, but I guess old Bob decided I was the best candidate for Tier II after all." She beamed as she pulled the wine and cheese wheel out of a paper bag.

"That's great, Becca," Amy said with as much enthusiasm as she could. She forced a smile as she pulled two wineglasses from the cabinet and set them out. "I'm really happy for you. I know how much you wanted this promotion."

"Hell yeah, I did! No more gopher work from Mr. Stick-Up-His-Ass. You got a corkscrew?"

"Um, yeah. Just a sec." She turned around and rummaged through her utensil drawer. How had she accumulated this much junk? Honestly, how many spatulas did a girl need?

"Ah, here we are." She fished the corkscrew from the back of the drawer. She handed it off to Becca, who deftly skewered the cork and yanked it free with a *pop*. She poured them both a glass.

"That's enough for me," Amy said once it reached halfway.

Becca raised a brow but stopped pouring. "What's wrong? I thought you liked red wine."

"I do." She adored it, actually. "It's just, I have somewhere I have to be later, and I don't want to get too buzzed for it."

"Oh?" Becca popped the cork back in after she poured her own glass. "And where is the famous Amy heading off to this evening? Do you have a second boyfriend I don't know about?"

Amy laughed. "Hardly. I have, um, to swing by the art museum to talk to the curator about another gala."

"Another one?" Becca's eyes grew big. "That's great, Ames!" She raised her glass. "Cheers to our awesomeness."

Amy smiled. "Cheers."

They clinked glasses and took a sip. "Hmmm." Amy took another gulp, this one much more generous than the first. "This is good."

"It's a sweet red. I know you don't like the dry stuff." Becca wrinkled her nose. "Neither do I."

Amy had an insatiable sweet tooth, evidence of which clung to her body in soft curves. She drank some more. They settled back into a familiar routine, laughing and drinking. For twenty precious minutes, life almost seemed normal. Amy glanced at her glass. Damn, was it almost empty already? She'd been so wrapped up in having a moment of fun with Becca that she hadn't been paying attention. She blinked, and her vertigo skewed. "Whoa." She gripped the counter for support. "What's the proof in this?"

Becca shrugged. "Not sure. Same as any other wine. All I know is that it's old as hell. You know what they say—the older the wine, the better."

"Hmmm." Amy tipped back her head and finished off her glass. "Wow." She shook her head and blinked a few times. Was her vision blurry? "That was good."

Acute drowsiness took over, weighing her eyelids down. She always felt relaxed after drinking a glass of wine; she usually enjoyed a glass while taking her Friday-night bubble baths, a relaxation treat. Yeah, sleepiness usually followed in such a relaxed state, but this seemed to hit awfully fast.

Becca watched her silently from across the counter, a slight smile on her lips. Her dark eyes glittered.

Amy knew something was wrong when she went to take a step and collapsed onto the floor. The glass shattered, flinging broken shards across the kitchen floor. She tried to get up but couldn't move. It was as if her limbs were made of cement.

"What's...happening?" she stuttered as she stared at the ceiling. Even her tongue felt heavy, making it difficult to enunciate.

Footsteps echoed in her head as a pair of black heels approached from the corner of her eye. Her eyes dragged upward, seeing Becca's silhouette standing over her.

Becca smiled. At least, Amy thought she did. Her vision grew blurrier, and white sparkles started to fill the edges.

A buzzing filled her head, making it hard to hear.

"It's all right, Amy." Becca sounded far away. "It'll all be okay soon."

THIRTY-FOUR

I T TOOK HIM a full five minutes to calm down. Damn, he was going to be exhausted before the punches even started to fly.

A cold sweat coated his body. Icy droplets trickled from the ditches of worry lines on his forehead into the hollows of his eyes, making them sting. Every muscle ached, as if he'd just run a marathon. Hell, even breathing was a chore.

He closed his eyes and ran his hands over his face. *If you're done freaking out now, can we continue with to-night's scheduled ass kicking?*

Tension tightened his jaw. That son of a bitch Ghost was going down.

Scott smiled darkly.

And he will never see it coming.

Harsh banging rattled the door, making Scott jump. "Five minutes, pretty boy," barked Trevor.

Scott's heart tripped over a few beats before it resumed its frantic thrumming. Okay. He had to stay calm. He'd get through this. The feds probably already had a lock on him. All he needed now was time.

And to not get killed.

"No problem," he muttered.

Changing clothes was a lot harder with numb fingers, but he managed. He'd just laced his other shoe up when the door opened without preamble, and in strolled Ghost.

"Ah, good." Ghost looked him over as if appraising a prized stallion. "You're ready."

Scott glared back at him. "You gonna give me any gear?"

Ghost smiled. He looked like that big-ass Aussie shark from *Finding Nemo* when it smiled at a cowering Dory and Marlin. "No gloves or a mouthpiece tonight. I want it raw and bloody in my coliseum."

"Yeah, I bet people are willing to pay a premium to watch two men literally beat the living hell out of each other," Scott said dryly.

"What can I say? It's good business. I aim to give the people what they want." He started out the door.

Scott didn't have to be told he was supposed to follow, though it took some effort to make his leaden feet move. "I guess some things never change. The wealthy are just as bloodthirsty as they've always been."

The dark halls brightened every few feet with pendant lights that hung from the shadowy ceiling. "Oh, don't think it's just the wealthy," Ghost said over his shoulder. "Men and women both rich and poor like to see blood spilled. It's the animal in us all. But it would appear bloodthirst only affects the wealthy, since they are generally the only ones who can afford tickets to my events."

Scott grunted. *It's always about the money.*

The low roar of the crowd, dulled by the metal doors they approached, thrummed in Scott's blood. They chanted something he couldn't quite make out.

Ghost's step didn't falter as two tuxedo-clad men opened the doors and he strolled through. "You remember the Underground?" Ghost raised his voice to be heard.

Now that he looked around, Scott started to recognize the place. It was the old, antique theater they built the auditorium over. It was called "the Underground" because it was literally built underground. The building was contracted by a young investor who'd hit it big on Wall Street. The Underground had catered to Los Angeles's elite, since it doubled as a swanky restaurant. The investor had built it underground for acoustical purposes, as well as adding to the uniqueness and allure of the establishment.

An elegant hallway with red-carpeted flooring and antique bronzed sconces led them to the main floor. The theater stage itself was at the center of the room, the base of which was outlined in old gas lamps. Glimmering wire ropes were stretched around its perimeter, creating a barrier. Stadium seating rose on all four sides of the stage, adorned with red velvet cushions. The place could easily hold up to five hundred people.

Jeremy was already in the ring. His shoulders slumped forward, as if already admitting defeat.

As if Ghost would ever allow it.

Men in tuxedos guarded the doors and formed a perimeter around the ring. Scott wouldn't put it past them to

Taser him, or worse, should either he or Jeremy try to escape.

An announcer decked in a sequined gold suit stood in the middle of the ring. With his oily hair and mustache, he looked more like a used-car salesman. Sounded like one, too. His overly cheerful voice echoed around the hall as Scott and Ghost approached. "And here he is, the king of the jungle himself—the Lion!"

The crowd stood and roared; their clapping sounded like thunder. Scott looked around. Everyone was dressed in their finest. Tuxedos, expensive suits, ball gowns, cocktail dresses...not a single person wore casual attire. He'd wager all the glittering trinkets adorning the women's necks, hair, and ears that there was enough money in expensive gemstones here to buy a small country.

The VIPs, of course, were given the best seats, directly next to the arena. Scott recognized some of the faces.

The mayor.

A judge.

The district attorney.

The CEO of a famous conglomerate.

They cheered for Scott as he passed them. He met their enthusiasm with a glare. Ghost's influence, as well as the corruption in the city, went a lot further than he'd thought. It sickened him to see so many high-ranking officials participating in something like this, an illegality they supposedly passed the bills for themselves to outlaw.

Hypocrites. Spoiled, rich pigs. Doesn't anyone have any damn integrity anymore?

The feds were going to have a field day with this. That is, if this crazy-ass plan worked. He felt like the star of a *Jack Ryan* flick, only this wasn't fiction.

This was pounding-heart, break-out-in-a-cold-sweat real.

The sound of the crowd chanting his name faded away as he took one heavy step after another toward that fateful ring. Already, he could imagine its surface marred with their blood and broken bodies.

Ghost climbed into the ring with Scott and took the mic from the announcer. He raised a hand, and the hall quieted down.

"Thank you, esteemed patrons, for coming out this evening. Both of these men have impressive track records in the arena, and I know you'll be in for a treat."

Scott silently fumed in the corner of the ring parallel to Jeremy's. Ghost made it sound like the crowd was a bunch of kids waiting for a cotton candy at the fair instead of about to witness a fight to the death.

"Don't forget to place your final bids in the pot before the bell strikes." Ghost smiled. "Enjoy tonight's entertainment!"

The crowd applauded and whistled as he handed the mic back to the announcer. He walked over to Scott. "Don't disappoint me," he said, a knife-like edge to his voice.

Scott smiled tightly, thinking of what the look on Ghost's face would be when the feds busted this place. *Oh, I won't.*

"Fighters, ready!"

Ghost pushed past Scott and exited the ring as Scott reluctantly stepped forward. Jeremy did the same, head hung low like a beaten animal.

Scott's heart rate picked up, as did his breathing. Adrenaline coursed through his veins as he stared at Jeremy, who refused to look at him. His heart sank. Before the bell even rang, he knew what Jeremy was going to do.

Or rather, not do.

"FIGHT!"

The bell sang, and the announcer quickly stepped out of the way of the two fighters. Neither of them moved.

The crowd waited in silence, watching for a minute before they grew restless.

Scott shifted his weight, flexing his fingers before he curled them back into fists. "Jeremy," he hissed.

His friend's eyes remained lowered onto the stage.

People began to boo.

Scott remembered Ghost's warning. He took a step closer to Jeremy. "Dammit, man, fight me!"

"No."

Scott froze.

Jeremy's answer had been near inaudible and yet seemed to carry across the ring. Ghost cursed and snapped his fingers, fury on his face.

The biggest man Scott had ever seen stepped into the ring, a leather whip curled in one hand. Scott's heart pitched into his stomach.

"Jeremy—" he started, but with snake-like speed, the man unfurled the whip and cracked it against Jeremy's back. He cried out and staggered forward.

"Fight," the man commanded in a deep voice.

Jeremy regained his footing; his nostrils flared as he sucked in tight breaths. He turned to face the man, glaring defiantly at him. "No."

The whip arched through the air and snapped downward in an arc across Jeremy's chest. A bright-red welt rose where the whip had bitten him. He clamped down on his lip to keep from crying out, and his knees trembled.

Scott rushed forward, putting himself between the man and Jeremy. "Stop it!"

"I'll stop when he fights," the man bellowed. He raised his hand again, prepared to strike.

Frantic, Scott whirled and grasped Jeremy by the arms. "You have to fight me."

Jeremy shook his head. Pain gathered in his eyes. "No."

"Yes, dammit, you can! You don't have a choice! Neither of us has a choice!"

The whip cracked. Nothing could have prepared Scott for the blinding pain that seared into his back. His back arched, and a strangled cry climbed up his throat as he stumbled, bumping into Jeremy.

"Son of a bitch!" Scott spat, feeling the burning mark on his back. If they didn't do something, they'd be whipped to death.

Reining in the pain, Scott formed a fist and cracked his knuckles across Jeremy's jawline. The feel of flesh pummeling flesh was familiar to him. Jeremy's head jerked to the side, but other than that, he didn't budge.

"Fight me!" Scott screamed. "Come on!" He hit Jeremy again and again. Temple. Chest. Abs. It didn't matter where he hit; Jeremy remained standing, looking away as Scott drove his fists into what felt like solid rock.

The backs of his hands burned, making his joints ache. Scott racked his mind. It was cruel, but it might be the only chance he had at saving them both. "This is pathetic," Scott snarled as he stalked around Jeremy. "No wonder your family couldn't depend on you."

Jeremy's head jerked around, disbelief in his widened eyes.

"You heard me." Scott felt like shit for being such a dick. "You couldn't save your wife because you were too much of a pussy to fight!"

Something in Jeremy's eyes snapped. With a roar, he swung for Scott's head. The crowd cheered as Scott narrowly missed the punch by an inch.

"That the best you got?" he sneered.

It was like pitching gasoline on a fire. Jeremy snapped, lunging at Scott with a roar that cut through the growing noise from the crowd. People cheered and shouted as Jeremy and Scott danced around the ring, fists and feet flying in a flurry of punches and kicks. It was all Scott could do to keep from getting his face smashed in. Jeremy might be bulky, but God was he quick.

With every barely evaded punch, every last-minute step to the side, Scott felt his energy draining. That, or Jeremy's punches were growing more accurate.

Shit.

BOOM!

It felt as if someone had whapped him upside the head with a sledgehammer. Stars fired before his eyes, and his vision blacked out for a terrifying second. The world spun, and he crashed into the rope. By the time his vision corrected, someone had thrown him back into the ring and directly into the arms of a very pissed-off Jeremy. Well, more like in the way of another helluva punch that sent him sprawling across the floor.

God, his face hurt. His jaw squealed in pain when he tried to open his mouth. Probably broken.

A kick landed in his side; he swore he felt a rib crack. Excruciating pain tore through his torso, and he nearly screamed. All right, maybe pissing Jeremy off wasn't the brightest idea, but he'd been desperate. He couldn't let him get whipped to death simply because he was too stubborn to throw a punch or defend himself.

Another kick sent Scott flying into the rope so hard the air left his lungs. He collapsed onto the mat and spit up blood. *That can't be a good sign.*

Every bone and muscle in his body hurt. He'd suffered some beatings in the ring before, but never like this. Then again, he'd never fought the Destroyer before, either.

Two hands clasped him and hauled him up. Before he could regain his senses, he was flung across the other side of the ring. His nose hit the railing, taking the brunt of the fall. Hot blood poured down his face. Great. Now that was broken.

"Jeremy," Scott rasped, trying to get up as heavy footsteps thudded closer.

Scott managed to lift his head high enough to glance at Jeremy's eyes. What he saw made his blood freeze.

Rage. Nothing but pure, unbridled bloodlust and anger.

Jeremy was going to kill him.

He knew his friend had anger problems. Hell, it'd been one of their bonding points, a familiar pain to both of them. Why, oh, why didn't Scott think this through before?

"Don't." Scott scrambled to get up. The blood from his nose had slicked the mat, making it harder to find his footing. "You don't want to do this."

"Don't I?" Jeremy picked him up and hoisted him above his head. Scott flailed, trying to break free. Jeremy raised his knee.

Oh God. Scott's heart stopped. He'd seen this move before, when Jeremy had killed that one fighter. The moment that spawned a lifetime of regret and sleepless nights for him.

He was going to break Scott's back.

"Don't!" Scott shouted. "Jeremy, snap out of it!"

His friend blinked several times. His heavily muscled arms remained locked above his head. Scott's fate hung in the balance.

Though he was hanging upside down, he caught several dark, armed figures moving in from the exits. The guards. Something had them in a flurry.

They shouted to one another, bellowing commands into their headpieces. The spectators were too enthralled with what was happening in the ring to pay attention to the exits.

That is, until gunfire erupted.

Screams broke out, and patrons ducked as black-armored figures stormed the room. Scott caught flashes of white FBI letters stamped to the backs of their vests.

Oh, praise Jesus!

The guards were quickly overpowered. There had to be three feds to every goon Ghost had under his employment.

"What the...?" Jeremy sounded more like himself as he looked around, baffled.

"Hey!" Scott shouted, writhing. "Set me down!"

"Oh shit! Sorry, man!" Jeremy gently lowered Scott.

Scott swore as his full weight went to his feet. It seemed like with every pulse, his body throbbed.

"Whoa." Jeremy's eyes, widening, scanned Scott from head to toe. "Holy shit. Holy *fucking* shit. I am so sorry!"

"There's no time for that! We have to find Ghost, now!" Thank God for adrenaline; otherwise, Scott might not be able to withstand the pain.

He looked around, as did Jeremy. People were trying to escape, but by now, the feds had the crowd contained. Everyone's hands were raised in the air; hundreds of wide, frightened eyes stared back at the guns pointed at their faces.

Jeremy helped Scott out of the ring, just in time to greet a tall, lanky man with graying hair and steely eyes—Agent White. "We got him."

Scott stared. "Ghost?"

Agent White's answering grin made Scott's heart skip for joy. "Trying to sneak out the back, through one of the more secluded emergency exits. Cocky son of a bitch." He looked around, amused. The mayor scowled as he was cuffed and led off by federal agents. "I see we have a lot of paperwork to do."

"You sorry?" Scott asked wryly.

Agent White shook his head, eyes twinkling. "Nah. Just happy." He frowned as he looked Scott over. "Jesus, you look like shit."

"You can blame this guy." Scott elbowed Jeremy in the abs. Jeremy's shameful look had him adding quickly, "Not that it was his fault. He was forced to fight me. Ghost all but threatened to kill us if we didn't put on a good show."

"All to line that son of a bitch's pockets, I'll bet." Agent White sighed. "Come on. Let's get you both checked out by a paramedic."

They followed him out to the main hallway, where two feds were barely holding on to a livid Ghost. His face was bright red, and it was the first time Scott had ever seen a hair out of place on his perfectly styled head.

He looked like a man possessed, his teeth baring at Scott when his wild eyes landed on him. "You! I know it was you! What the hell did you do?"

Scott innocently raised his brows. Well, as much as his sore-as-fuck face would allow for, anyways. "I'm just a peon. What could I possibly do?"

It looked as if Ghost's head might explode. "Gah!" He lunged for him, snapping his teeth like a piranha. Agent White stepped forward and clocked him across the temple. Ghost's eyes rolled back, and he immediately slumped, unconscious.

Agent White gave the two men a curt nod as he rubbed his reddening hand. "Get that disgusting piece of filth out of my sight. Jesus," he muttered, shaking his hand. "His head's a lot harder than it looks."

"Always the case," Scott said.

"You were working with them?" Jeremy pointed between him and Agent White.

Scott figured it couldn't hurt. Jeremy had been a victim as well. Reaching up, he pulled out a tiny hearing aid from his ear. "When he brought me here, Ghost took my cell phone."

"As we knew he would," Agent White chimed in.

"But what he didn't count on was this." Scott held out the tiny skin-colored piece of technology. "It's a transmitter, emitting a homing signal for up to a twenty-mile radius." He squished his nose at the broken hardware. "Or, at least, it was. Must have taken a beating, too, during the fight."

"Sorry," Jeremy mumbled, looking guilty as hell.

Scott gave him his best attempt at a smile. It was hard to make his mouth move when he was pretty sure his jaw was broken, or, at least, bruised like hell. It was getting harder and harder to talk by the second. "Don't worry about it. Anyway, the feds were waiting near my apartment building for Ghost to come for me. They followed us to the location, and once there, used the homing signal to pinpoint where we'd gone inside the building."

"Ghost tried using the fundraiser as a cover, which would have worked had we not had Scott helping us out." He slapped him on the shoulder, making Scott groan in pain.

Agent White rescinded his hand and winced. "Sorry. Forgot."

Scott raised a brow. "You forgot I was covered in bruises and cuts?"

Agent White shifted his weight. "Anyway," he said pointedly, "about that paramedic."

"Actually"—Scott grabbed his arm to stop him from walking off—"can they treat me in the ambulance?"

"Well, yeah, I suppose. Why?"

"I want to get back to my girlfriend." Nerves twisted his gut as he said it. Hopefully, Nathan hadn't had a chance to get to her in the time he'd been gone. It felt like an eternity, even though it had only been a few hours. "She's being stalked, and I don't like leaving her alone."

Agent White frowned. "Stalked? By whom?"

"Can I explain on the drive home?" Scott asked, impatient.

"Sure, sure. I'll get our ride arranged."

On the drive to Amy's apartment, Scott could barely sit still. Jeremy stayed behind to be checked out, considering his injuries didn't nearly match Scott's in severity. The paramedics poked, prodded, and tested until he thought he'd turn blue in the face. Some things were obvious, like the broken nose, the gash on his back, and other apparent injuries. Others, not so much, though they suspected he'd earned at least a bruised rib and jaw. They wouldn't know until they got to the hospital. They kept insisting they take him there immediately, but Scott flat-out refused. He wasn't going anywhere else until he made sure his Amy was okay.

Before the ambulance even drew to a complete stop, he'd opened the door, rushed inside the building just as someone was coming out, and loped up the stairs at as fast a pace as he could manage.

I'm coming, baby. I'm home.

He couldn't get to Amy's fast enough, injuries be damned. Nothing else mattered except making sure his beloved was safe. Lifting his fist, he went to knock. The door opened the second his knuckles brushed the door.

Scott tensed.

Why was the door unlocked?

Dread whispered horrible things in the back of his head as he tentatively stepped inside. "Amy?" he called out. God, it hurt to move his mouth.

Silence.

Braveheart greeted him. "Hey, buddy." Scott stepped around him. He was trying hard not to move his jaw much, which made his words sound smeared. "Where's your mommy?"

The kitten purred and then batted around something shiny on the kitchen floor.

Scott bent to retrieve the object. "Ouch!" He swore, nearly dropping the glinting material. It was sharp, like glass.

His eyes scanned the rest of the floor, where Braveheart was happily playing. A large chunk of a mostly shattered wineglass lay on the floor, along with several tinier pieces.

He checked the countertop and the sink, but there were no other glasses.

Scott's heart sank deeper in his chest.

A knock came from the door. Agent White stepped inside. "Everything all right?"

"No." Scott still stared at the broken wineglass. "Amy's missing."

A grave look overcame Agent White's face. "Any signs of a struggle?"

"I haven't been able to check the rest of the apartment, but I found this." He pointed to the broken glass.

Agent White walked over and knelt, slowly examining the immediate area with a critical eye.

"The door was open, too, when I came in," Scott added. "She wouldn't just run off and leave the door unlocked. Nor would she leave all this broken glass here for Braveheart to get into."

"Braveheart?"

"Her cat," he said, not without irritation. Scott pressed his lips together, thinking. "Hey, do you think one of your guys could ping her cell phone?"

"It's worth a shot." Agent White stood and whipped out his own cell. Less than two minutes later, he said, "We got an address. Monroe and 8th?"

"Monroe and 8th?" Scott repeated, startled.

"Sound familiar?" Agent White's eyes narrowed.

"Yeah." Scott nodded. His brows furrowed. "It's her best friend's place. Rebecca Dawson. But I don't know why she'd be over there."

"Only one way to find out. You up for playing detective?"

"I'm up for finding the love of my life," Scott said, steel in his voice.

Agent White smirked. "That's the spirit." He started toward the door. "Come on, killer. Night's not over yet."

THIRTY-FIVE

WHEN AMY FIRST came to and opened her eyes, she thought she might still be dreaming. The memory of hitting the floor, her body so heavy and her vision so blurry, while Becca stood and watched, doing nothing, had to be a dream—or a nightmare.

Amy groaned and blinked several times as her eyes adjusted to the darkness. From what she could tell, she was in a basement. Stairs led up to the next floor, and an old washer and dryer stood against one cement wall. Dancing yellow light flickered from beneath a closed door to her right. The floor was concrete and cool. Amy shivered. Her head pounded from whatever Becca had drugged her with.

Why? Why would she do that?

Her skin tingled from the coolness of the air. Her clothes were missing, leaving her bare, save for her panties and bra.

The air smelled funny. It had a metallic tinge to it.

Amy tried to sit up but flopped against the floor. She winced. Her shoulder was sore from landing on it earlier in her apartment. Thankfully, it didn't feel displaced or broken.

Her wrists scraped against something rough when she tried to bring her hands in front of her. It had to be rope. Judging from her inability to move her legs apart, she was also bound at the ankles.

Tears pricked her eyes. Why was Becca doing this? Was this some kind of sick joke?

Panic began to set in. Ropes. Basement. Kidnapping.

Oh God.

A table sat alongside one wall, a curtained window above it. On the table sat knives, hammers, and other workman's tools.

She writhed against the ropes, fighting to sit up so she could stand and hop over to the table to get the knife. She didn't even know whether she was coordinated enough to attempt sawing through her binds, but she had to at least try.

She finally managed to sit up. Carefully, she tried to stand, but her ankles wobbled, and down she went. The drug must still be in her system, making her shaky. Or was that her terror?

She fell backward this time and smashed into something heavy. Biting down a cry, she arched her neck to see what she had landed on.

All the breath left her. Choked noises sputtered from her mouth as her lungs fought to take in enough oxygen to power a scream.

Nathan stared back at her, eyes devoid of life, his throat slit from side to side.

Whimpering, because that's all the noise she could make, Amy scrambled away from the body as fast as she could. Her eyes remained glued to the man who'd haunted her nightmares for so long, the man whom she thought she would kill tonight.

But, apparently, someone had beaten her to it.

What the hell was he doing in Becca's basement? What kind of violent activity had Becca become involved in?

Amy wasn't watching where she was going, because all she could do was stare at the body. Her back bumped into the table; tools crashed to the floor in a loud ruckus.

A door opened, and light poured down the stairwell, spilling onto Amy.

She squinted as a silhouetted figure stalked down the steps.

"Well, well, I see you're finally awake," came Becca's voice. Only it was wrong. It was deeper and harsher, almost like how a man would speak.

"What did you give me?" Amy rasped.

"Rohypnol," Becca said casually, as if this was no big deal. "Don't worry. I didn't give you much. Just enough to take you under for a bit. You might feel a little shaky until it wears off."

Becca reached up and pulled on a chain. A tiny light-bulb clicked on. The light illuminated the contours of an oversized leather jacket around Becca. She stared at Amy, head cocked to the side, hair pulled back in a ponytail. A smile lit up her face, but it wasn't friendly. It was the smile Nathan wore, and Ghost.

The smile of a monster.

Amy stared at her. "Becca...what's going on?"

"Becca?" she barked. She blinked. "Oh, that's right. The girl." She grinned. "Just call me 'Watcher.'"

"What?" Amy wrinkled her eyebrows. "What the hell has gotten into you? What's happening?"

"Isn't it obvious?" Becca circled her. There was a swagger to her step, like how an overconfident man would walk. Becca always seemed smooth and elegant. Very girly. Now, she wore men's work boots and jeans that were too large for her. "I saved you." She stopped in front of Nathan's body and kicked it, hard. "Now that this son of a bitch is dead, we can finally be together."

"What are you talking about?"

Becca approached her and knelt. Amy shuddered as Becca drew one long finger along Amy's jawline. "I have a surprise for you." Becca stood. She grabbed Amy and hoisted her up.

Jeez, she was strong.

Half-dragging Amy across the room, Becca opened the door with the flickering light.

Amy's heart stopped.

At least one hundred candles filled the tiny room, all twinkling from shelves that went from floor to ceiling on two of the walls. Hundreds of pictures of Amy and Becca, mostly of Amy, plastered the wall that sat parallel to the door.

It took Amy a moment to recover from her shock. "What is this?" Amy whispered, horrified.

"My shrine. To you."

"To...*me*?"

Becca turned her and caressed her cheek. "You're perfect, Amy. You're the only one who's ever noticed me. You deserved to be worshiped, as I intend to do."

Amy stared at her. "Are you mad? What the hell are you—?"

Becca's face contorted in rage. Before Amy could finish the sentence, Becca's hand flew out and smacked her across the face so hard she tumbled backward.

Amy's elbows cracked against the floor, making her eyes water. Stunned, she lay there, gathering her senses while Becca towered over her.

"Look what you made me do!" screamed Becca. She pulled at her hair and began to pace. "Stop hitting her! You can't hurt her!" Becca shook her head and muttered to herself. "Shut up! Just leave me alone!"

Amy went cold all over as she watched her friend compose herself and at last look at her.

Becca's shoulders heaved as she took deep breaths and let them out. "Is it so hard to believe we could be together?"

Amy had no idea how to answer that, for fear Becca might hit her again. "I…it's just…overwhelming."

Becca blinked and smiled, as if Amy had paid her a compliment. "I know. I still can't believe you're here, with me. Now we can be together the way I've always wanted." She reached into her jacket pocket and produced a familiar bottle.

It was Amy's lotion, the one that went missing the night someone broke into her apartment.

She remembered what Nathan had told her, about how he'd gotten into her apartment. "'I know a little bird,'" Amy muttered. She looked up. "It was you, the first night," Amy whispered as Becca popped open the lotion bottle lid. "And when Nathan cornered me and held a knife to my throat. You let him in. You betrayed me."

Becca rubbed her palms together and spread the lotion over her hands. "I just needed him to scare you enough so you'd turn to me for help. Which you did. Sort of." She sighed. "You, of course, were so wrapped up with that fool Michael to even notice me."

Amy stilled. "You said Michael."

"No, I didn't."

"Yes, you did. Michael died. I'm with Scott now..." Her voice trailed off as she put the pieces together. "Did you...did *you* kill Michael?"

Becca stared at her, an amused smile on her face.

Amy's lip trembled. "Why?" she croaked. "You knew how much I loved him!"

"Oh, please, Amy. Save me the waterworks. He was cheating on you. You can't tell me that's love, not like what we have. He kept talking about moving away after the wedding. I couldn't let him take you away from me."

"But you took everything away from me!" Amy screamed.

"And now I'm giving it all back and more." Becca leaned over her, hunger in her eyes as she stared at Amy's breasts. Her hand massaged the lotion into Amy's thigh. Amy squirmed, disgusted, but Becca pinned her bad shoulder to the floor to hold her still. "I've imagined doing this for so long..." Becca kissed a trail down Amy's throat to her navel. Amy whimpered when Becca grabbed the top of her underwear with her teeth and pulled.

Amy struggled to breathe. A million thoughts raced through her head, jumbling her thought process and preventing her from making a cohesive escape plan.

Then she didn't have to, because the door splintered open and in stormed Scott, along with about three cops.

"Freeze!" shouted a stern-looking man with graying hair as the cops raised their guns. Scott's eyes found Amy's, lingering there. Fear raced through them.

Becca growled and jerked Amy up, using her body as a shield. She pressed a knife to Amy's throat. "You can't have her. I'm not going to let you take her away!" Becca screamed.

"Just calm down, Becca," Scott said soothingly, holding his hands up as he took a step forward.

The knife bit into Amy's flesh, making her yelp. Hot blood drizzled down her throat. Scott immediately froze.

"Not another step, asshole," Becca said. "Or I'll split open her throat in front of you."

Amy fought not to whimper. All she could see was red, red, red, coating Michael's throat in her memories and coating her own. Stars fired around her eyes—she was on the verge of hyperventilating and passing out.

Becca backed up, taking Amy with her. She stopped suddenly; her back must have hit the wall. Frantically, she looked around. The only exit was blocked.

Becca kissed Amy's clammy forehead. "Don't worry. We'll be together soon. I'm taking us to a place where no one can hurt us ever again, where we can finally be together. And no one else can have you."

Becca raised the knife.

Amy drew in a breath, eyes frozen on the object that would deliver her death.

Time seemed to stop. She barely heard the gun go off from the ringing in her ears. Barely felt the bullet whiz by as it implanted itself in Becca's hand. Becca screamed and dropped the knife.

Amy blinked and snapped out of it. She bit Becca's

other hand, the one that held her, as hard as she could. Another screech tore from Becca's mouth as her grip loosened, and Amy kicked her hard in the gut before she scurried into Scott's arms.

Becca, eyes filled with rage, roared and started after her.

Pop! Pop!

Two bullet holes spewed blood from Becca's chest. Stunned, Becca glanced down at her chest. Two rivers of blood stained her clothes. She reached up to touch it and stumbled backward, landing hard on the floor.

Her body trembled as she lay there; a pool of blood grew wider under her.

Amy cried from Scott's arms, shaking so badly she could hardly stand. When she took a step forward, toward Becca, Scott said, "Wait."

Amy kept going anyway. Scott followed close behind.

Becca gasped and sputtered as Amy knelt about a foot away from her, just on the edge of the blood pool.

Becca stared up at her with wide, frightened eyes. The color was already draining from her skin. A tear rolled down her cheek. "I just wanted you to love me." She reached a bloodstained hand, the one that had been shot, for Amy. Before it could touch Amy's face, her hand fell limp, and Becca's last breath left her.

THIRTY-SIX

BECCA'S FUNERAL WAS quiet but beautiful.

Several of her coworkers came; even her bosses showed up. No one could understand why she died, who could possibly want to kill her. All they knew was that she'd been murdered in her own home.

Amy sat during the ceremony, lips sealed tight. It didn't matter she'd sworn an oath of silence to the feds. She wouldn't be the one to tell Becca's coworkers, bosses, and friends otherwise.

That the woman they knew might not have even been the real Becca.

She understood it now, why some people were content to live in a fantasy world. As sad and pathetic as it sounded, sometimes a lie was more attractive than the truth.

Earlier that week, Amy had received an invitation to chat from Becca's psychologist.

The woman seemed nervous but sympathetic as both Amy and Scott sat down across from her in her office. "Thank you for coming," she said. "At the request of your doctor, Amy, I felt it necessary to inform you of what I know from my sessions with Becca."

"Isn't this a breach of confidentiality?" she asked.

Dr. Lamb shook her head. "I've told the police everything you are about to hear. I thought it might be best you hear it from me, in case you had any questions. What I have to say can be a bit...shocking." She cleared her throat and clasped her hands on top of her desk. A moment of silence passed as she searched for words. "Becca was...an unusual client of mine. She suffered from dissociative identity disorder or, as it's more commonly known, multiple personality disorder."

Amy blinked. "Becca had split personalities?"

"Several, in fact. As I worked with her throughout our sessions, I met a total of four distinct personalities. There may have been more. I'll never know.

"One personality was a child. This is common with this disorder, since many victims first develop split personalities when they are children, usually in response to some severe trauma. This could be repetitive physical, sexual, or emotional abuse. Since there is a record of Becca's mother having physically abused her due to her own unstable mental state, it's safe to assume this personality formed when Becca was between the ages of six and twelve."

"Jesus," Amy breathed, horrified.

Dr. Lamb's kind blue eyes softened. "One personality was adult Becca, which I believe is who she was most of the time. We call this the 'host' personality. It's the truest form of that person's character, and the personality that tends to show most of the time. That is, until a more dominant personality emerges." A shudder rolled through her. The doctor tried to hide it, but Amy's eyes narrowed. "'Adult Becca' was the personality you most likely dealt with while the two of you hung out," the doctor went on quickly as she leaned back and crossed her legs. She fiddled with the placement of her hands on top of the desk. "That is, until recently."

"What happened recently?" Scott interjected.

She sighed deeply, taking off her glasses and massaging the bridge of her nose as she squeezed her eyes shut. "Normally, the personalities switch due to a trigger. This can be an event that reminds the victim of a traumatic event, or even something as simple as a sound, picture, or smell. The alternate persona takes over for a while, dealing with the situation at hand before letting the host resume control. The host usually has no memory of the hours they spent while donning the alternate persona. We call these 'blackouts.' There will be a lapse of not only memory, but time."

Amy winced. That had to be scary. She couldn't imagine the terror Becca felt. Surely, she'd noticed the time lapses and had questioned her sanity.

"Sometimes, however," Dr. Lamb said, "one of the personalities is so strong that it suppresses the others, including the host. This one is usually accompanied by rage. It represents all the bottled resentment, anger, and despair the victim has felt. It generally emerges later in life, after these feelings have had time to fester. It also forms from the victim's intense desire to become stronger than the trauma haunting her, an indestructible force. Becca had one such personality." The blood drained from Dr. Lamb's skin. "He called himself 'the Watcher.'"

"Wait a minute," Scott said. "You said 'he'?"

Dr. Lamb nodded. "Just because the host personality, and the human being itself, is female does not mean all the personalities will share the same gender. The Watcher was volatile and male. Becca would even come in wearing men's clothing from time to time."

Just like she was the night she drugged and tried to kill me, Amy thought.

"That explains the men's clothing at her place," Scott said grimly.

"Unlike Becca, the Watcher liked women," Dr. Lamb said. "And unlike Becca and the Watcher, the third personality—Scarlett, she called herself—liked both men and women. She was a promiscuous and seductive woman, a femme fatale, if you will."

"Oh my God." Amy gripped the armrests of her chair for support.

"What?" Scott gazed at her with worry in his eyes. He placed a hand at the small of her back.

"The police... They said Nathan hadn't been sleeping with his parole officer and paying for her house, like Becca had said. It was Becca who had been sleeping with her. Becca's mother had several investments, the majority of which she transferred to Becca's and Zach's names when she hospitalized herself. She wanted to make sure her children were taken care of, financially." Finding out Becca's mother was alive and not dead was also a shocker. Amy shook her head. "Scarlett must have used some of the money to pay for the parole officer's house."

"Scarlett was also the personality who lured Nathan out, most likely," said Dr. Lamb. "They have several recordings of their phone conversations together. Scarlett has a habit of chewing gum while she's talking because she thinks it makes her sound sexier."

"Becca hated chewing gum," Amy blubbered. "Said it made her jaw ache."

"Thus, another habit particular to the personality wearing the body," said Dr. Lamb. "Scarlett might have been the most recent personality, brought on by Becca's intense desire to protect the object of her obsession"—she pointed to Amy—"you."

"So this is all my fault." Amy's shoulders slumped.

"No, honey," said Dr. Lamb kindly. "It's no one's fault but the disease."

Amy couldn't remember much of what was said after that. She couldn't help but keep thinking about what Dr. Lamb had said. Those words haunted her for days.

How could she miss the signs? Becca's mood swings, her headaches… What Amy had dismissed as a weird personality quirk, or stress, had been so much more. She should have pressed harder to help, to get Becca to open up to her. Nathan had never tried to pursue her after Michael's death, so far as she knew. It had been Becca who'd drawn him out, convinced she was protecting Amy somehow.

So, in a way, didn't that make Amy responsible for not one but two deaths?

"It's no one's fault but the disease," she mumbled, staring ahead.

Scott nudged her.

She blinked, and the funeral home came back into view. She'd been staring at the casket, replaying Dr. Lamb's conversation in her head. Guilt gnawed at her.

Scott leaned in. "What's up?" he whispered.

Amy shook her head. "Not now."

The rest of the ceremony went by in a blur. Amy barely felt present, as though she was there but not actively participating. It was the same sense of disconnect that had overcome her when she'd sat through Michael's funeral, the sense that this horrible thing wasn't real somehow. As if thinking that would make it any better, would take away her pain and guilt.

Amy didn't linger once the pallbearers began to haul the casket out the side door to the hearse. She touched Scott's arm as they stood. "Can we go?"

"You don't want to watch the burial?"

She shook her head. She couldn't watch them lay her friend in the ground and pretend as if it wasn't her fault. It was.

Oh, God, Becca, I'm so sorry.

Tears pricked her eyes. Scott frowned and ushered her outside.

Amy cast one last look at the casket before it slipped out of view.

Becca's little brother, Zach, stood in the front row, watching the casket go without a single tear shed. His face wasn't quite stoic. It was...almost peaceful.

A lump formed in Amy's throat. She'd heard...Becca had abused Zach. The bruises, the welts: his running away made sense now.

I should have seen the signs. I should have done something.

Their steps were hurried as they passed through the lobby toward the doors. Amy's knees almost buckled as her guilt racked her. Scott swore and held her up, pulling her to him. "Come on, baby. Just a little bit farther."

Amy clung to Scott as if he were a life raft. Her legs felt like jelly, and she shook all over.

When they were almost to the car, a well-dressed elderly man intercepted them. "Excuse me, but are you Miss Amy Miles?"

Scott immediately stepped in front of her. "Sorry, but if you're a reporter—"

"I'm not, young man," he said with a knowing smile. "I'm Becca's lawyer. It appears a letter was found in Becca's apartment, labeled for Amy. Becca had a living will. She told us where to find the letter and whom to give it to." He reached into his coat pocket and produced a long scroll secured with a red ribbon. "Do with it as you wish. But please take it so she doesn't come back to haunt me for not following her last will. You do not mess with the dead's wishes, the law be damned."

Amy stared at the letter. With a trembling hand, she reached for it.

"Amy—" Scott started, but she already had it.

"Thank you," she rasped, standing straighter and clutching the letter in her hand.

The man nodded. "If you have any questions"—he handed them a business card—"this is my contact information." He started to turn and then paused. "Just between us," he said quietly, "the police don't know about this letter. If anyone asks, say it was left under your windshield wiper, because that's what I was about to do."

Amy stilled and softly smiled. She nodded, unable to speak.

He tipped his fedora to them and hobbled off to a BMW down the street.

"Interesting," Scott murmured, still frowning. "Superstitious geezer."

Amy and Scott silently walked and got in Scott's car. They sat there for a few seconds.

Amy didn't need to ask to know what Scott was waiting for. Holding her breath, she delicately slid the ribbon from the scroll and unfurled the letter.

The handwritten note was dated about six months ago.

Dearest Amy,

I'm sick. Not cancer sick, though it feels like it sometimes. I'm talking out-of-my-mind crazy.

No, seriously. I need help. I'm trying to get help, but I can't trust myself sometimes. And God, I'm so scared to tell you.

What will you think of me? Will you hate me? Will you abandon me too?

I think I'm getting worse. I've started losing time. Mom did. Now she's in a mental health facility.

That's right. I never told you that, because I lied and said my mother was dead. My father really is in prison, but my mother is alive. I'm so sorry for all the lies, Amy. I'm sorry for hiding the truth. Know I only did it to protect you.

I never meant for this to happen. I've kind of accepted it, you know? I mean, I knew there was a chance I could inherit my mother's disease. It runs in her family.

But I'm scared. I'm so damned scared, and I don't know where to go anymore.

So I'm writing this letter to clear my head, and in case something happens to me. Because crazy people do crazy shit, right?

I don't want to hurt you. If I ever do, know that it was never my intention.

You've been like a sister to me. You're one of the kindest people I know.

I met you, once. A long time ago. We were both kids sent to the same summer camp. I was weird and awkward, but you befriended me anyway. I thought, "What a nice girl. I wish she could be my friend."

Years later, when we met again in college, you were. I looked totally different, so you wouldn't recognize me. But I remembered you.

For your smile. Your kind heart. Your passion to help people.

I think I fell in love with you the first time I saw you paint. You were so lost in it. I'd never seen anyone pour that much love into anything in my life.

You looked out for me when no one else would. I pretended to be a popular girl in college, because I thought that's who I had to be to get attention. But around you, I could be myself. You saw me for me, and I'll never forget that.

I hope wherever you are now, things are better. You spend so much time being sad and thinking every single bad thing that happens is your fault. But it's not. Sometimes, shit just happens. And that's okay. There's nothing you can do about it.

So stop beating yourself up. If you get this, I know I'll already be dead. And you'll probably find a way to blame yourself for it, too.

So stop. Love yourself, Amy. Go live your life to the fullest, and know I'll always be watching over you.

Love Forever,

Becca

Tears darkened the paper around the signature. They flowed in torrents down Amy's cheeks, unstoppable as she read the letter again.

A huge weight lifted off her.

Becca didn't blame her—she was blaming herself. Had blamed herself for Michael's death, too. And Nathan's, in a strange way.

She had to let go of the guilt and move on. Dr. Lamb was right. None of this was anyone's fault.

It was the disease's.

Scott set a hand on her shoulder, giving her a look that said, "Are you okay?"

Amy smiled and wiped at her face, nodding. "Yeah," she said at last. "I'm fine now."

THIRTY-SEVEN

Two years later

THE BOOKSTORE WAS crowded. Like, wall-to-wall crowded. The fifty seats the staff had managed to squeeze onto the floor were filled within thirty seconds of them opening their doors. Three minutes after that, all the floor space near the podium had been occupied, as had every inch of wall space.

It still blew her mind how far she'd come. Four years ago, Amy Miles was convinced she'd never set foot in front of a crowd again. Now, she couldn't seem to stay out of the spotlight. And she hoped she wouldn't. She had a message that needed to be heard.

And, apparently, there were scores of hurting, broken people who needed to hear it, too.

The first time she spoke in front of a crowd on her press tour after her memoir/self-help book was published, her voice warbled. Her palms sweated, her skin turned clammy, and she felt as if puke was trying to climb up her throat.

Seeing the hope, the desperation, and the heartache in the eyes of the hundreds of people she'd spoken to gave her courage. They believed in her. Some later told her at the book signing that they'd driven hundreds of miles to hear her speak. That kind of unwavering devotion and encouragement was staggering.

She couldn't let them down. And she hadn't, if her fan mail and chart-topping success were any indication.

"What happened to me is not a unique story," she read, starting the last paragraph of the opening chapter. "Every year, thousands of people fall victim to senseless violence. My goal is not to seek pity, but rather to spread the message that you're not alone. I wish I had known that. It might have saved me a world of tremendous grief, as I hope to do for you." She closed the book with a warm smile. "Thank you."

The crowd applauded. Some people had tears in their eyes. So far at every stop on her press tour, she'd made no fewer than a dozen people cry. The staff had started to keep boxes of tissue out because of this.

A question-and-answer session followed, along with a book signing. She still couldn't believe this was her life. That she was actually helping people. She'd been allowed to do her own cover art, and she'd brought along several paintings to sell, as well as prints and other merchandise. People told her: "They were moved by her." "She inspired them." "She gave them strength." On and on the praise went. With every kind word, her backbone grew that much stronger. Her soul and heart mended. She'd even started a support group for assault victims back in Los Angeles, and she donated twenty-five percent of her royalties to charities supporting her cause.

She'd always thought art was her purpose in life, but now she knew she had a far greater calling—to help people, to give them courage when they couldn't find any, to be the beacon in a sea of darkness.

Though the bookstore closed at nine p.m., Amy stayed to shake the hand of and talk to every single person who showed up. It was nearly ten thirty before she and a very tired and somewhat irritable closer left the building. The taxi she'd asked to pick her up wasn't outside, but that was fine.

Because her closest confidant, her best friend, stood in front of a used black 2009 Jetta. She'd used some of her book advance money to purchase it for a steal from a local dealer back in California.

Scott smiled at her as she ran to him. "Whoa! Easy there. Wouldn't want to squish Emma."

"Sorry." Amy blushed. She ran her palm over the bump along her lower belly, where their child rested. Amy couldn't wait to meet her. She'd always wanted a family to call her own, and now she had one. Life sometimes seemed too good to be true.

"Don't be, gorgeous." He kissed her forehead. "You're perfect."

"When did you get in?" she asked as he opened the car door for her. Her second trimester was drawing to a close. Sometimes, she felt bigger than a whale, even though she knew the pregnancy journey was far from over. She buckled in as Scott walked to the other side and got in.

"Little over an hour ago," he answered. "I found your cab driver sitting here when I pulled in. Being the gentleman that I am, I, of course, happily sent him on his way." He grinned and wriggled his eyebrows.

Amy laughed. "Well, you're better than the cab ride. I wasn't expecting to see you until I got back."

"Eh, I thought I'd surprise you." He winked. "Plus, I missed you."

"Aw."

"Aw," he added in his goofy voice. They took off, driving through the quiet streets of the sleepy seaside town of Hope, North Carolina.

It was beautiful here. Amy would love to move to North Carolina. She'd always loved the South. The idea had been mentioned to Scott more than once, and he was keen on it. There were a lot of painful memories for him, too, in Los Angeles. Besides, she could write and paint from anywhere, and he was working on getting transferred to the Charlotte branch of his employer. Plus, it would only be about a four-hour drive to Myrtle Beach, which she positively loved.

They talked about the signing as they got on the interstate. "I'm getting better at it—public speaking, that is." Amy leaned her head back and closed her eyes with a satisfied smile.

"Oh yeah? No more feeling like you're going to hurl all over anyone?"

She playfully shoved him. "No. I mean, I still get a little nervous right before I go on. Somehow, waiting to speak is way worse than the actual act itself."

"So I've heard from a lot of people in showbiz." He cast her a sidelong glance. "You seem happier."

"I am happy." She clasped his hand. "Because I have you."

Something flashed in his eyes. She frowned. Why was his hand sweaty?

"You okay?" she asked.

"Yeah," he said quickly. His voice rose slightly in pitch and came out breathy. "Why?"

"Well, it's just that your hands are clammy. And your forehead has a bit of sweat."

"Eh, it's hot in here." He turned on the AC. "Aren't you hot?"

She winced, shivering. "No, for once. I'm actually freezing."

"Oh shit. Sorry." He turned the AC down again. "Sorry, babe."

"It's okay." She quirked a brow. "Everything all right?"

He took a deep breath and stared out at the road. "I hope so."

Hope so? "Did something happen?" she pressed after a beat of silence.

"No, no. Everything's fine." He smiled brightly, the smile that had lit up her life and brightened her days since she first met him. "I'm just nervous, that's all."

Aha. "About?"

He gulped. "You'll see. It's a surprise, okay?"

It had been a half hour since they'd left the bookstore. Not many cars shared the interstate at this time of night. Scott exited onto a country road. Nothing but farms and green pastures spread out on either side of them. "Where are we going?" Amy looked around. "My hotel's not for a few more exits."

"We're not going to the hotel."

She blinked. "We're not?"

347

"Nope." He grinned. "We're going home."

Home?

He put his blinker on, despite there not being any other cars for miles, and turned on to a little gravel driveway. It took her a moment to recognize the place they'd visited about a month before, when they'd used a bit of his quarterly bonus to go on a Southern vacation.

The little Victorian farmhouse was quaint but roomy. At about two thousand square feet, it was a cute two-story, with white vinyl siding and sky-blue trim. A charming white picket fence outlined the property, about ten acres' worth of farmland.

It was a lot of land, with a lot of money attached to it, which Amy was initially against looking at. However, Scott convinced her otherwise when she learned she'd earned out her advance and then some, so she'd be receiving a hefty royalty check. Plus, Scott had just gotten a promotion. Having quickly advanced in his new company, and being completely free of debt and all criminal charges, he had managed to save a nice little sum himself.

Scott pulled in front of the house and parked, killing the engine. "Ta-da," he said, getting out.

Amy followed suit. "What do you mean? What are we doing here?" Her eyes landed on the SOLD sign posted in front of the house. She quickly put two and two together. Her eyes widened, shooting to Scott. "You didn't."

"What do you feel about spending the rest of our lives, or most of them, anyway, in this 'dream home,' as you called it?" He walked over to her, love in his eyes as he gazed down at her.

Amy's mouth dropped as she gasped. "You mean this is *ours*?"

"I just closed earlier this week."

Amy looked from the house—her house—to her amazing boyfriend. She'd say, "Hell yes!" if it weren't for one thing. "What about your job?"

"They were actually looking to grow their Charlotte office. I interviewed and found out I got the job last month. I start at the end of the month."

"When our lease runs out on the apartment," she breathed. They'd since graduated from the shitty little apartments they met in. Though it was a far cry from the ritziest places in town, the modest one-bedroom apartment they shared now was definitely a step up. They'd opted to keep it cheap and stay in an affordable neighborhood, in order to save up money to buy a house.

Tears stung her eyes, and she laughed. "Oh my God, Scott." She hugged him. "This is wonderful."

"There's only one thing that would make it better." He cupped her cheek and stared into her eyes with intense emotion. His voice turned quiet, raw. "Amy, I wasn't living before I found you. I thought I was damned, and you stumbled into my life, like an angel come to lead the way. You stood by me when a lot of women would have run. I owe you everything."

Reaching into his pocket, he knelt and held out a small black box.

Amy's heart stopped as he opened it, revealing a sparkling ring. A pretty little round diamond was set in a silver band that looked as if it had been carved with vines. It was beautiful and simple, the type of vintage jewelry Amy so admired.

"Julia Amy Gray, mother of my child, keeper of my heart, will you marry me?"

349

She cried, smiling and laughing through her tears. "Yes. Oh, Scott, yes."

He swept her up in a hug, kissing her fiercely and twirling her around. At last, he set her down and placed the delicate band around her ring finger.

Amy stared at it, unable to believe what had just happened. After going through the heartbreak of losing Michael the night before their wedding, she thought she'd never want to see another ring on that finger again.

But now she couldn't take her eyes off it, because it made her so happy. So intensely, stupidly happy.

She thought her heart would burst from joy as they shared another passionate kiss.

"Do you want to see our house, Future Mrs. Meyers?" Scott asked.

Her lips stretched into another silly grin. "I indeed would, Mr. Meyers."

He ducked his head, and his lips brushed her ear. "Someday soon, I'm going to pick you up and carry you, my blushing bride, over the threshold and into our new lives."

"I can't wait," she whispered back. And she couldn't.

Hand in hand, they walked toward their future.

Even though the shadows were thick around them in the quiet, dark countryside, she never once looked over her shoulder—because her eyes were only on Scott.

THE END

CALL FOR RATINGS AND REVIEWS

T HANK YOU FOR reading my book! If you have a moment, I'd really appreciate an honest rating and review. They help authors stand out in a busy marketplace, plus they give browsing readers the nitty-gritty on books they're shopping. Everyone wins when you rate and review, so please do! Your opinion counts!

NEW RELEASE NEWSLETTER

Want to be notified when I have a new release?
Then sign up for my new release newsletter!
It's free and I promise not to spam you.
Visit www.lolataylorbooks.com for more information,
or http://bit.ly/1WAw9gT to sign up!

ABOUT THE AUTHOR

"LOLA TAYLOR" IS a pen name created for the romances I can't show my grandma without blushing. My favorite genre to write is romantic suspense, usually involving hot werewolves, warlocks, or any other type of paranormal creature. Keep the action hot and the romance hotter—that's my motto! I'm a horror film junkie, I still love Halloween as an adult (seriously, I think I get more excited for it than some kids do), and what precious spare time I have is spent with my family, reading (everything from sci fi to middle grade), playing the flute, painting pretty pictures, or screwing around on Pinterest or Etsy. Hailing from the South, I currently live in the Midwest with five fur babies and my hubby.

You can connect with me on Facebook, Google +, Pinterest, or my email. Learn more about me and my books at www.lolataylorbooks.com, and sign up for new release notifications via my free New Release Newsletter.

OTHER BOOKS BY LOLA TAYLOR

The Her Dark Desires Trilogy
Carnal
Sinful
Soulful (coming soon)

Blood Moon Rising
Fever
Protector
Betrayal
Captured
Sacrifice
Ritual (coming soon – final book!)

Blood Moon Rising companion novels
Lust
Forever (coming soon!)

Standalone novels
Shatter

For a full list of titles, please visit
http://www.lolataylorbooks.com/